THE
WITCHING
ELM

BOOK 1 OF THE

MEMENTO MORI SERIES

BY C.N. CRAWFORD

THE WITCHING ELM

BOOK 1 OF THE MEMENTO MORI SERIES

Copyright © 2014 C.N. Crawford

ISBN-13: 978-1505669282
ISBN-10: 1505669286

Edited by John Hart
Cover art by Carlos Quevedo
Interior design by C.N. Crawford

www.cncrawford.com

Give feedback on the book at:
cncrawfordauthor@gmail.com

Twitter: @CN_Crawford
Facebook: cncrawfordauthor

Third Edition

Printed in the U.S.A

About the authors

C.N. Crawford is not one person but two. Christine (C) grew up in the historic town of Lexington, and has a lifelong interest in New England folklore—with a particular fondness for creepy old cemeteries. Nick (N) spent his childhood reading fantasy and science fiction further north during Vermont's long winters. Together they work to incorporate real historical events and figures into contemporary urban fantasy novels.

To Corinne Crawford and all feisty women.

I

Fiona - Mather Academy

The way Fiona saw it, there were two options: either magic was real, which meant she could one day become a powerful sorceress with a legion of sexy demons at her fingertips, or it wasn't—and she would end up working in an office with fluorescent lighting, having to smell her coworkers' lunches.

Of course, the first scenario was considerably more appealing. Each time she and her friends gathered for a séance, she felt a spark of hope at magic's possibility. *Maybe this time, a witch's spirit will flicker before us, ready to spill her magical secrets.* But Fiona wanted something definitive. She wanted a translucent crone to emerge from the closet, clad in a black woolen dress and gripping a spell book. Or at the very least, a cup of tea could fly across the room. So far, she'd seen nothing more than a vague fluttering of the curtains to suggest magic's existence.

She sat on her floor, her back against her bed. The acrid smell of burning sage filled her tiny dorm room. She watched as her roommate, Celia, lit white candles and incense on her tidy desk, blonde hair cascading over her school uniform. Celia was unwavering in her enthusiasm for communion with the spirits.

1

To her, every flickering candle or shift in temperature heralded a ghost's arrival.

Probably every school had a girl like Celia—the classic beauty who turned all the guys into gibbering idiots. Fiona twisted a brown curl around her finger. No, that wasn't right—every school had a girl who looked like Celia. There couldn't be that many Grace Kelly clones who spent their free time trawling through websites about obscure occult practices.

She cast a glance out the large window above Celia's desk. Iron-gray storm clouds gathered in the late afternoon sky. The weather forecast had predicted at least a foot of snow for Boston. She shivered in her thin sweater. They never seemed to get these rooms warm in the winter.

"Where's Mariana? We're supposed to start soon." Celia lowered herself to the floor, sitting cross-legged against her bed.

"The last time I saw her, she was stuck in a goth music video loop on her laptop. Every time one video ends, another one pops up, and she has to watch it."

Celia raised her eyes to the ceiling in resignation. "The goth thing is so ridiculous. She's so pretty without all the black eye makeup." Her scrutinizing gaze turned on her friend. "I think it's quite brave that you never wear any makeup."

Fiona narrowed her amber eyes. "Brave?" That has to be an insult.

"I mean you don't need it. Your skin is tan and perfect. And your hair is attention-getting enough, with all the—" She waved a hand at Fiona's head. "It's just that most girls our age aren't confident enough to go au naturel." She cocked her head. "But you would look really good in a plum lipstick."

The door swung open, and Mariana held up a hand in a greeting. "Hi guys. Sorry I'm late." She had dressed up her uniform with black and white striped leggings and a silver pentagram pendant. She dropped down to join them on the floor, her black hair hanging in her eyes.

"That's fine." Celia straightened. "We haven't started."

Mariana blew her bangs out of her eyes. "Who are we calling up this time? Can we do Ian Curtis?"

Celia scowled. "Who?" She shook her head. "Never mind. I know he's some depressing musician. And I have another plan."

Mariana arched an eyebrow. "Another dead witch?"

Celia smiled. "Yes, as a matter of fact. Goody Glover. She was killed just over there." She pointed to the window. "In Boston Common. I have a good feeling about this one."

"Fine. Whatever you want." Mariana opened her palms to the ceiling. The three girls clasped hands, closing their eyes.

"Goody Glover." There was a note of hope in Celia's voice. "We call on you in the spirit plane." She gripped harder, her nails digging into Fiona's palm. "Goody Glover. Speak to us and move among us."

"Goody Glover," they chanted together. "Speak to us and move among us."

Fiona strained her ears. Was someone whispering?

Celia raised her voice, a slight tremble in her tone. "Goody Glover. Answer our questions and tell us our fates."

Fiona's skin tingled, and she opened her eyes. The sky grew darker, now the color of a blackened cauldron. She was used to Boston's blizzards, but something about the unnatural pulsing of these storm clouds raised the hair on her arms.

"Goody Glover." Celia chanted. "Answer our questions and tell us our fates."

Fiona swallowed, staring out the window. The clouds seemed to writhe, sick and angry. Her heart beat faster. She glanced at

Celia, whose eyes snapped open. Her voice changed, now low and soft, and her blue eyes were unfocused. "Another Boston. Another Common. A panicked mob. He's coming for them over the cobblestones—through the alleys in Crutched Square. He wants philosopher blood. He wants us."

Fiona's pulse quickened. *What is she talking about?* Something rattled behind them, metal against wood, and then a creaking noise, like a—door. Her head whipped around.

The dorm mother, Ms. Bouchard, stood in the entrance to their room. She crinkled her delicate nose. "What *is* that smell? Are you—smoking something?"

Fiona loosed a breath, unsure if she was relieved or disappointed. "It's sage, Ms. Bouchard."

Celia withdrew her shaking fingers from Fiona's grasp.

Mariana's hand flew to her chest. "I have asthma. I'd read it would help open up the lungs."

Ms. Bouchard's jaw tightened, and she nodded at Mariana. "We need to get you an inhaler. This—" She pointed to the desk. "Is a fire hazard. Put it out, and get back to your room."

While Mariana blew out the candles and incense, Fiona ran the back of her hand across her forehead. Maybe they had been close this time. Her roommate's face had paled, and there was a sadness in her eyes.

She bit her lower lip. Or maybe Celia had just been putting on a show.

2

Tobias
Maremount - Present Day

Tobias approached the darkening Common with a growing sense of dread. Panicked shouts echoed off the stone temples surrounding the park as a small mob swarmed toward him. He searched for a familiar face, nearly falling onto the snowy cobblestones when the crowd surged past.

Spotting his neighbor's grizzled jowls, Tobias stepped forward and gripped the pie-man's arm. "Anequs, what's going on?"

Anequs's eyes held a terrified look that he'd only seen on horses—strained open to show the whites. There was no sign of the cheerful man who used to bring Father corn pudding.

Trembling, Anequs whispered a single name: Rawhed.

At the two blunt syllables, Tobias's stomach dropped. Rawhed—the monster—was hunting outlaw philosophers like him.

And I left home without a weapon.

Racing with the crowd, he sprinted through northwestern Maremount's winding alleys, desperate to bring home the news and grab his pike. Tonight, there were no foxfire orbs to illuminate the streets, nor candles flickering in bedroom windows. Rawhed's approach had left the neighborhood shrouded in profound darkness. Still, Tobias could navigate these streets blindfolded if needed. He had grown up in this labyrinth of alleys and passages, hawking fresh cornbread alongside the steep-peaked timber houses.

As he climbed the steep incline of Curtzan Hill, silver moonlight briefly illuminated the edges of the ramshackle, top-heavy buildings. Outside a tavern, iron birdcages clanged fretfully in the wind.

Is Eden safe? Tobias increased his speed, his locket thudding against his chest as he raced up the hill. Frigid air pierced his lungs and stung his arms through his wool sweater. The temperature had plummeted in the last hour.

Close to the top, glass shards gleamed in the snow. Above him, shutters slapped against weather-beaten walls. Just as he reached the summit, a woman's agonized scream rang out. He turned, his hands on his knees as his lungs heaved. Rawhed was interrogating someone back near the Common.

It was his duty to aid those in danger. But he was also supposed to have a plan before taking action, and running unarmed into Rawhed's army wasn't much of a plan.

A thinning crowd fought its way up the hill, the women hoisting their skirts as they fled alongside the men. Crooked rooftops and chimneys were silhouetted against the glow of a spreading fire. Just as he caught his breath, the woman's screams cut out. His throat tightened. There was no point trying to help her now. The decision had been made for him.

He turned north again, sprinting toward his home. His arms whirled as he slid downhill over the slick paving stones, hurtling toward the frozen sludge of Crutched Square. The smell of smoke thickened.

Despite the cold, sweat soaked his brow by the time he reached the top of Black Bread Lane. A trail of blood spread across the fallen snow. Some of Rawhed's army must have been through here already, in search of underground covens. Arriving at his own doorstep, he slipped on the cobbles. Sprawled in the snow, his face lay inches from a child's blood-spattered hat.

He pushed himself up and banged on the door. "It's Tobias. Let me in!"

The door edged open, and his father's strong hand plunged into the winter air to yank him in. A single candle lit the cramped wooden room, guttering and wavering where it stood on a cast-iron stove. Its light flickered over shelves of baking tins and a long table, dusty with flour.

Father pushed his straight, dark hair off his face. He clutched a spell book and a brown envelope. "Do you have any idea what's happening?"

"Rawhed is coming from the south."

His friends Oswald and Eden rushed down the stairs, and Tobias let out a shaky breath. *They're safe—she's safe.* Eden's blond hair trailed behind her tiny frame as she hurried toward Tobias, stumbling over the ragged hem of her skirt. She hugged him, burying her head in his shoulder before pulling away.

Across the room, Tobias's crow squawked near the ceiling. Oswald swatted at the bird with a lanky arm, his sandy blond hair hanging in front of his face.

Tobias looked between Father and his friends. "They were interrogating people. We need to gather the Ragmen—"

Father shook his head, a worry line etched between his thick, black brows. "Not now. We're evacuating the youngest philosophers. You three are going to Boston for safety, to Mather Academy." He pulled a few papers from the envelope and stared at Tobias. "Do you remember what to do?"

Tobias's jaw tightened. "Of course we know what to do, but I don't see the point." He and his friends were to fly through the schism that divided Maremount and Boston—sister cities split through powerful magic long ago. Tobias hated the idea of leaving his home. The Ragmen needed him here. No one could wield a pike like he could. "We should stay."

Smoke from the streets seeped through chinks in the wall as Father paged through the spell book, ignoring him. The fire was spreading fast, and fumes stung Tobias's eyes.

Father pointed to a page before pausing to give Tobias a hard look. "The Ragmen have voted on this. It's not up for discussion now. You must go to Boston. If Rawhed sacks Maremount and hangs the outlaw philosophers, you will need to carry on our work. We need you three alive." He returned to the book. "I'll chant the traveling spell while each of you transform. Tobias, you'll go first. You know what to do when you get there."

Tobias scowled, the floor growing hot beneath his ragged leather shoes as Father intoned the traveling spell. The magical aura rippled over Tobias's skin before black feathers sprouted from his body, and wings burst from his elongated fingers as he compressed.

A blast of frigid air rushed in when Father pushed open the door, holding out the papers. Tobias grasped them in his talons before taking flight into the smoky Maremount sky.

For a moment, he could see an orange blaze across Crutched Square before darkness enveloped him.

3
Tobias

Tobias had soared into the biting winds of a nor'easter, and then even higher above the storm. While black clouds convulsed like an unquiet spirit below, the Milky Way arched majestically above him. As he'd flown, the winter air had crept into his flesh, overtaking one body part at a time—numbing his head, his feet, then his wings.

The traveling spell had better work, or my final transformation will be from crow to corpse.

When he could see the Great Bear's three starry hunters pierce the horizon, he plunged back through the churning clouds. As he did, a magical charge sparked and sizzled over his feathers, singeing the tip of his tail. It had worked; the spell had sent him through the schism.

And yet a dark sea seethed beneath the storm, no land in sight. Tears streamed from his eyes in the glacial winds. For a moment he considered giving up and gliding to a watery grave, until he caught a glimpse of a narrow island dusted in white. The panic in his chest unclenched a little, and he dived lower toward the harbor islands. Before him, a jagged coastline came into view—the legendary city of Boston, with its electric lights and towering buildings.

Gliding over the city, he recognized the flat, white expanse of Boston Common. Its pentagonal shape was unmistakable, so similar to Maremount's central park. He could almost feel the warmth of a fireplace on his skin as he arced over the yellow pinpricks of light around the park.

He angled his pinions toward a wooden building surrounded by a brick wall. The school stood across from the Common. Connected to its gabled main building, two long wings faced each other across an open courtyard.

Tobias swooped over the wall toward a stand of yew trees shielding a snowless patch of ground. Dropping the papers, he pointed his feet, landing with an undignified thump on the frozen earth. He shook with fatigue.

As he puffed his feathers, he scanned the stormy sky for Oswald and Eden. They must not be far behind, though he hadn't seen them on the journey. He shivered and glanced at his gray talons. He should wait in the courtyard, but his feet were flirting with frostbite.

In the shadows, he began the transformation from crow to young man. In a matter of seconds, his stomach descended, his lungs ballooned, and his heart lurched upward. As feathers retracted his skin stretched over swelling muscle and bone. For a brief instant, he felt as if his muscles might rupture out of his body, until the transformation completed with a throbbing and buzzing in his skull. Overcome by nausea, he bent over and retched, one hand pressed on the frozen ground for support.

His tattered shoes, soaked through with melted snow, still covered his feet. When he touched his throat, he found the locket of Eden's hair. With shivering hands, he reached down for the papers scattered on the earth. Snow smudged some of the words, but they were still legible. He rose, brushing off a few remaining feathers, and crossed the schoolyard. As he did, he double-checked the name above the oak door: Mather Academy.

A handwritten note hung over a metal button, reading, "Push for entry." He did as instructed. With chattering teeth, he considered what he was about to undertake. His knowledge of schools was limited, but he doubted anyone expected new students to arrive during overnight snowstorms.

He held his hands in his armpits and racked his brain for a simple distraction spell. It was much easier to convince an absentminded person of something absurd. Hopefully, Oswald and Eden would remember this when they arrived. Oswald was always forgetting his lessons.

At last, the door opened, and a silver-haired man peered out. He wore a rumpled T-shirt embroidered with the words MIT Crew 1970 and blue pajama bottoms. A pair of sheepskin moccasins warmed his feet.

He glowered at Tobias from beneath an unfortunate single eyebrow. "What on earth are you doing?" he barked. "How did you get past the gate? And the alarms?"

Off to a great start, Tobias. He gazed into the man's blue eyes and uttered the spell, pushing his dark, wet hair out of his eyes as he chanted the words. The stranger's pupils dilated, his eyes drifting to the falling snow.

"I'm Tobias Corvin. I believe I'm expected. I'm from England." It was the lie his coven had come up with. He'd never been to England. In fact, he knew less about England than he knew about Boston. But he couldn't exactly say he was from a magical city forged from colonial Boston, and the lie would help to explain his accent.

"Tobias Corvin?" the man murmured, admiring the drifting snowflakes. He raised his lone, hoary eyebrow. "You're expected, you say..."

Tobias exhaled, relieved. The spell worked best on those who were easily confused; this man seemed a perfect subject. Tobias thrust the papers forward, eager to be in the warmth of the building. "Everything's in the paperwork."

Hopefully his underground coven had cobbled together the appropriate documentation. He hadn't been paying much attention to the planning himself, too eager to practice pike fighting to listen to details about paperwork.

The man looked the documents over and, as though recalling a distant memory, he nodded. "Right. The new student from England. Come in. I'm Mr. Mulligan, the principal."

He opened the door wider, and Tobias stepped into a vestibule. In the dim light, he could see a saggy-eyed marble bust that stared vacantly into the courtyard. *Richard Mather,* it read.

Mulligan led Tobias into a small, paper-littered office. "Follow me. We'll do the forms. I know there's a time difference, but really, showing up at all hours."

Slush soaked the bottom of Tobias's pants, and he glanced enviously at Mr. Mulligan's slippers. He hugged his arms around himself as the principal rested against a desk, closing his eyes. Perhaps the distraction spell had been a bit too effective. Tobias cleared his throat.

Mulligan's eyes opened, and his gaze alternated between a glazed stare and an irritated grimace. Tobias smiled faintly, pleased with his work.

Mulligan coughed. "You don't have any belongings? Where are your bags?"

"I lost them on the way."

Mulligan flipped through the papers in his hand. "The new student... They're supposed to give test scores, you know, to put into our computer system. People just don't follow the rules. I tell them over and over, the paperwork needs to go in this box here." He waved toward an empty inbox on his desk. "It's quite simple. Documents in order, and no paperclips. They take up too much space in the folders, and it's not like we have..." He glanced at the door and closed his eyes again.

Melting snow dripped between Tobias's toes, and he shifted from one foot to another. *Am I supposed to respond?* "I don't like paperclips either."

Mulligan's eyes snapped open again. "Paperclips? What are you talking about?"

Wrong answer, Tobias. He was tempted to just knock the man out with a sleep spell, but that could be awkward in the morning.

"Seventeen. You'll be a junior," Mulligan grumbled, "although it's not as if we have room for more juniors. I'll get your uniform." He turned to open a large wardrobe, half full of shirts and jackets that hung over a sparse layer of folded pants and sweaters. After rummaging for a few moments while muttering about "people around here," he pulled together two uniforms for Tobias.

With a scowl, he handed them over. "Don't lose these, or you'll have to buy new ones. I'll show you to your room."

Mulligan shuffled out of his office, and Tobias followed. In the vestibule, Tobias turned for one last glance out the door's window but saw only shadows. He could already hear Mulligan creaking up the stairs.

Tobias shivered up the winding stairwell, hugging his new clothes.

Mulligan shouted down to him, "They don't like to spend money on lighting, so you'll be lucky if you don't break your neck."

After two flights of stairs, Mulligan turned to Tobias. "We're in the central hall." He pointed to a closed door to his right. "At *that* end of the central hall, the girls' wing begins. Young men aren't allowed in there." He fixed his gaze on Tobias, raising his eyebrow in caution before shoving open the opposite door. Apparently he and Eden would have to get creative to steal time together.

Turning left, Tobias followed him through a high-ceilinged hallway, glancing through tall windows overlooking the courtyard. No birds lingered in the snow.

At the end of the central hall, they turned left into another dark corridor, its white walls hung with portraits interspersed between doors. A few steps from the end of the hall, Mulligan stared at the name on one of the doors, wheezing.

"Alan Wong," he muttered, reading the handwritten sign. "He'll do." He opened the door, revealing a small corner room with two single beds. In the bed to the right, Alan's snoring body was bundled under blankets. Black tufts of hair sprouted out from the sheets, pulled up tight around his face.

Mulligan cleared his throat. "There you are. Good night." He disappeared into the dark hall, shutting the door behind him.

Tobias dropped his uniforms on the empty bed. He rubbed his eyes and scanned the room. Between the beds, a bay window looked toward the Common, while to his left, another window overlooked the courtyard. Its panes were glazed with frost, but Tobias could see that the storm still raged.

His new uniforms fell to the floor as he crawled into

bed, making a nest of the heavy blankets. With a view of the courtyard, he stared into the silvery landscape, thinking of Rawhed's attack—the smoke, the woman's screams, and the red trail of blood through Black Bread Lane.

When he was little, he'd chanted nighttime charms to ward off the devils and hags that crept into children's rooms at night. He'd been stupid to think they might work. And yet the odd rhymes always popped into his head in moments of danger. *Heigh diddle diddle, a nighttime riddle...*

Wrapped in his warm blankets, his throbbing muscles began to relax. Normally, he read in his bed before falling asleep. In fact, since he was little, he read books about Boston. Ever since his father had given him his first contraband *Viscount Brad of Boston* book, he'd wanted to visit the city. As a boy, he'd dreamt of Boston's metallic, subterranean monsters winding below the streets, their bellies full of people traveling to work. And when he'd grown older, he'd pored through murder mysteries about a detective named Danny Marchese. Straining to keep his eyes open, he muttered the exotic name: "Danny."

Alan shifted, groaning at the noise.

Tobias inhaled sharply. *What am I doing? I'm half-delirious with exhaustion.* He pulled his blanket tighter, squinting as he searched for his friends descending through the sky. He would wait up all night if he had to, listening to the gentle rattling of the windowpanes near his bed. *The fire wasn't close enough to burn them, was it?*

He rested against his pillow and closed his eyes for just a moment, melting into the soft blankets. Soon, he would scan the skies again for Oswald and Eden. Any number of things could have killed them after he'd escaped.

4

Tobias

A hand tapped his shoulder as a deep voice interrupted his sleep. "Who are you?"

"Tobias," he mumbled. "I'm Tobias."

He opened his eyes. Someone tall—Alan, it must be—stood in a stream of pearly morning light, his dark hair still rumpled from sleep. His athletic build suggested that the young people here were better fed than their Maremount counterparts.

Tobias rubbed his eyes, sitting up to gaze out the window. No new footprints marked the snow.

"Are you supposed to be here?" Alan scratched at black stubble on his angular jawline. "No one told me I was getting a new roommate."

"I arrived from England last night," he managed. "I'm Tobias. Mulligan brought me here."

"Oh." Alan nodded, looking at the floor while he thought. "From England. That's cool." He stared at Tobias again, folding his arms. "Anyway, breakfast is starting. They have French toast on Tuesdays."

What in Blodrial's veins is French toast? What he really

needed was to go outside to find some ravens. The messengers from Maremount might be able to tell him what had happened to his friends.

He flung off his blankets, gathering his clothes from the floor. "I need to go outside." He slipped into his new blue pants.

Alan rubbed the back of his neck. "Go outside? You can't. You have to get breakfast, and then class starts. We're supposed to be up at 7."

At the word "breakfast," Tobias's stomach rumbled. He hadn't eaten since he'd left Maremount, and then it was just corn pudding and well water. *The ravens will still be around after I eat.*

His stomach growled as he pulled on his new blue sweater. His friends had probably roosted near a warm chimney on one of the harbor islands to wait out the storm. It had been a difficult flight, but Oswald had pulled through worse situations.

He slipped into his leather shoes and followed Alan out the door into the corridor. The starched collar chafed his neck, and he loosened one of the buttons, shuffling toward the central hall behind other students.

As they descended two flights of stairs, the students jostled around a tall guy with curly brown hair and ruddy cheeks the color of overripe peaches. Over a square set of shoulders, his neck was as thick as his head. They spoke in shouts.

"You think they got that sausage today?" asked a short boy with close-cropped black hair.

"What's wrong, Jared? Not getting enough sausage?" The pink-cheeked guy jerked up his chin, grinning.

"Shut up, Sully."

"Yo! Jared likes hot sausages!" Sully cupped his hands

around his mouth as he yelled up the stairwell.

Jared scowled up at him. "I said shut up!"

They broke into guffaws.

Idiots. Still, hot sausages sounded delicious to Tobias. Alongside Alan, he reached the ground floor and hurried toward the smell of baking bread. As he rounded the corner into the dining hall, he knocked into a girl with flame-red hair.

"I beg your pardon," he said, looking down at the back of her head.

The girl turned to look up at him. Her vibrant hair reminded him of the fire goddess, though no warmth shone from her striking features. She stared at him with eyes the color of a stormy sky. "You must be new here. I'm Munroe."

Her milky white hand flew to a pendant at her throat. It was a silver chalice, shining with tiny rubies made to look like drops of claret. He couldn't fathom how it was possible, but it looked like something he'd seen in Maremount.

5

Tobias

Voices echoed off the vaulted ceiling as students continued to file into the hall. Across from Alan, Tobias scanned the room. It seemed less like a dining hall and more paintings he'd seen of cathedrals. Colored light streamed through stained glass images of scholars and plants. Under the windows, portraits hung on dark wooden walls. The paintings alternated with hunting trophies—an array of grimacing deer heads that overlooked students as they ate. Rows of wooden tables crossed the room beneath brass chandeliers that must be twenty feet long.

Tobias cut into another piece of eggy bread. Dripping with maple syrup and tiny pools of melted butter. It wasn't as good as his father's baking, but a million times better than his own shoddy attempts to woo Eden with soggy blueberry bread.

He had just sipped his juice when Mulligan's voice boomed through the hall. "Students—uh—*students!* Good morning," he thundered from the opposite side of the hall. He stood on a platform before a great stone fireplace, nearly the width of an entire wall.

The students' conversations hushed, and a few voices mumbled "Good morning, Principal Mulligan."

Clearly the distraction spell had dissipated. Mulligan was all business this morning as he thrust an open hand into the air. "I'd like to introduce our new student, Tobias Corvin. Tobias, please stand."

Tobias rose, staring out over twenty rows of tables, half filled with students eating breakfast. A few latecomers entered the hall, grabbing trays. Chairs shifted as students turned to look at him. A cough echoed through the room.

"Tobias arrived late last night from England. He'll be a member of the junior class."

Someone a few rows away called out in a mock-English accent, "Please sir, may I have some more?"

It was the guy who'd been shouting about sausages. Sully, they called him. Munroe leaned into him, laughing into her hand. He'd known people like him before—the well-heeled young men who made fun of his clothes—the smirking fatheads who drunkenly shoved Tatter children into barrels, rolling them down Curtzan Hill. He frowned, returning to his seat. He didn't much care what they thought.

Alan shook his head. "Those guys are idiots. This school is full of idiots. That's why I usually sit alone."

At least he had something in common with Alan. Tobias nodded, biting into a sausage as three girls strode toward them holding trays. Unused to seeing skirts cut above the ankle, Tobias stared at their legs as he chewed.

Alan turned to look at them. "Hey, Celia!"

"Hey Alan," replied a blonde girl in the trio. Her hip stuck out as she stood by the edge of their table. "Tobias, was it?" A welcoming smile played on her glossy pink lips. "I just heard your introduction. I'm Celia." She nodded toward a girl whose straight black hair was cut in an odd style: short on one side, and long on the other. "That's Mariana." The third girl's hair was a wild mass of honey-brown curls. "And that's Fiona."

They were all pretty, and Tobias struggled to pull his eyes away from the smooth olive skin on Fiona's strong-looking legs. He swallowed.

"Hello?" Fiona said, and he forced himself to look up at her. She struggled to balance her tray in one hand and eat toast off it with the other. "You're English, right? I just saw a documentary about British drinking culture. It was something to do with social anxiety."

He nodded with a faint smile. *Is this supposed to make sense?*

With her heavily made-up eyes, Mariana looked askance at her friend. "Fiona, you're freaking him out. He just got here."

"But apparently meditation helps." Dark lashes framed Fiona's amber eyes.

"Thanks for the suggestion." He had the feeling he was being insulted.

"We should sit." Celia tilted her head. She reminded him of a society beauty with her small, pointed nose and wide-set blue eyes. The three girls strolled to an empty table.

"That was awesome." Alan leaned in. "Celia never talks to me for that long. I only know her from Biology."

"They're very pretty." Tobias touched the locket of Eden's hair at his neck—the blonde hair, so unusual for a Tatter. She hadn't even arrived yet, and he was already staring at other girls. He closed his eyes to clear his mind.

Alan squinted at him. "You don't really look English. You look sort of American... what's the word... indigenous."

Tobias's mind raced. He couldn't exactly say that he came from a land created by English and Algonquian sorcerers centuries ago (though, as he would tell anyone who'd listen, they preferred to be called *philosophers*).

"English people don't all look the same." He shoved another forkful of French toast into his mouth.

Alan seemed satisfied with his answer and nodded solemnly. "Right." He stared at Tobias. "Do you play an instrument? My friend Joe and I have a band, but we don't have enough instruments. He goes to Boston Latin. I'm on trumpet, and Joe's on drums. We're called Drumpet."

"I play the lute."

"Awesome! We could be called Lump... Lumpet..." He scratched his chin. "I need to think about the name more."

"Sounds interesting. Well, I hope you don't mind, but I must go." He stood and picked up his crumb-filled tray. He was desperate to find out news of his friends.

Alan shook his head. "You can't miss English. You can't skip classes on your first day. Ms. Ellsworth's is the worst class to skip. Mulligan will kick you out if you start off wrong."

"I'd be kicked out of school?"

"I think so. You can't leave the building until classes have ended."

He needed to find out what had happened to his friends, but if he got expelled, he'd be forced into the Boston winter on his own. In exile, a person's ears could turn black and fall off from frostbite.

"I'll be to class in a minute. I must use the bathroom." Tobias's stomach rebelled against the sudden influx of rich food.

"English is in Room 202. You've got two minutes."

Two minutes. Apparently they're awfully preoccupied with scheduling here.

He clenched his jaw as he strode toward the bathroom. With no sign of his friends, he began to worry that something had gone terribly wrong.

6

Tobias

By the time he'd finished in the bathroom and found Room 202, nearly twenty minutes had passed. He creaked opened the classroom door into a dark-walled room that smelled of old coffee. Students sat at desks crammed together in three rows. Tall, rounded windows overlooked the icy courtyard and the yews where he'd transformed.

A petite woman stood in front of a chalkboard beside a desk covered in tidily stacked rows of paper. Her brown hair, streaked with gray, was scraped into a tight knot at the back. "You're late. Do you have something better to do with your time than attend class?"

Very much so. "Not at all."

Heels clacking on the hardwood floor, she stepped closer to him, fixing her hazel eyes on him over the rims of her glasses.

"I'm Tobias."

Her mouth twitched at the corner. "I'm Ms. Ellsworth. I was only told you were joining my class this morning." She turned, pulling a printed sheet of paper off her desk and handing it to him. "We're discussing this poem today. I hope

Mr. Mulligan told you that this is a rigorous class and that I have high standards. I suppose you'll need extra help catching up. Sit with Munroe for the partner work." She pointed to the back row. "Sully, you'll have to move."

Munroe blinked her gray eyes at him, smiling as she fiddled with her chalice pendant. Beside her, Sully shuffled his collection of crumpled papers to a nearby desk, dropping his book on the floor. He glared at Tobias as he reached down to pick it up.

"As I was saying," Ms. Ellsworth resumed while Tobias took his seat in the back, "The Tempest is believed to be one of Shakespeare's final plays."

He looked around the room as Ms. Ellsworth lectured in front of a chalkboard. The classroom had the same walnut walls as the dining hall, and bookshelves lined the entire right wall. He'd never seen so many books in one place.

Most of the other students bent over their desks, scribbling in notebooks. Searching for writing implements, he found that Sully had left a half-eaten apple and a crude drawing of the male anatomy, but nothing he could use to write.

He wanted to stand up and scream that this was a waste of time and he needed to find the ravens. Instead, he leaned toward Munroe and whispered, "Do you have a pen?"

"What?"

"A pen—do you have an extra?"

"Tobias." Ms. Ellsworth's heels clacked toward him. "In the future, I will expect you to come prepared. When people are unprepared, you waste my time and yours. Now I will ask everyone to turn to your partner, and discuss Browning's poem in relation to The Tempest."

Tobias glanced at Munroe, who rolled her eyes. Her lips were painted a deep red.

"Ms. Ellsworth is always talking about time." She reached inside her bag, pulling out a pen and handing it to him. "We're always wasting our time and hers, like we care about time-wasting. My dad went to school here. We've been at Mather forever." She nodded toward Ms. Ellsworth. "She wanted to be a singer, but she ended up back here, freaking out about passing time. It must be depressing to have failed at your dreams." She bit the end of her pen, turning to Tobias. "Can you imagine having to be a teacher? It would be the worst."

When he was little, he'd dreamt of what it would be like to stand before a classroom of wide-eyed students. Once or twice he'd draped himself in a blanket, attempting to create a teacher's robe. He lectured to chalk drawings about herbs and astrology.

He raised his eyebrows. "It would be awful."

"Have you read *The Tempest?*"

"A few times." Maremount citizens considered Prospero an important philosopher. Some noble families claimed him as an ancestor.

"Oh, good! I haven't finished it. Shakespeare is so boring, and I don't know why we're reading about disgusting old warlocks." She arched a thin, red eyebrow. "But it would've been fun to live in Tudor times. Like when the men wore those big lacy collars, and the women had golden gowns."

"If you were rich, it might have been been fun. Otherwise you'd live a brutish life."

She frowned at him, chewing on the end of her pen and then turned to jot notes in silence. Tobias picked up the Browning poem on his desk, pretending to read it while he ran through the possible scenarios that might have detained his friends: the fire, the storm, the bone wardens, and Rawhed himself.

"OK, class." Ms. Ellsworth clapped her hands together. "Let's begin." She glared at Tobias over her glasses. "Tobias, what did Munroe teach you?"

The students in the front rows turned to stare at him. Silence descended as he scanned the poem. After a minute, Sully threw back his head and gave an exaggerated sigh.

"Ms. Ellsworth?" Fiona spoke from across the room.

"Yes?"

"He's British, and I think he..." She dropped her voice to a stage whisper. "He's socially anx—"

"Language is magic," he said, interrupting Fiona. "Caliban sees Prospero at his books, peeling a wand and calling it by a name. When he named it, he imbued it with magic. But Caliban knows that language is a curse and a blessing."

Alan's hand shot up. "Can we talk about the staff? I thought that was the best part. In a universe where matter could be transformed by magical energy directed by a wooden medium, a staff could transmit way more energy than a wand—"

"Alan, we're discussing the poem now," Ms. Ellsworth clucked.

Thirty minutes later, class ended with the clanging of a bell. Tobias felt stuck in an odd dream, severed from the world he knew. He'd seen Mather Academy many times before—only he'd seen it in Maremount, and he'd never been allowed within its gates.

When the Great Philosophers created Maremount, it had begun as a replica of Boston, hidden through powerful magic. Because the school had been built before the Great Schism, it was one of the few buildings that continued to exist in both worlds. He'd often walked past the Mather gates, gazing in at the courtyard. And yet, right now he could think of nothing but getting out again.

At lunch, he sat with Alan over bowls of vegetable soup. Alan assured him there was no time to leave for a walk before History. As Alan rushed through his homework at the table, Tobias thought of Oswald and Eden tumbling through the blizzard. What if Mishett-Ash, the gray-faced storm god, had chased them out of the skies?

In History, his teacher described the early days of Massachusetts. She explained how the pilgrims befriended the Wampanoag King, who'd helped them survive the harsh winters. She said they'd thrown a thanksgiving feast to celebrate their friendship.

Tobias noticed there was no discussion of what happened next; how the pilgrims feared the Natives were devils and burned villages full of heathen children. There was no mention of how, when Massasoit's son had arrived for a Plymouth thanksgiving years later, it was in the form of a severed head.

7

Fiona

Before lunch, Fiona stopped by her room to try her hand at accessorizing. Today, she would speak to Jack Hawthorne. Ever since he'd arrived in September, she thought of his face every night before falling asleep. His appearance was a study in contrast: black eyelashes and pale blue eyes, porcelain skin and pink cheeks, unruly dark hair and a sober, almost severe dress sense. She'd seen him earlier today, and since he was hardly ever in school, she had to take her chances when she could.

Yesterday's clothes formed misshapen mounds beside her bed, draped over books and an empty mug. As usual, Celia's side of the room was pristine, her books alphabetized and her blanket tucked in neatly.

Fiona looked at her reflection in the closet mirror. Her brown ringlets formed a bushy halo around her face. On the plus side, her hair's volume gave her the illusion of having a gigantic head—a look that celebrities could only attain through starvation. She rifled through Celia's cosmetics for purple eyeliner. Celia had told her it would bring out the gold flecks in her eyes, but after a few minutes of fumbling through plastic tubes, she gave up as her rumbling stomach seized control.

On her way out, she grabbed a beaded hairclip from the end of her bed, securing her curls off her face. She wove her way through the dense packs of girls in the corridors and stairwell. In the dining hall, she loaded her tray with pasta and plopped down across from Celia and Mariana.

Mariana wore her usual black eye makeup, and she'd drawn a skull on the back of her hand in pen. The only thing about her that didn't scream "goth princess" was her healthy, golden complexion. She stared at Fiona. "You changed your hair. It looks good."

Fiona smiled. "Good. I'm talking to Jack after school."

Celia picked at her lunch. "I don't know why you like him. I get that he's cute, and it's cool that he's related to Emmanuel Hawthorne—"

"Nathaniel," Mariana put in.

"—but he's been here for over a year, and he never talks to anyone. He's weird."

"Yeah, but he's hot." Mariana shrugged.

Fiona took a sip of orange juice. "He just needs someone to bring him out of his shell."

"Enough about him." Celia waved her hand dismissively. "What do you think of the new British kid?"

Fiona drummed her fingers on the table, looking up to the ceiling. "He's kind of hot, too. Skinny, maybe, but he has nice lips."

"It's about time we had some fresh blood." Mariana raked black fingernails through the air.

Celia wrinkled her nose. "You guys are scary. Oh, do either of you know if we're being tested on *The Tempest* tomorrow, or are we still talking about it? I never finished it."

"Still talking about it," said Mariana.

Celia groaned. "I'm never gonna finish it."

"I really liked it," said Fiona.

"Did you actually read it this time?" Celia narrowed her eyes. "You're not just relying on your freakish memory to spit out everything from class?"

"What makes you think I do *that*?" Fiona twirled her pasta around her fork.

Celia sighed. "Anyway, I wish we could learn more *real* magic."

Fiona looked up, frowning. "It seemed like something was happening at our last séance. You really don't have any idea what that meant? About the cobblestones, and the philosophers?"

Celia shook her head. "No idea. But you could tell *something* happened. That's all the evidence you need."

Mariana lowered her chin, staring at Fiona. "Fiona. Magic is real. Last year, my aunt Carolina put a curse on us, all the way from Rio. She's still mad at my mom for moving to the states. My cat died." She rested her chin in her hand. "Lucas started getting bad grades, and I kept getting eczema on my elbows." She straightened up again. "But then we put salt around the house, and my rashes cleared up. The cat stayed dead though, and Lucas is still failing."

"Poor cat," said Celia. "What was her name?"

"A couple of years ago, I renamed her 'Dog is Dead.' It was a tribute to one of my favorite philosophers." She chipped at her black nail polish. "Before that, she was Ms. Mittens."

"Interesting." Fiona forced a smile.

"Well, that proves it. Magic is totally real." Celia lowered her voice to a whisper. "You know how I used to be friends with Munroe?"

"Before you stole two of her boyfriends?" said Mariana.

"Right. Well, she doesn't have to worry about Sully. That guy's a jerk." She shuddered. "The point is, Munroe's dad is a senator. He knows all kinds of stuff. She told me the government has a whole anti-witchcraft task force. Only they don't call it witchcraft, because they don't want people to know about it. It's called 'crimes against the state' or something."

Fiona frowned. "I don't know if I believe anything Munroe says. She acts like she thinks she's better than everyone. She's so proud of her stupid chalice emblem."

"You can get a family crest off the Internet for like ten dollars," said Mariana. "I designed my own with a cat wearing an Elizabethan ruff."

"Well, I believe her about the witchcraft thing." Celia's voice was emphatic. "Have you guys heard about the Mather Adepti?"

The others shook their heads.

"There are rumors about a group of sorcerers who studied here a long time ago. There's supposed to be a secret room someplace, where they practiced spells. *Ghost Hunters* did an episode on it. They walked into the library, and their EMF meters beeped like crazy. Plus, the rooms were all cold and drafty. Mather Academy is full of spirits."

"That, or they're stingy with the heat," Fiona said after swallowing a mouthful of pasta. "How many times have we had séances and not seen a ghost? We'll have to face the fact that none of us will ever earn a living as psychics. We're just going to work in offices, like everyone else. It's going to be awful."

Celia flared her nostrils. "Don't be ridiculous. We have the perfect opportunity to try something different. We can sneak out tonight and try a séance right on the spot where they used to execute people."

Mariana's black-rimmed eyes widened. "How are we supposed to sneak out?"

Celia lowered her chin, hunching forward as she spoke in a conspiratorial tone. "Apparently, one of the seniors paid an MIT freshman to disable the alarm system for a party. Mulligan doesn't even know about it yet. We can get out the front gate. We just have to get past Ms. Bouchard's room."

Mariana's jaw dropped open and closed again. She slapped both hands down on the table. "We have to do this."

Fiona shook her head. "I'm all for sneaking out, but if we're going to do it, we should do something worthwhile. Like a party."

Mariana scowled and continued prattling on about séances with Celia, while Fiona attended to her lunch with an enthusiasm found only in the very athletic.

When the bell rang, she positioned herself near Jack as she trudged out of the dining hall behind a stream of students. She tried to catch a glimpse of his shy blue eyes from beneath his mop of black hair. For a moment, she thought he smiled at her, and her cheeks burned red.

In Algebra, instead of working through word problems about driving speeds, she spent the class mentally rehearsing her conversation with Jack. Music was always a good conversation starter.

In Art, her last class of the day, she stared around the room at the students' crude imitations of impressionist paintings. By the end of class, Ms. Bouchard stood nearby, bent over Sully's desk to chat about his project. She'd given everyone too much time to read an article about the Fauvists, and now students hunched over their desks, whispering and texting.

The art teacher's smooth brown hair draped over her rainbow blouse. She had declared today Fun Colors Day, which was an improvement on last week's Sparkle Day. Ms. Bouchard lived for the opportunity to wear decorative clothing and jewelry. There were silky autumnal leaf shirts, pumpkin earrings for Halloween, and, demonstrating an unfortunate misunderstanding of local history, there was the feathered war bonnet for Thanksgiving. Somehow, with her statuesque body and shiny hair, she made all of these costumes and baubles appear seductive.

Fiona glanced at the clock again. After school, Jack sometimes lingered around the courtyard, scribbling in his notebook. That was the most likely place to find him.

She looked down at her papers, grabbing the oil pastels to sketch an approximation of her favorite poet's face: Lord Byron's large eyes, straight nose, and curling hair. She marked his eyes and skin with bright colors, like the Fauvists—crimson hair and green smudges under the eyes. She lined below his mouth with an electric blue, but couldn't quite get the curve of his lips right. She glanced at the clock again.

At last, the second hand rounded past the six. The bell rang, releasing her from her academic purgatory. The class heaved a collective sigh of relief.

"All right, class," Ms. Bouchard projected. "Finish the reading, if you haven't already. And draw something beautiful for me."

A wild giddiness rose in Fiona's stomach as she hurried out of classroom. While she walked through the halls and down the stairs, she unbuttoned the top of her shirt and rolled the top of her skirt to shorten it as she had seen Celia do.

A few piercing rays of light escaped from behind the clouds when she opened the large wooden doors leading to the courtyard. For a few seconds the sunlight blinded her, but her eyes adjusted as she searched for Jack. Melting snow seeped into her canvas shoes. With a sinking feeling, she realized that Jack was unlikely to be outside in this weather.

Then, she squinted in the sunlight and saw him standing in a corner of the brick walls, bent over a small notebook and covered in a light dusting of snow. He wore a gray woolen pea coat over his uniform. His rosy cheeks and full lips reminded her of a painting of Dionysus. She could picture him bare-chested and reclining on pillows, surrounded by grapes. She took a deep breath, plunged her hands into her pockets, and walked toward him. He looked up from his notebook. Fiona caught a playful half-smile as she approached.

Her voice caught in her throat she tried to think of something to say. "Hi, Jack."

"Hi. Fiona, is it?"

He knows my name. She smiled. "Yes."

She swallowed as he looked at her from beneath his long lashes.

Her toes numbed. What was she planning on saying—something about music? "What are you working on?"

"Just some drawings, though the snow is smudging them a bit. And a poem."

"A love poem?" *Why did I say that?*

"Not really. Why, do you like love poems?" He closed his notebook, stuffing it in his pocket.

"Well, I like Lord Byron. But he didn't get too schmaltzy. I mean, you can't be obsessed with love."

He held up his hand to lean against the brick wall. "Is that your theory? Love should be in moderation?"

"I mean, you need to stay your own person, right? You have to let the other person keep their identity or they're not interesting or worthwhile anymore. It's like when Germany planned to invade England, they wanted to keep the most impressive buildings intact, so they never bombed St. Paul's. It's no good taking over a city full of rubble." *Christ. What am I talking about?*

He smirked. "I see. So in your love metaphor, are you Hitler?"

"I don't..." She trailed off, biting her lip. She squinted up at him. "Do you like jazz?"

"Fiona!" A familiar, high-pitched voice sliced through their tête-à-tête.

She froze as Jack's attention shifted to somewhere behind her. "I think the Latin teacher is looking for you."

"Fiona Forzese!" Fiona's mother's voice grew louder. "You need to wear a hat in this weather."

Her eyes clamped shut. Opening them, she turned to see her mother looming closer, brandishing a woolen hat and scarf. Her mother's curly, strawberry blonde hair caught in the wind, dancing in the air like a lit match.

"Honestly, Fiona. I know you're at the age where you like talking to boys, but you need to cover up. It's January!"

"Mom!"

"*Salve*, Ms. Forzese," said Jack.

"*Salve, Ionannes.*" Ms. Forzese raised her hand in a Roman salute. Turning to her daughter she continued, "Fiona, why don't you ever wear this hat your grandmother knit for you?"

She placed the lumpy red hat, complete with pink pompoms, on Fiona's head and wrapped a bulky blue scarf around her neck. She started to move away, and then squinted as she scrutinized her daughter again.

"Have you rolled your skirt up?" she demanded.

Fiona turned to Jack. "Um, I've got to go."

She rushed past her mother, eager to escape the disaster before Jack saw the tears in her eyes.

8

Tobias

I t was dusk when Tobias stepped outside the school gates, and the setting sun's light pierced the clouds before disappearing below the horizon. Scattered snowflakes continued to fall. He hurried across the street. In the Common, blood-red lines marked some of the cleared paths. On the far side of the park, where abandoned temples stood in Maremount, elegant, castle-like buildings graced the hill. Their windows, orange-hued with electric lights, punctuated the wintry landscape. They looked like the type of places where Viscount Brad might attend a dinner party in one of his old children's books. As Tobias strode through the park toward the ravens, he looked out for the great elm. But where its jagged branches should have been easily visible, he saw instead a swirl of falling snow.

In Maremount, they were hanging people at the elm again, like the old days. He dug his hands into his pockets, looking at the ground as he walked. *What if Rawhed captured everyone after I flew away?* He'd seen what Rawhed's Harvesters could do to someone. Once, he'd seen John Ursin standing atop a tree trunk on the Maremount Neck. His head was covered in a black hood, his arms outstretched. The Harvesters used magic to ignite the surrounding air, so that if he moved even an inch, he would electrocute himself. John's body shook all over. By the time Tobias had run to gather members of his coven to fight alongside him, John was missing, only to turn up later as a mutilated corpse in the harbor.

He glanced at the murky clouds. Until he reunited with his friends, he wouldn't be able to talk to anyone here. Not *really* talk. He fiddled with the locket around his throat. He'd miss Eden's hands rubbing his neck when he worried. He'd miss his father's rambling stories of his youth. He'd even miss the early-morning squawking of Ottomie, his crow. He felt an overwhelming sense of isolation.

Outside the northern border of the Common, he quickened his pace toward the King's Chapel cemetery. The ravens were most likely to appear there. As he drew nearer, he saw that the black gates had closed.

Rows of of gravestones rose in uneven lines from the snowy ground, comforting in their irregularity. Everything else in Boston seemed to be made of straight lines. He gripped the gates' iron spikes, waiting for a messenger. For hundreds of years, ravens had traveled between Maremount and Boston, delivering news.

A group of ravens was called an unkindness, but they weren't unkind really. Just indifferent. Oswald and Eden transformed into meadowlarks, and the phrase "exaltation of larks" fit them better than "murder of crows" suited him. One medieval philosopher with a corvine familiar murdered a few monks, and suddenly all crows had a bad reputation.

A single raven fluttered from a maple tree. It landed on the gate between his hands, blinking its black eyes up at him.

"Hello, Contcont." Tobias addressed the raven by its formal name. "Can you tell me what happened to Oswald and Eden Larkin? The last time I saw them, Father was about to chant the traveling spell from the philosopher's guide."

The raven puffed its chest. "Burned, unfortunately."

A flash of pain gripped his stomach. "They burned? They're dead?"

"No, your friends are alive. The *philosopher's guide* burned. Your friends are merely stuck in Maremount."

His chest relaxed as he exhaled. "Thank the gods. What are they doing?"

"They're in hiding with your father, trying to fight Rawhed from the Tuckomock Forest."

"Who's winning?"

"No one." It puffed his feathers, shaking its head.

Tobias looked down at the ground, biting his lip. It was hard to think of what to say to a raven.

He glanced up again. "What can you tell me about Rawhed?"

The raven cocked its head, blinking at him before emitting an irritated croak. The ravens were reluctant to get on the wrong side of powerful leaders.

"Can you tell me what he looks like? The Tatters named him after a monster in a children's story. *Rawhead and the Bloody Bones*. Is he a real monster?" Tobias pictured Rawhed with an emaciated face and long, bloody fangs.

The raven blinked, opening his beak and closing it again soundlessly.

"Can you tell me what he's searching for? He's not just after the illegal covens—is he? He's looking for something else." Impatience crept into his voice. He knew the raven wouldn't answer. It was a messenger, not a spy.

It shook its body.

Tobias sighed. "Thank you."

With a twitch of its head, the messenger hopped along the fence, and then extended its wings to fly back toward the maple. That was it, then. He'd be stuck here on his own, perhaps for the rest of his life.

As far as he knew, Father had owned one of the few philosopher's guides that existed outside of the schools. With the book destroyed, no one could recite the spell for traveling between worlds. Tobias's link to Maremount had been severed.

9

Fiona

Fiona marched through the Common with tears stinging her eyes. Her friends didn't have to worry about embarrassing mothers who worked at the school, covering them in woolen pompoms and bulky hand-made scarves. Sure, Mom's employment there meant that she received discounted tuition, but her presence was stifling. The only thing worse would be if her mother *lived* at the school, like Ms. Bouchard.

The sky had darkened to a muddy gray. She needed to return before curfew, but she kept marching through the snowy park, only slowing her stride when she approached an old man who tottered through the snow with a cane. She'd always thought it disrespectful to walk too quickly past elderly people. It felt like showing off.

Few people lingered in the park today. Fiona tightened her scarf against the cold as she crossed Park Street, trudging past the church and the crimson-robed woman who always sermonized there.

"All must submit to the King of Terror! When we defy God, the world of the living becomes the world of the dead!"

Fiona trudged on, beyond the fading rants of the hoarse-voiced woman. As she neared King's Chapel Burying Ground, she saw someone without a winter coat leaning with his back against the gates, dark hair falling into his eyes. He stared at the ground. As she drew closer, she recognized Tobias.

"Hey!"

He lifted his chin, his dark eyes meeting hers. "Hello."

"You know, you're supposed to be back in your room at dusk."

"Oh?"

She shrugged. "You wouldn't know. It's your first day."

"Why are you out at this time then?" He stood up straight. "You don't look very happy."

She shook her head, looking down. "I've had an awful afternoon."

"What happened?"

She took a deep breath. "I was trying to talk to a guy I like, and it turned into a disaster." She wiggled her freezing toes in her shoes. She should've worn boots today.

"Oh. It probably wasn't as bad as you think."

"Trust me, it was. What about you? You don't look particularly happy either."

He shrugged, glancing toward the cemetery. "Just homesick already, I guess."

"For England?"

He nodded. "Right."

He wasn't giving many details away. "Aren't you cold without a coat?"

He gave a little laugh and nodded, his eyes glistening. "Yes. I'm cold."

As the Park Street Church bells pealed, she pulled off her chunky blue scarf, wrapping it around his neck. "There you go. All yours."

"Thanks." He glanced at her with a weak smile. "Should we go back to the school?"

"I guess." Her breath misted in front of her face. "But I don't really want to. How about some hot chocolate first?"

She led him across the street to the nearest coffee shop and bought a large cup for each of them. Heat from the paper cup warmed her hands as they tromped back toward the Common. Tobias was quiet, sipping his drink and looking at the snow.

"What's the hot chocolate like in England?"

He frowned. "Not this good. I don't think I've ever tasted anything so good."

They stepped into the park, where shrieking children pelted each other with snowballs.

Fiona peered over at Tobias. He had those cheekbones people described as *chiseled*. "What part of England are you from?"

He sipped his hot chocolate. "The west."

"Just 'the west'? Is there a city?"

He shook his head, frowning. "You know, it's not that interesting. How about I tell you a story as we walk back? Something I've been writing."

"You write?"

"When I have time."

"I happen to like English writers." Tobias was even more interesting that she'd initially thought.

She followed him on a path that diverted toward the right. The thrill of being out in the dark brought a smile to her lips, and giddiness rose in her stomach.

"Picture a place that looks like Boston." He looked into Fiona's eyes, gesturing with his paper cup. "There's a Common like this. Around it are crowded alleys that wind below people's windows. At night, the streets are lit with floating lanterns of foxfire."

They walked west through the darkening Common, past the snow-covered tennis courts. Fiona peered at him over her hot chocolate. This was an unexpected turn.

"In this place, ordinary people can't read, so there are painted signs on the taverns in blue and red and gold paint. There are symbols of ravens and stars, king's-heads and fire-breathing dragons."

"Why can't people read?"

"Well, the wealthy can read. In Maremount, the aristocrats practice magic, but for everyone else it's illegal. There are a few secret covens for poor people, but the King wants them disbanded."

Fiona wrinkled her forehead, glancing over at him. "This place is called Maremount?"

"Right. It's just imaginary."

They now stood at the edge of the park, as cars inched forward in gridlock along the icy street.

"You see these streets?" He looked down at the slushy pavement. "They were filled in with land from the nearby hills. In my story, these streets remain a bay, full of cod and lobster. There's water all around. There are crabs here, and sometimes at night there are flickering sparks on the waves. Those are the Nippexies—the water spirits. They're still here underground, I think."

"Maremount sounds lovely."

He kicked at an icy chunk of snow. "Well, except for the civil war."

"Civil war?"

He adjusted her scarf on his neck. "Just part of the story."

"Boston's not as beautiful as the place in your story, but

there's the garden in the summer, and you can see fish in the aquarium."

"The aquarium?"

"They've got a tank that you can walk under. You can see the fish from underneath. It's beautiful."

"That sounds nice."

"We should go with Mariana. She knows all the fish names."

"We should get back now, right?" He gazed at her with a hint of a smile. "I guess my story didn't really go anywhere. But it was nice to talk to someone."

"I guess we should get back." By now she could picture the sparkling bay he'd described and was loath to leave it for her dreary room.

Tobias started to walk toward the school, and she followed, glancing back at where the water spirits might be. She usually hated this time of year, when the trees looked like skeletons and her feet were always cold. But their stroll after curfew had refreshed her, and Celia's proposed adventure started to seem more appealing.

IO

Tobias

In the warm glow of his desk lamp, Alan sat on the floor wearing a large pair of red headphones. He held a sketchpad in his lap, absorbed in drawing pictures of sea monsters. Tobias had finished his homework an hour earlier. Unsure of what else to do, he lay against his pillows trying to read one of Alan's books: *The Golden Dragons of Llanwyon.*

He could usually lose himself in a good story. It hadn't been easy, though, learning his letters—an endeavor forbidden to the poor. As a child, he'd stayed up late with his father every night, reading by candlelight. What's more, he'd had to practice the dialect of the literate classes. Even Oswald and Eden didn't speak it; book words weren't the language of the Tatters in Crutched Square. But his father had taught him the language of wealth, of schools, of lavish dinners, and fictional heroes like Danny Marchese.

Though he'd learned how to read, the complicated genealogies at the start of Alan's book sapped his focus. He glanced out the window. Snow fell from branches in cloudy gusts that sparkled in the streetlights. Wind rattled the old windowpanes, and drafts seeped in through their cracks.

Oswald and Eden must be sheltering somewhere in the Tuckomock Forest now, among the few shabby houses in the wilderness. He pulled the blanket around his shoulders.

Alan looked up from his drawing, pulling off his headphones. "You never explained what happened at your old school. Why did you leave partway through the year?"

Tobias's eyebrows shot up. He didn't even know enough about schools to come up with a reasonable answer, but he found it worked best to stick as close to the truth as possible when he lied. "I was educated at home." *Is that something people do?*

Alan nodded slowly. "Homeschooled. With your mom?"

"My father."

"And it wasn't working out?"

"Exactly." He exhaled. It seemed like Alan knew what he was talking about. "You know how it is."

"I wouldn't last a week at home with my parents." Alan reclined against the base of his bed, folding his hands behind his head. "But what happened to all your stuff? You don't have any clothes or a computer or anything."

Tobias's jaw tightened, and he pulled his blanket closer around him. He and his coven had obviously overlooked a few things when they'd talked about blending in. "Everything was lost on the way."

"On the flight?"

"Right. The machine—the airplane lost it."

Alan stared. "You have to buy new clothes and everything?"

He looked toward the window. "I would, except the coins were lost." *That's not right.* He waved his hand. "Not coins. I mean, the money. The dollars. 'Coins' is English slang for money." With any luck, his classmates knew less about England than he did.

Alan eyed him quizzically. Still, there was always the distraction spell if he really needed it.

"Huh." Alan shifted the sketchpad off his lap and stood up. "I have an extra coat you can borrow. And my mom sent me some Christmas and Valentines Day underwear there's no way I'm wearing." He opened the top drawer of a dresser, rifling around until he pulled out two unopened packets of underwear. He tossed them to Tobias.

"Thanks, Alan." He held the packages in his lap. In one, cupids and hearts decorated the fabric, while the other featured an apple-cheeked old man with a white beard. At least this would save him from the awkward nightly ritual of washing a single pair of underwear in the bathroom sink and holding it under the electric dryer.

"And socks." Alan threw a package of red and white striped socks into his lap. "I read that girls like boxer briefs. Hang on." A buzzing noise interrupted their conversation, and Alan pulled a small, square device out of his back pocket. He stared down at the screen. "It's Fiona. She wants your number." He glanced at Tobias. "Do you have a phone?"

"Lost. By the airplane." He hugged his blankets. Apparently, Fiona had enjoyed his story.

A smile spread on Alan's face. "Sweet. Fiona says someone disabled the alarms on the front gate." He glanced at Tobias. "She, Celia and Mariana want us to sneak out with them for a séance. Are you in?"

"Someone knows how to conduct a séance?"

"Celia does, apparently." Alan returned to the floor, crossing his legs. "Anyway it's not real, it's just for the hell of it, like Ouija boards. We're supposed to meet them at the corner of Boylston and Tremont at midnight. What do you think?"

What did he have to lose? There were no bone wardens here to tear him to pieces for practicing casting spells; no king to hang him in the square. Sure, magic always created *some* danger. A spell's aura could summon spirits, and not always the nice kind. Magic could lure a wrathful mattinitock wearing a human-skin cape, or one hungry for possession of a living body. *Demons*, they called them in Boston.

But the risk of encountering a mattinitock was very small, and a Ragman like Tobias didn't hide in his bed worrying about demons. And anyway, he wasn't going to let people dredge up spirits without him.

He smiled. "I'm in."

"Nice. We just have to sneak past Mr. Grunshaw, plus Mulligan's room by the entrance."

Tobias stretched his arms over his head. "Who's Mr. Grunshaw?"

"Math teacher. Sweats a lot. Always has food in his beard. Sleeps in a room at the end of the hall."

It was ten minutes before midnight when Alan pulled his coat from the closet, and a yellow raincoat for Tobias. Alan flicked off the lights and pulled open the door, leading Tobias down the hallway. The floor creaked a few paces before Mr. Grunshaw's door, and Alan froze, peering back at Tobias with a grimace. The Math teacher's rhythmic snoring filtered through the door.

They tiptoed on, turning into the central hall and peering out its tall windows into the dark courtyard. They crept into the stairwell. Tobias bit his thumbnail as they snuck down the rickety stairs, half regretting his decision already. If Mulligan expelled the others, they still had homes, but he'd be left to wander in the streets, earless from frostbite and begging for food.

Then again, he was willing to risk a bit of danger to observe a séance. He and Oswald had once spent an evening crawling through the sewers to spy on a medium in the Throcknell fortress, though, to Tobias's disappointment, the sewers merely led them into a rat-filled cistern below the dungeons. He never saw the spirit of the great alchemist John Dee materialize before the philosophers.

At the bottom of the stairs, the vestibule was almost completely dark. Alan turned to Tobias, mouthing the words, "Are you good?" He held his thumb up, waiting for confirmation. When Tobias nodded, Alan stepped backward into the marble bust of Richard Mather. Tobias's chest tightened as Richard's torso wobbled on the wooden base, and a rolling noise filled the vestibule. Alan's hands shot up, steadying it. They stood only a few feet from Mulligan's room. *Did he hear?* In the silence, Alan's breath sounded deafening, as if it echoed off the walls.

After a minute, when nothing stirred behind Mulligan's door, Alan tiptoed toward the front door. He looked back at Tobias, biting his lip, and cracked the door open. A cold blast of air stung Tobias's face.

As he followed Alan on the snowy path through the courtyard, he was grateful for the striped socks warming his feet and for Fiona's bulky scarf under the raincoat. He glanced back at the school building, relieved that no lights shone from the windows. He stuffed his hands in the pockets, exhaling a shivering breath.

Within the high brick wall that surrounded the school, a wrought-iron gate blocked their exit. If the alarm was going to sound, it would happen here. Alan took a deep breath, his gloved hands hovering in the air as if casting a spell while he built up the resolve to open the gate. He grasped an iron bar, gently pulling the gate inward. As it edged open, they heard only a creaking sound. They hurried through to the other side, letting the gate click shut behind.

The girls waited for them at the corner of the Common wearing heavy coats and scarves, steam rising from their faces. They huddled on the sidewalk before a squat stone building that looked like a mausoleum, only with doors that swung open as people passed through.

Fiona waved as they approached. "You made it," she smiled.

Mariana squinted at Tobias. "You're wearing a raincoat."

"Airline lost his luggage." Alan swung his arms, trying to stay warm. "This is awesome, by the way."

"It is, but I'm freezing." Mariana jumped up and down.

"Let's get going then." Celia beckoned them into the park with a white-gloved hand, her blond hair streaming from a fuzzy white cap.

They plodded after her on one of the ancient, crooked cow-paths that meandered into the center of the park. On the path, the snow was only a few inches deep. The trail followed the same course as one in Maremount, unchanged over the years. Lined with bare maple and oak trees, it led them through the flat terrain of the Common.

Tall, black streetlamps lit the path with gauzy circles of light. In the distance, warmly lit buildings stood against a dark sky. Almost no one else was in the park in this weather. In fact, Tobias could only see one person tottering away from them, a wine bottle swinging in his hand.

He glanced at Celia. "How did you learn to call on the spirits of the dead?"

"I have a book on it. I've been trying to raise spirits forever. It hasn't worked really, except once I think Zelda Fitzgerald might have knocked over my iced tea. Or it might have been Mariana."

Fiona sidled up to his left. "We had a séance for Kurt Cobain that didn't work. We tried using an old ripped flannel to draw his spirit."

"And Courtney Love didn't work either." Celia pulled her scarf tighter around her. "But it turned out, she's not dead."

"Whose spirit are we calling up tonight?" Tobias scrunched his hands up in his pockets. *Shame Alan's mother didn't burdened him with any embarrassing gloves.*

"I thought we should call up the spirit of someone who was executed in the park," said Celia. "A woman named Ann Hibbins was hanged for witchcraft forty years before the Salem Witch Trials."

"They used to call it the Witching Elm." The air froze in front of Fiona's mouth. "Then it was rebranded as the Liberty Tree."

To their left stood a circular stone building with elegant columns like an outdoor temple.

"The Witching Elm," Tobias repeated, tucking his chin into Fiona's wooly scarf.

Fiona trudged closer to him. "During the Salem witch trials, Cotton Mather said Ann Hibbins had cursed Massachusetts, and that's why witches plagued Salem."

Tobias shivered as a gust of wind blew snow into his face. His pants were now damp and cold up to his knees. As they waded through the snow, their footprints wove unsteady patterns behind them.

Fiona turned to Tobias, looking him over. "How's the scarf treating you?"

He smiled. "It's wonderful. I don't know why you didn't hang on to it."

"You needed it more than I did. I think the Witching Elm was somewhere around here."

"It was just over there." Tobias pointed to a snowy corner of land near the partially plowed paths. The elm site rested at the base of a small incline, gently rolling up toward Beacon Hill. Through bare branches, the top of the State House was visible. Snow dusted its gold dome, lending it the appearance of an iced butter cake.

Celia turned to Tobias, wrinkling her nose. "How do you know that's the spot?"

He shrugged. "I looked at a map."

"Hmm." Celia pivoted to lead everyone into the unsullied snow off the path. It was over a foot deep.

When they stood together, shivering in the drifts, Celia held out her hands to either side. "Everyone get in a circle."

They did as they were told. In the heart of the park, the only noise was the muffled sound of distant traffic. Pulling some tea candles from her pockets, Celia asked everyone to hold hands. She made several attempts to light them, but the wind snuffed them out.

"Can we move this along?" Mariana rubbed her gloved hands together. "I'm freezing."

Celia stood again. "Fine." She grasped Tobias's hand on one side and Fiona's on the other. She tilted her face up to the night sky and began to lead the group in a chant: "Ann Hibbins—we call on you in the spirit plane."

With chattering teeth, they chanted the words after her. Tobias tucked his chin into his chest, peering around. Celia didn't give him a strong impression of knowing what she was doing. He should have stayed in his warm room with the heavy blankets. Shame he hadn't learned more Angelic. All he could call to mind from the magical language were a few minor spells, the kind with subtler auras.

Celia raised her voice. "Ann Hibbins—speak to us and move among us. Answer our questions and tell us our fates."

Snow drifted through the lamplight. *What's the formula for auras?* He was never good at the alchemical sciences. *It was something about the power of one aura multiplied by the other aura, and then distance—*

A breeze picked up around them, spraying clouds of snow into the air, and a tingling sensation caressed his skin. Nearby, the electric lights flickered and dimmed. *Is it actually working?*

While the others chanted with their eyes closed, Tobias searched his mind for the Angelic words. He didn't know any full necromancy spells, but he could remember the words for spirit and appear. He whispered them under his breath. Perhaps together, as a coven, they could be as powerful as the great philosophers of Sortellian College. As he spoke, the frigid wind intensified. His neck hairs stood on end.

"Ann Hibbins—we call on you," chanted the others in unison.

The park lights flickered, now burning brighter. The wind whipped up eddies of snow, swirling into a vortex that filled the center of the circle. As Tobias stood transfixed by the whorl of flakes, a gap appeared in the center. In the squall, a human silhouette emerged. It was as deep and dark as the entrance to a cave. Tobias's muscles froze. Silence fell. In the snowless space, a faint image of a woman appeared, her gaunt face downcast. She wore a cap over snarled gray hair and a baggy black gown with a large white collar. When she looked up, her dark eyes shone.

Celia's jaw dropped. She spoke in quavering voice: "Ann Hibbins, thank you for coming."

The somber spirit remained motionless in the maelstrom.

"Ann Hibbins, we have questions for you."

Tobias stood stunned. He hadn't actually expected this to work.

"Maybe we should—" Fiona stammered, but the specter interrupted her, speaking in a deep voice.

We wait beneath corrupted frozen ground.
Unconsecrated, tangled roots enshroud
our crumpled necks and long-smothered embers,
where the hours fly, and death is remembered.

In nameless hollows, Philip's men await.
The unlamented—

The apparition's eyes bulged as she choked out the last words, and strangling noises filled the air. A thick tongue lolled out of her mouth. Her face withered to the color of a rotten plum before she disappeared. Before anyone had the chance to speak, another form emerged: an elongated human figure, its body pale as bone. Ribs protruded from its chest, the skin between them as taut as a rawhide drum. Instead of a nose, a ragged, triangular hole marred the center of its face. Tobias's breath left his lungs as a spark of recognition ignited in the back of his mind.

He looked into the creature's cavernous eyes. As they stood mesmerized, antlers sprouted from its head.

Fiona whispered, almost inaudibly, "What..."

The spirit pointed a skeletal finger toward Tobias. Its mouth opened to reveal a dark hole, and it spoke garbled words in a raspy growl, swinging its head from side to side. Its maw gaped open further, emitting a piercing howl. Tobias clamped his hands over his ears and fell to the ground. As he lay in the snow, a cold, gnawing dread rose and filled his chest. At last, the noise subsided.

His face half-sunk in the snow, he uncovered his ears. The spirits were gone, and the snow fell gently again. He stood up, looking around. Mariana and Fiona huddled together with Alan, while Celia stood gaping.

"What the hell *was* that?" Mariana shrieked. "Did we summon a demon?"

Fiona clung to Mariana and spoke with labored breaths. "I think we did. I didn't think they were—I thought it was all—"

Celia's voice was barely a whisper. "We should go."

She ran. The rest followed, fighting their way through the heavy snow. Tobias's arms flailed as he ran after them. He could hear the others' panicked panting as they scrambled forward, their arms swinging into each other.

When their feet made contact with the plowed sidewalk along Tremont Street, they picked up speed, hurtling toward Mather Academy in an avalanche of feet, knees, and elbows. Fiona sprinted ahead across Boylston Street, narrowly missing a car. As she approached the school, she rushed through the gate and held it open for the others while they darted through.

With shaking hands, Mariana tried to lock it behind her. "There's no lock."

"There's just the alarm that someone disabled," said Alan.

Mariana gripped his arm. "Well, I'm not going to my room by myself."

"Then come to my room." He waved her forward. "But let's get the hell inside."

One by one, they snuck across the courtyard and through the large oak door. They tiptoed up the stairwell and through hallways to Alan and Tobias's room at the end of the boys' wing. Once inside, Alan turned on a desk lamp. Fiona and Mariana rushed to the bay window, checking to see if anything had followed them.

Tobias flopped backward on his bed, catching his breath, while Celia and Alan threw themselves across Alan's bed, gasping.

"There's something out there," Mariana said between heavy breaths. "Oh, it's a student, I think. I guess we're not the only ones who knew about the alarms."

"What the hell was that?" Celia demanded from Alan's bed.

Alan sat up, hissing, "We need to be quiet. Grunshaw's going to hear us if everyone's talking at full volume."

Fiona and Mariana joined Tobias on his bed, slumping against the wall in a daze. For a minute, no one spoke.

Celia broke the silence, pushing herself up on her elbows to stare at Tobias from Alan's bed. "The demon pointed at you. Why did it point at you?"

"I don't know. I've dabbled in the magical arts, but I've never called up a spirit before." He unwrapped Fiona's scarf.

"What do you mean, magical arts?" Fiona folded her arms. "Like séances and tarot reading?"

"Right."

Alan rose, pacing in the small space between the beds. "Did you guys see the antlers?"

They nodded.

"There were two spirits, right?" Alan gripped the back of a chair, staring at the floor. "Who were we trying to call up?"

"Ann Hibbins," said Mariana. "She was executed in Boston Common for witchcraft."

"Any idea what she said?" asked Alan.

"Yeah." Fiona straightened. "'We wait beneath...' Hang on." She closed her eyes, taking a deep breath. "'We wait beneath corrupted icy ground... Unconsecrated tangled roots... enshroud crumpled necks and long-smothered embers... and hours fly, and death is remembered... In nameless caverns someone's men await.'" She held up her index finger. "'*Philip's* men await... the unlamented...'" She opened her eyes. "And that's when the choking started."

"Good memory." Alan smiled weakly, returning to his seat on his bed. "Who is *Philip*, though?"

Tobias ran the tips of his fingers along his jaw, staring at the floor. "Maybe King Philip."

"Oh—Metacomet," Alan murmured.

Mariana folded Tobias's blanket over her legs. "What was he King of?"

Tobias stood, pulling off Alan's raincoat. "He was a Wampanoag leader in the 17th century. The English called him Philip." He opened the closet, pulling out a hanger and tucking it into the coat. "His father helped the pilgrims survive in the 1620s. But during Philip's reign, the English provoked a war. Thousands of people died." He closed the closet door and returned to his bed, sitting cross-legged.

Celia crossed the room toward him and sat on the floor, plucking off her white gloves and resting her hand on his knee. "Can we get back to how you dabbled in the magical arts?"

"Oh my God. You have to teach us." Fiona's voice rose in pitch, her cheeks reddening. "I didn't know demons were real. But they are. And they're trying to kill us!"

"Keep your voice down," Mariana scolded. She turned to Tobias. Her black eye make up was smudged from the snow. "Will you teach us?"

The girls looked at Tobias with pleading expressions, and their three pretty faces made a compelling case. But it wasn't a demon they had summoned, and no spirits lurked in the Boston streets—at least, no more than usual. The apparition they'd encountered had been sent as a warning. He wasn't about to drag his new friends into a dangerous world of magic without their full understanding. It would be like bringing lambs to a wolf festival.

"I'm sorry. I don't really know much about it." He shook his head. In a way, it was true. Without a philosopher's guide to read from, there wasn't much he could teach them.

Celia pouted, turning to her friends to talk about Ann Hibbins's withered face.

As he lay back against his pillows, Tobias stared past the girls into the darkness outside, pulling the blanket over his legs. It seemed that someone from Maremount was watching his use of magic, even here.

I I

Tobias

Tobias waited for Alan on a faux-leather gym bench. It had been a week since the séance—a week of keeping his head tucked into books while he thought about Maremount: swimming in the bay with Eden, the summer quahog festival, and Father's spiced apple cakes.

While he stretched his arms, he looked forward to physical exertion. It had been only nine days since his arrival, and already his muscles had started to soften. Normally he'd spend a few hours each day practicing with pikes in single combat matches. He couldn't let his body atrophy as he stuffed his face with pancakes every morning. Still, he was unfamiliar with most of the equipment. On one side of the room, machines with wheels and levers towered over the glistening blue floor mats. On the other side, rows of shelves with dumbbells stood against a mirror.

A towel over his shoulder, Alan strode in, smiling. "You're here!"

Tobias rose, stretching an arm behind his back. "I'm here. Not sure what to do with most of this equipment, though."

Alan nodded toward the dumbbells. "You could always

start with the free weights."

"Good idea." Tobias walked over to the rack, picking up twenty-pound weights from the top shelf. "How often do you come here?"

"Most days. I have to keep up with it. I used to get bullied before I started working out." Alan jumped on a machine and eased into a jog. With a few beeps, he increased his speed, and the machine's whirring grew louder. "Are we gonna go forward with this band? We need to get you a lute."

Standing near the mirror, Tobias curled the weight into his arm. "Just so you know, I'm not very good."

"Doesn't matter. I'm still working on a name. Maybe we could call ourselves the Necromantic Fools."

Tobias cocked his head. "I guess that's appropriate."

"At my last gig, there were only two people." Alan spoke through labored breaths. "But now we've got the girls hanging out with us. Ever since—you know. I bet they'd come to our show." He wiped sweat off his forehead with the back of his hand.

Before Tobias could reply, Sully sauntered in with a friend. In contrast to Sully's square, chiseled face, his friend's face was round—almost cherubic. The boy's blond curls only enhanced the angelic impression.

Rubbing at the back of his broad neck, Sully threw his towel over the weight rack. He smiled, clapping his hands together and rubbing them. "Oh good, it's the affirmative action crew." A picture of innocence, he widened his blue eyes at Alan. "Did you earn your spot on that treadmill, or did someone give it to you because they felt bad for you?"

The cherub giggled, walking toward another machine. "You can't *say* that stuff in public, dude." He turned to Alan. "He doesn't mean anything by it. He's been hit in the head too many times in football."

Sully stood a few feet away from Tobias, near the rack of weights. He held up an elbow behind his head, pulling on it with his other hand. "What? I'm not racist, Connor. I love Asian girls." He smirked. "They're hot, *and* they can do your math homework for you."

Connor gave an embarrassed laugh. "Tone it down, man."

With a beep, Alan stopped his machine. With beads of sweat trickling down his face, he gripped the bars. He turned, glaring at Sully.

Sully's sneering tone had made Tobias's jaw clench. He put down his weight and stood beside the blue-eyed football player, looking him over. He was over six feet tall and muscular, though not any bigger than Alan. And he was probably too stupid to know how to fight.

Ignoring Tobias, Sully grinned at Alan. "Seriously though, I need some help with math. You got a sister you can lend me?" He straightened, holding his palms out in a welcoming gesture. "I'll take your mom, too. I'm not picky. Just don't tell Munroe." He winked.

Alan stepped off the treadmill, striding toward Sully who stepped backward, laughing and holding up his hands.

"What, you can't take a joke? Oh crap, do you know judo?" He backed up, grinning. "My bad. What is it? Jiu-jitsu?" As Alan pressed in on him, he took another step back, knocking into the weight rack. Losing his balance, Sully toppled backward into the mirror, arms over his head. Weights rolled from the rack, thudding to the floor.

With a reddening face, Sully sprawled over clanging dumbbells. His lips pressed into an angry line, and he breathed hard through his nose. His flared nostrils reminded Tobias of an enraged bull as he pushed himself up from the rack. "What the hell?" He stepped toward Alan, pushing him hard.

Alan returned the shove, knocking him into the rack a second time, but this time he remained upright. The bull gnashed his teeth and swung at Alan, smashing his jaw. Dazed with the blow, Alan stumbled back, his eyes glazed.

Red-faced, the bull shouted, "Do *not* mess with me!"

Tobias stepped in front of him, blocking Sully's path before he struck Alan again, but Sully grit his teeth and shoved him. Instinctively, Tobias swung for his nose. He landed the punch, and Sully stumbled back, bringing his hand to his face. He stared for a moment at the blood trickling down his hand, then lunged for Tobias, knocking him to the floor.

A flash of pain shot through Tobias's skull as Sully punched him in the temple, but then something tore Sully away.

Gripping his throbbing head, Tobias rose. Alan pinned Sully's arms behind his back.

The cherub hovered by them now, hands outstretched. "Okay, guys. Everyone just relax."

Restrained, Sully's face turned a deeper shade of red. Connor was right. If they didn't calm down, someone would end up seriously hurt.

Spittle flew from Sully's mouth as he struggled to free himself. He shouted, "You're *dead*, you swarthy fu—"

Tobias stepped forward, grabbing on to Sully's reddened jaw, whispering a distraction spell into his ear. The bull's breathing shallowed, his chest rising and falling more slowly. Tobias stepped back, watching as Sully opened his mouth and closed it again, shoulders relaxing. Sully's attention drifted to the rowing machines.

"Okay?" Alan released his arms.

Sully glanced at Connor before stumbling out of the gym.

Connor stared after his friend. He turned to Tobias,

narrowing his eyes. "What did you *say* to him?"

Catching his breath, Tobias shrugged, a hand over his aching forehead. "I just told him he needed to calm down."

Connor nodded slowly. "Huh." He grabbed his towel and marched out.

Alan ran the back of his hand over his sweating forehead. "*Dabbled in magic*, was it?"

Tobias swallowed. Had he been hit too hard in the head? Perhaps his spell-casting hadn't been as subtle as he'd intended.

12

Fiona

Fiona blinked at the schools of sea creatures floating in the glass tank above them. With Tobias in tow, she and Mariana had trekked down Milk Street to the aquarium. As they gazed at colorful fish and turtles, Tobias wanted to know the name of each creature. With a chipped black fingernail, Mariana pointed out the angelfish, a blacktip reef shark, and a small clownfish hiding in a sea anemone.

Tobias stared up at a large green sea turtle as it drifted through the water. "There's a legend that turtles are heralds between humans and water spirits. They straddle the worlds of water and land, the living and the dead."

Mariana spun in a circle as she looked up at the animals swimming overhead. "That's so cool. And did you know turtles are more closely related to birds than to lizards?" She stopped twirling to glance at Tobias. "At least, that's what I read on a science blog."

"That makes sense. Birds are messengers, too."

During the frigid walk back to Mather Academy, Mariana thrilled Tobias with descriptions of all manner of species: arctic foxes, scarlet macaws, and Komodo dragons that could cripple a man by severing his Achilles tendon.

As they approached the iron school gates, Fiona couldn't help but recall their frantic run through Boston's streets and the skeletal, hollow-eyed demon.

She hugged her arms around herself as they neared the school's wooden entrance. "Tobias." She turned to look into his deep brown eyes. "You said you dabbled in magic. You said you don't know a lot about it. But let me ask you one thing. Are we safe? Nothing's coming for us?"

He spoke softly, leaning toward her. "Nothing's coming for you. I think someone just wanted to scare us."

She exhaled. "Thanks." She opened the front door, greeted by a gust of warm air in the vestibule.

At the top of the stairs, they said their goodbyes, and the girls veered off toward their wing.

While they approached Fiona's door, Sadie sauntered toward them from the other direction. A smatter of freckles crossed her pert nose, and blond curls bounced over her shoulder as she walked. Fiona avoided eye contact. Sadie had a habit of launching into diatribes about her shin splints and rambling deliberations over breakfast choices. As Fiona opened her door, Sadie pressed her hand against the doorframe. Fiona's heart sank.

"Hey, guys!" Sadie smiled.

"Hi, Sadie," they mumbled.

"Do you know that new kid from England? I saw you talking to him the other day."

"Yeah, I know him. Tobias." Fiona pushed her door open further, edging into her room. She took off her coat, hoping to hurry things along.

Sadie shifted closer, threatening to enter. She spoke in a low voice, her eyebrows moving up and down. "Well, I heard that Tobias was in the gym using free weights, and he punched Sully in the face. He broke his nose." She crinkled her nose. "Do you think Sully's okay?"

"Tobias didn't mention that." Stepping further into the room, Mariana glanced at Fiona.

"So you don't know what his deal is?" Sadie gripped either side of the doorframe. "Not to be rude, but does he have, like, a mental problem?"

"Sully probably started it." Fiona hoped that would end the conversation.

"Yeah." Sadie nodded solemnly. "You're probably right." She turned to Mariana. "Tell your brother I said hi. He's been helping me get up the stairs because of my splints. I might also ask Jack. My shins are like—"

Fiona cleared her throat, inching the door shut. "You know, I would love to hear about that, but we have so much homework."

Mariana nodded eagerly. "So much."

"Okay, well, I'll catch you up later!" Sadie waved as Fiona closed the door.

Mariana plopped down on Celia's bed. "Wow. Tobias punched Sully? He didn't say anything about that."

Fiona folded her arms. "I'm convinced he knows more than he's letting on about magic."

"What makes you say that?"

Fiona stepped over a pile of clothes by her bed. "He described a story he's writing when I hung out with him in the park, something about an imaginary place with magic. But what if it's not a story? What if it's real?"

"What was it called?"

"I'll tell you, Mariana, but you can't tell anyone. Not even Celia for now. He didn't *say* it was a secret, but it sort of seemed like a secret. Promise?"

"You know I can keep a secret. I never told anyone you pretended to be a robot."

Fiona blushed. In sixth grade, she'd tried to impress a boy named Kieron by dropping metal nuts and bolts around his chair, hoping to convince him she was a cyborg. "Tobias told me about a place called Maremount, where they have sorcerers. He said it was like Boston—like another dimension of Boston where most people can't read, because if everyone practiced alchemy, it would screw up the inflation rate of gold."

"No way."

"The aristocrats learn magic in the schools, but the peasants aren't allowed, so they do it in secret. And there's a civil war."

"Where's it supposed to be?"

"I think it's like—another plane. But it's connected to Boston somehow."

Mariana gripped the edge of Celia's bed, eying her intensely. "We need to look this up." She sprung up, crossing to the door. "Come with me to the library."

The old Caldwell Library constituted the entire second floor under the dorm rooms. It was named after a Mather student who'd died in the Great Molasses Flood of 1919. Ernest Caldwell's mother had donated money to the school for a restoration of the library, under the strict provision that molasses could never be served in the dining hall. As they passed a bust of the Caldwell boy near the entrance, Mariana's brother Lucas rounded the corner.

"Hey, *irmãzinha*."

"What are you doing here?" asked Mariana. "You don't do homework."

"How could you say such a thing? You know I love sitting around reading about birds and dinosaurs. Oh no wait, that's you."

Mariana rolled her eyes.

He turned to Fiona, a playful smile on his lips. "Your hair is kind of cool and wild."

Mariana groaned. "Would you *please* stop flirting with my friends?"

He blinked his large brown eyes. "Speaking of which, I'm supposed to meet Celia now. You don't mind if I hang out with her, do you?"

"Whatever." Mariana looked toward the ceiling.

"Cool. See you two." Grinning, Lucas bounded past them up the stairs.

"New boyfriend. That explains why Celia's been busy all week," said Fiona as they entered the library. "Kind of awkward that it's your brother."

Long desks with lamps lined the center of the room, and painted ceilings arched over two levels of books, connected by spiral staircases. They found a quiet alcove below the pallid, oil-painted face of Sophronia Hastings, a patron of the school.

Fiona glanced around at endless rows of books that filled two wings and the central hall. "I don't know where to start."

"I'll look online." Mariana pulled her laptop from her shoulder bag. "You could look at the card catalogue."

Fiona bit her lower lip as she ambled over to the library's ancient, hand-written card catalogues, trying to remember how the library was organized. The Caldwell Library's unique cataloguing system had remained unchanged since the early Victorian era. After fumbling through the drawers, she found a *Legends of New England* title in the "Folklore" cards.

She closed the drawer, and passed through rows of oak bookshelves until she arrived at the end of the eastern wing. Tall, arched widows looked out toward the Common. On the right wall, a six-foot memorial plaque listed the names of Mather alumni who'd fought in American wars, while on the ceiling high above, painted gold stars and silver moons glimmered in a sea of dark blue.

On the left, a brass staircase led to the folklore section. She climbed the stairs and scanned the titles. An amber glow from ceiling lights illuminated the books' spines. She moved past a few books about hauntings and a row about witchcraft before she spied her title. A death's-head engraving adorned the slim gray volume.

Skimming the back cover, she found a listing of the topics covered:

- *European Traditions*
- *Indigenous Lore*
- *Salem's Legacy*
- *The Great Elm*
- *Merrymount*

Clutching the book, she thumped down the stairs and rushed back toward the central hall.

"Mariana!" she called out as she approached the alcove. "I found something."

Mariana looked up from her computer. "Me too! What have you got?"

Fiona pulled out a chair to sit across from her friend. She opened to the index, skimming for the word *Merrymount*. She paged through to the chapter.

"What does it say?" Mariana peered over the book, trying to read upside down.

"Hang on... Okay, so this says Merrymount started as a Native town. Then an English guy named Thomas Morton began colonizing. He renamed it Mare-mount. Now it's a neighborhood in Quincy..." She looked up. "Just south of Boston." Fiona resumed skimming. "The Mare-mount colonists mixed with Natives. They had pagan ceremonies together. Like the Maypole festival."

"They sound way more fun than the Puritans."

Fiona skipped to the end. "Then the Puritans got more powerful, and after ten years they destroyed the whole colony. Jerks." She closed the book. "What did you find?"

Mariana hunched over her laptop. "There's a Ph.D. student named Thomas Malcolm who studies these legends. He sounds cool. Here's his bio: 'Thomas Malcolm grew up in both South London and Jamaica, where he developed an interest in folklore. Since completing his bachelor's degree at Queen Mary in London in 2010, he has researched folklore and mythology at the University of Massachusetts in Boston.'"

"Does it say anything more?"

"He has a website." She clicked a link. "He's cute." She swiveled the laptop to face Fiona. At the top of the screen was a photo of a young man with a goatee, his brown eyes framed by thick-rimmed glasses. His dark skin was striking against his crisp white shirt. She turned her laptop to face her again.

"He *is* cute, but what does it say about his research?"

Mariana squinted, clicking another link. "On top of the legit history, he describes a legend that the Maremount Colony was made up of English sorcerers. They shared magic with the Natives. Over time, they tried to blend in when the Puritans got more powerful. After the Salem Witch Trials, they wanted their own colony again."

"This is awesome." Fiona's eyes went wide. "What else does he say?"

"The sorcerers created their own land with magic in the late 1600s. It was just like Boston, but limited to English and

Algonquian sorcerers. It was called the Great Schism. They've been isolated for over 300 years."

"Is that it?"

Mariana scrolled down. "Then it's mostly accounts of people who claim to have been there."

Fiona slapped her hand on the table. "We need to find Thomas Malcolm."

At breakfast the next morning, Fiona found Mariana sitting with the guys, grilling them for details about their confrontation in the gym.

"You should have seen how it ended." Alan glanced at Tobias. "He calmed Sully down with his voice."

Fiona sat down at the long wooden table with her tray of pancakes and stared out at the dining hall. Something seemed off today. Two boys she recognized from the football team sat with their heads in their hands at a nearby table; other students huddled in groups, wiping tears from their eyes.

Fiona frowned. "Guys, I think something's going on."

Her friends' conversation subsided, and they glanced around the hall. Sadie approached, red-eyed. She stopped directly across from Fiona, propping both hands on the edge of the table. "Did you guys hear what happened?"

Fiona shook her head. "What's going on?"

Sadie shook her head. "I can't believe it. He was such a good athlete." She sobbed, covering her face.

Fiona held out her hand, gently touching Sadie's arm. "Who? Who was a good athlete?"

"Sully was found dead this morning." She pulled her hands from her pink and blotchy face, wiping her nose across the back of her hand.

Tobias's color drained.

Alan swallowed. "Do you know how it happened?"

"Someone said there was an empty bottle of vodka on the floor, and it was alcohol poisoning. But Munroe saw the body and totally flipped out. She thinks he was cursed. She said his skin was, like—*mummified*." She sniffled, turning to Tobias. "Oh, I'm sure it's nothing to do with your fight. At least, I don't think so."

Fiona's stomach dropped. What if it *was* a curse? And what if the séance had unleashed it?

13

Thomas

An icy breeze from Dorchester Bay picked up the tobacco from Thomas's unrolled cigarette, scattering it across the harborwalk. He sighed and turned his back to the wind as he pulled another lump of tobacco out of his pouch. He'd just finished a three-hour lecture about African-American folklore, and he desperately needed nicotine. Of course he shouldn't smoke, but he could always offset the lung damage with some speed bag work at his boxing gym later.

As he rolled and lit his cigarette, he looked up to see two uniformed schoolgirls marching quickly across the courtyard. His years of living around London hooligans had bestowed in him a habit of avoiding teenagers at all costs, as though at any moment they might scream "pedo" in his face, or smash a glass bottle over his head for no reason. He'd just turned to leave for the buses when one of the girls called to him.

"Professor Malcolm!" yelled the one with a mane of brown curls.

He started as they marched directly in front of him.

"I'm Fiona. This is my—*associate*, Mariana."

"Nice to meet you. I'm not a professor yet, though." He glanced around for the quickest escape route.

"We have some questions about your research," added the goth one—Mariana.

"My research? Sorry, but—who are you?"

"We're students," said Mariana.

"Here? At UMass?"

The girls looked at each other.

"We're from Mather Academy," said Fiona finally.

"Ah." He nodded slowly. "Are you working on a project? It's a bit cold out. Maybe we can discuss this over email?"

Fiona knitted her brows. He had the feeling that he wouldn't escape this encounter easily. His experience with graduates of posh boarding schools had led him to believe that these privileged kids generally got what they wanted. A bottle to the head no longer seemed like such a terrible alternative.

"It's very important that we speak now." Fiona crossed her arms. "People could be in danger."

"We can walk you to your car." Mariana smiled hopefully.

"I take the bus."

"Great." Mariana rubbed gloved hands together. "We'll ride with you."

"You know, people might think it's a bit weird for a grown man to hang around teenage girls," he ventured as they plodded over the snowy walkway.

"Why?" Mariana gave him a perplexed look.

"Never mind. What's going on, then?"

Fiona took a deep breath. "We have reason to believe that Maremount isn't just a legend. It's a real place. We might know someone from there, and we might've dredged up some kind of curse by messing with magic."

Thomas looked sideways at the girls as he walked, taking a long drag of his cigarette. "I promise you, Maremount is just a rumor." He blew smoke away from them.

"At one point, the danger of smoking was just a rumor." Mariana peered over at him, black hair hanging in her eyes.

"Yeah, thanks for the reminder. I mean, there's no evidence that Maremount is a real place. It's just a folk story, like Avalon or Atlantis."

Fiona turned and blocked Thomas's path, staring into his eyes. "Magic is real. We summoned the spirit of the accused witch Ann Hibbins. She appeared and recited a poem about King Philip, and then she turned into a demon. And then someone at our school died. Possibly from a curse."

"That sounds like quite an adventure." He wondered if they'd been sampling hallucinogens. And yet... "Hang on, you said a poem about King Philip?"

Metacomet was the leader who'd first sparked Thomas's interest in New England. Family legends tied his own ancestors to the King—from New England, to slavery in Bermuda, to Jamaica, to Britain. And here he was, back in New England.

Fiona closed her eyes. "The ghost said, 'In nameless chasms Philip's men await—the unlamented...'"

"And then it was cut off by choking sounds. When she disappeared, a demon showed up."

He took another drag on his cigarette. "All right, come back to the library with me for a minute. I've been researching King Philip legends." He turned back to the school, tossing his cigarette in a snowy ashcan on the way. The girls followed.

Inside, they walked up several flights of stairs, and he led them into the book stacks. The folklore section stood in the back by a dripping water fountain. Beneath the flickering fluorescent lights, a student dozed in a folding chair.

After running his finger along a row of books, reading through the titles, he pulled out a small volume entitled

The Reckoning of the Indian Killers. "Have you heard of the Angel of Hadley?"

"Sounds like a superhero." Mariana pulled off her black gloves.

Thomas glanced over the book. "He was a mythical adversary of King Philip. During a battle, someone known as the Angel of Hadley mysteriously appeared, defeated the attacking Wampanoag and then disappeared. Some think he was the man who beheaded King Charles I, hiding out in Massachusetts. Others claim he was a powerful sorcerer." Thomas skimmed. "The Boston poet Robert Lowell described him. Here it is—*Who was the man who sowed the dragon's teeth, that fabulous or fancied patriarch, who sowed so ill for his descent, beneath King's Chapel in this underworld and dark?*"

Fiona squinted at him. "What does that mean?"

"Sowing the dragon's teeth references a Greek myth about raising a supernatural army. This legendary sorcerer possessed an army of the dead. If he wants, he can call them up from the dark garden of King's Chapel Burying Ground. They'll rise up from the underworld—from the corrupt roots of the nation."

Fiona moved closer. He was beginning to understand that she had no concept of personal space. "Do you think that's related to *our* poem?"

"It's just a legend. Well, really a metaphor for the violent early days of New England. You know, the type of history that doesn't get as much attention. You seem like nice kids, and it's an interesting story, but... well, to be honest, I'd really rather not believe that demons and sorcerers are real." He closed his book. "I can barely keep up with normal life, and I'd like to get a job at some point." He took a card out of his wallet and handed it to Fiona. "If you want to learn more about this stuff, I can get behind that. Email me if you find out anything, or if you have any questions about whatever supernatural beings you summon up after school."

As they walked away, an image flashed in his mind of a shadowy sorcerer raising a Puritan army from ancient and moldering mass graves. It was just a rumor, of course. So why was it that his stomach had lurched when he'd read the other lines of the poem—about the *dark enigma* and the *jerking noose of time*?

14

Fiona

"**M**arcus Sullivan's death shocked us all." Dwarfed by red oak walls, Ms. Bouchard paced on a wooden stage in front of a brick fireplace. The art teacher's heels echoed through the amphitheater-like room, known for centuries as the Round Chamber. Marble statues of orators flanked the platform.

Near the stage, Fiona shifted on a hard wooden bench. Shocked students sniffled in their seats around her and in two levels of wooden balconies above.

Ms. Bouchard wrung her hands as she lectured about bereavement, decked in a tight black dress and a veiled hat. With her fashionable clothes, she was a striking change from the former art teacher. The portly figure of Mr. Wormock had always been covered in food stains. Fiona had even once caught him hiding Italian pastry in a secret stash above a ceiling panel. It was sad but not surprising when their beloved teacher had suffered a heart attack, though the Mather boys were only too happy to welcome his well-toned replacement.

"And that's why, in times of tragedy, it's important that you find a trusted adult." Ms. Bouchard's hand flew up to her forehead as she closed her eyes, shaking her head. She glanced up again, green eyes glistening through her veil. "Anyone overwhelmed by Marcus Sullivan's untimely death should practice the relaxation exercises that we discussed. Stay in tune with your emotions." She paused near the front of the stage, tightening her hands into fists. "Remember that when you get very upset, at a level five on our scale, you need to check in with an adult."

Fiona glanced down at the stupid emotion handout they'd all been given before staring around the hall. The round walls of the chamber connected to the stage in a semi-circle. On the wooden walls above the benches, names were engraved in a curving line around the room, each nearly a foot tall: Wendell, Morton, Putnam, Cooper. *Who were these people? Former students?*

Ms. Bouchard pressed her fingers together in a steeple, resting her chin on the tips. "Please have a safe weekend. And remember, I'm always available to talk." Her red lips turned up at the corners in a sympathetic smile.

The hall swelled with students' conversations as they shuffled between the benches. In the chaos of exiting students, Fiona pretended not to see her mother waving. All the talk of death made her gloomy, and a conversation with her mom could push her to a level five on Ms. Bouchard's scale.

She glanced back at Tobias, dozing in the corner of a bench. She crossed over to him and tapped his shoulder.

He startled out of his sleep and slowly focused on Fiona.

"You were dreaming."

"Oh." He sat up straight, blinking his eyes and looking around the emptying hall. "I haven't been sleeping well."

"Do you want some fresh air? I need to get out of here. It's too depressing. And I could show you to the best pizza in Boston."

He straightened, rubbing his hair. "Pizza? Oh, you mean the bread with the cheese? I love that stuff. They serve it on Tuesdays."

"Tobias." She placed her hand on his shoulder. "The stuff they serve in the dining hall is *not* pizza."

He joined her through the halls and the cold air, along the same sidewalk they'd sprinted down weeks before. Outside, the barren tree branches that clawed the winter sky deepened Fiona's desolate mood. She nestled her head into her coat against a strong wind. Tobias seemed content to walk in silence. As they passed the spiky gates of the King's Chapel cemetery, she glanced over and caught him distracted by ravens overhead.

Together, they wandered through the dense crowds of Quincy Market, on a road wrought from the stone ballasts of European ships hundreds of years ago. They walked past the jumbled stalls of Haymarket, and into the winding North End streets. A line trickled outside of a bakery as people queued up to buy cannoli. Nearby, fans crowded a café to cheer at a soccer match.

Fiona led Tobias into Galleria Umberto, and they waited in line as customers ordered square slices of pizza and small plastic cups of wine. They left with oil dripping down their hands as they ate, strolling the length of Hanover Street.

At the corner, Tobias studied the brick buildings as if trying to get his bearings. "The Old Way..." he muttered.

She wiped her hands on a paper napkin. "What?"

"Do you know how this street ended up here?"

"No idea."

"It was someone's shortcut to work. There was a shoemaker who lived by Haymarket in the 1630s. He also ran the Charlestown ferry from the North End. He trudged through the marshes on his way to the ferry. Then everyone started using it. It became a path called the Old Way. This big street is here just because a shoemaker took a shortcut to work four hundred years ago."

"Where did you learn that?"

"I used to have a lot of time to read history books." He took a last bite of pizza, crumpling up his paper plate and tossing it in a bin.

"You read a lot when you were homeschooled?"

"Right."

In her bleak mood, she threw caution to the icy wind. "Are you from Maremount?"

He frowned. "I told you. It's just a story."

She stepped closer to him, trying to catch his dark, almond-shaped eyes. *He's avoiding looking at me.* "I can tell when people are lying, you know," she ventured.

He narrowed his eyes at her, biting his lower lip. "Fine." He exhaled. "I guess it doesn't make a difference if people know, since I'm trapped here anyway."

It's real. Her mouth went dry, and her jaw dropped. She needed to sit down. "Really?" she whispered.

"You can't tell anyone. I'm in hiding."

She shook her head. *Is there any sensible reply?* "Did you say hiding?"

He glanced around to see if anyone was nearby. "Can we go someplace warm?"

She didn't know whether to smile or scream. She gripped his arm. "I know a place."

They spent twenty minutes walking in the cold. In hushed tones, Tobias told her of the ornate city gates and the winding streets of Crutched Square.

Fiona could do nothing to keep the excitement out of her voice. "How does magic work?"

"Mostly through language," he whispered. "Especially the Angelic language—the language of the gods. That's how the material universe was created. You know the word *Abracadabra*? It comes from the gods' language, meaning *I will create as I speak*. The universe was first created with a word."

"I *have* to learn Angelic. This is amazing."

"I'd like to learn more too. There aren't really any spell books outside Sortellian College."

Finally, the shivering duo arrived at 10½ Beacon street: The Boston Athenæum. They pulled open the large red door and flashed their Mather Academy ID cards at the guard. Tobias followed Fiona to a small red-walled gallery, empty of people. They sat on a chaise lounge, surrounded by an exhibition of stained-glass windows.

She scooted toward him. "So are you going to tell me who you're hiding from?"

He spoke close to her ear. "He's a powerful philosopher called Rawhed. At first, King Balthazar hired him to crack down on illegal magic. But then Rawhed created his own army through magic. His soldiers look like demons with glowing eyes. They've started ransacking houses. He's searching for something. No one knows what. Everyone he's interrogated has been killed, and the King's gone missing."

Fiona stared. This wasn't as nice as the water-spirits story. "He's called *Raw Head*?"

Tobias nodded. "No one knows his real name. They say he has a twisted face with long bloody fangs, and he feasts on children's flesh."

She shuddered. "So he's a monster."

Tobias nodded. "His soldiers are called Harvesters. They nourish the Deadly Nevergreen—the elm tree where they hanged people long ago. They're using it again. And there are other ways they hang people. When they're not ransacking homes, they're stealing people away to execute them. It's like some sort of ritual. No one knows what spell he used to create his army."

Fiona bit her lip. "Okay, don't get mad at me."

"What?"

"You mentioned Maremount the other day, and I looked it up. I found a British grad student who knows a lot about it. I told him that I thought I'd met someone from Maremount."

Tobias frowned. "Who is he?"

"He's a researcher. He believes Maremount is just a legend. But he said something about an evil sorcerer who can raise an army from the buried Puritan bodies. Like the ones at King's Chapel."

He ran his fingers through his hair, staring at the ground. "Rawhed could've called on one of the gods to raise an army of corpses. He could be a necromancer." He glanced at her, narrowing his dark eyes. "It makes sense. Their clothing is odd. The style is hundreds of years old."

"Was Rawhed after you? Is that why you had to escape?"

"I belong to a coven that practices magic illegally. Tatters— poor people— aren't allowed to learn magic. We can't cast spells within the city, or the bone wardens will come for us. Anyone they catch is torn to pieces. They leave nothing behind but lumps of flesh and broken bones. So we go into the Tuckomock Forest, outside the city. We call ourselves the Ragmen. We had only a stolen philosopher's guide, but it's burned now."

"Bone wardens... This keeps getting creepier. But why are you called the Ragmen?"

"When the rogue covens started long ago, there was a man who sold linens from house to house. He would hide coded texts in them—instructions on where to meet. That's how we started. After Rawhed came, the younger Ragmen were sent to Boston, but my friends didn't make it out in time. And now I'm stuck here, on my own."

"How many young Ragmen were left behind?"

"Just Oswald and Eden. They're siblings."

"Are you close with them?"

He nodded. "They used to be at my house a lot, because their dad drank too much. And as we got older, Eden kept getting prettier."

Fiona was almost too astonished to think of what to say next. "I can't believe all this is real. I mean, I wouldn't have believed any of it if I hadn't seen the demon with my own eyes. Don't you think it could have cursed Sully?"

Tobias shook his head. "It wasn't a demon."

"Are you sure?"

He gazed into her eyes. "It looked exactly like a bone warden, only smaller. Someone wanted to stop us from finishing the séance. Someone wanted to scare us."

15

Fiona

"**O**hhh diseases that plague you—the diseases that plague you, I think I've got, I think I've got the ague!" Alan wailed into the mike.

Tobias swayed at the front of the stage, plucking his lute and harmonizing. Colored lights danced on their faces as they played.

Fiona stood at the front of the meager crowd at the Keller to see the Chief Cocks. She'd unsuccessfully tried to convince Alan that their new band name might be a bad idea, but he'd insisted on keeping it. "Chief cock," he'd said, was a cool historical term for a boxer.

With a slight sense of trepidation, Fiona had made her way to the loud and claustrophobic all-ages show. The few times she'd come to the bar, she'd ended up pressed between sweaty college students, inhaling the stench of stale beer, though the black Xs on her hands prevented her from ordering anything more exciting than soda.

Tonight, only a few patrons lingered in the bar. Lucas and Celia had plenty of room to dance while the Chief Cocks played one song after another about historical diseases. Fiona had tried to join them during a song about leprosy, but her feet had stuck to something on the floor.

"*You know the kind of thing I need!*" Alan jumped up and down. "*Balance the humors when I bleed...*"

"Tobias and Alan are looking good," Mariana shouted to Fiona just as the song ended. The end of her sentence echoed through the room, and she hid behind her black bangs as the sparse crowd cheered.

"Thank you. We're the Chief Cocks!" Feedback pierced the room as Alan spoke into the mike.

When the set ended, Lucas and Celia said their goodbyes. Fiona grabbed Mariana's arm, and they hurried the stage where the Chief Cocks packed up their instruments.

"That was great," said Mariana.

Tobias pulled off his lute. "Thanks. I don't think we're very good yet."

"Should we meet you outside?" shouted Fiona.

"Yeah, I'll be out. Alan's going to help Joe take his drums home."

Fiona looped her arm through Mariana's, and they wrapped up against the cold, heading to the dark street in front of the Keller to wait for Tobias. The temperature had dropped while they were inside, and the girls huddled together.

As Fiona nestled into her friend's shoulder, she heard footfalls on the pavement. She looked up from Mariana's down jacket.

Munroe stood before them with her arms folded. Her deep red hair hung in a tangled ponytail, and she glared at them through red, puffy eyelids. Behind her loomed two tall jocks, one skinny and one very round, both wearing Mather varsity football jackets. The skinny one's chin jutted out, and he made popping noises with his gum.

"Where's Tobias?" Munroe's voice trembled.

Fiona didn't have a good feeling about the two jocks. "Is there anything I can help you with?"

Munroe stepped toward her, narrowing her eyes. "He cursed my boyfriend."

"I'm sorry about Sully," said Fiona. "Um, I haven't seen—"

Before she could finish lying, the door swung open and Tobias stepped out with his lute case. The thin football player lunged forward, punching Tobias in the jaw. Tobias dropped his lute as he slammed against the door. He sprung forward, swinging and landing a punch in return. As he did, the other jock rushed toward Tobias, pinning his arms behind him. While Tobias struggled, Munroe inched toward him, her arms crossed.

"I know what you did." Her voice was icy.

He took a deep breath, gazing at her. "I'm sorry he died, but I didn't have anything to do with it."

Tears filled Munroe's eyes as she grabbed his shirt collar. Her hair seemed to blaze under the yellow streetlamps. She hissed, "I know you killed him with magic." She stepped away and nodded toward the skinny boy, who punched him in the jaw.

"Stop it!" Fiona yelled. She grabbed the lute case from the ground and swung it hard into the football player's lower spine.

"Ow!" He turned to Fiona, towering over her. "Did you just hit me with a violin?"

"It's a lute," she said, brandishing the case. "And there's more where that came from."

The Keller's door opened again, and a bouncer poked his head out. "Everything okay out here?"

As the jocks released Tobias, a serene grin replaced Munroe's scowl. "They were just messing around. There's no problem." She turned to her lanky friend, stroking his jacket. "Let's go." They strolled off down Commonwealth Avenue.

Tobias straightened, rubbing his jaw as the bouncer disappeared.

Fiona gave him a worried look. "Are you okay?"

"I could have taken him if there weren't two of them. It wasn't really a fair fight."

"Well, you had *me* there to back you up." She stuffed her hands in her pockets as they began their walk to the subway. Ice on the sidewalk reflected the garish neon signs above.

"That's true. They didn't know my secret weapon. My lute-swinging avenger." He smiled, holding his jaw.

"Let me see the damage." Below the streetlights of Kenmore Square, Fiona appraised the growing bruise on Tobias's jaw and the blood running from a split lip.

"Hang on." After trawling through her bag, she brought out a package of tissues to wipe the blood off his chin.

"Do you still like the guy you told me about before? The one you had a disastrous conversation with?"

Surprised by the question, she studied his face. "Yeah. But I haven't really talked to him. Unrequited love is lame, isn't it?"

"Are we gonna get on the subway?" Mariana called, seemingly out of nowhere. "It's freezing."

Fiona started, spinning around.

"You forgot I was here, didn't you?" Mariana smirked.

16

Thomas

Thomas Malcolm had all but forgotten his recent conversation about Maremount as he swayed under the glaring lights in the boxing ring. He held his opponent, Adam "The Calculator" McCarthy, in a clinch, blocking out the crowd's noise. Thomas trapped the accountant's arms, almost catching his breath before his opponent broke free. Adam hunched forward, uncorking a wild right hook to the body that failed to connect. Thomas's limbs felt heavy and slow, as if he were fighting through a flood of molasses. A fat drop of sweat stung his right eye, but he tried to focus on the larger man across from him. Gritting his teeth, he forced himself forward, straining to maintain some kind of form as he threw a double-jab at his opponent. *Easy, Thomas. Come on.*

Adam telegraphed a haymaker and Thomas, reading the trajectory, pulled his chest back. Adam missed, losing his balance. As he considered whether he should move around or clinch again, the bell rang overhead. He shielded his eyes against the glare.

After a few moments, the announcer's voice boomed through the room, prolonging his words. *"We have here the former welterweight champion. And it has been decided, after a fantastic performance, and by unanimous decision, we have a new winner of the White Collar Boxing Championships, Thomas 'The Historian' Malcolm!"*

Adam stepped toward him, lifting Thomas's gloved hand. Closing his eyes against the bright lights, Thomas let himself fully absorb the crowd's cheers for the first time. A wave of euphoria swept through him before he looked around again. He didn't know a single person there.

He slid off his gloves, shook hands with Adam, and slipped quietly off the stage. As he found his way back to the empty locker room, he pulled off his headguard and wiped the sweat from his forehead. In the shower, he was alone with his thoughts. After the high of the arena and the screams of the crowd roaring for the champion, the locker room's silence unsettled him. Back in London, he would've had ten friends there, ready to celebrate into the small hours. Instead, he'd have to go out by himself and wait for a seat at the bar, surrounded by bankers.

The Champion. This word had been coming up a lot lately. After those two girls had visited him with a story about a King Philip poem, he'd continued reading about the Angel of Hadley. Hawthorne called him the Gray Champion—a mysterious old Puritan on a "shadowy march." That part he'd already known, but as he'd read more about the legends, he'd found something that nearly made him spit out his coffee. He didn't want to make too much of it. He was a researcher, not some fantasist. He wasn't one of the raving lunatics you saw in the park shouting into the air about conspiracies.

He finished dressing and zipped up his coat as he left the locker room. After pushing through the gym's crowd, he stepped into the cold. He pulled out his tobacco pouch and papers while he crossed the street into the park. Much of the snow had melted, and slushy water pooled in paths through the Common. He strode past the old site of the elm, marked by a small plaque set into the ground.

SITE OF THE GREAT ELM
here the sons of liberty assembled
here, jesse lee, methodist pioneer
preached in 1790
the landmark of the common, the elm,
blew down in 1876

That was only part of the story, but he supposed it would have been a bit morbid to mention the bodies that had swung below the tree.

As he continued toward Beacon Hill, his forehead tingled, like strands of hair brushing his skin. He smiled, shaking his head. When he was a kid, he used to think walking through a spider web meant you'd encountered a ghost. He rubbed his forehead.

Nearby, a woman wearing candy-cane earrings and pink tube socks shrieked at a bench. "They drink blood! Vampires! The people in the government—you think you know, but you don't know. The government drinks blood..." She tottered over, slumping onto the ground, defeated.

You got a lot more crazies around here than you did in London—a symptom of the dismantled mental health system, he supposed. At least the light in Boston was a significant improvement over the grim London skies. As he walked toward the State House, a tawny glow gleamed over the snow.

Toward the western edge of the park, the sun blinded him,

and he shielded his eyes. Someone was heading right for him. As she drew closer, he recognized one of the girls from the posh school. Fiona.

"Hey. What are you doing here?"

She nodded toward Boylston Street. "My school's just around the corner. I was gonna try to find you. Aren't you supposed to be in a boxing match? I saw your picture on the poster."

He beamed. "Just finished. Won the championship, as it happens."

"No way! I can't believe it! That guy looked so much bigger than you on the poster."

His smiled faded. "Right, cheers." He rubbed his hands together in the chilly air. "Well, it's been fun chatting, but I'm off to celebrate with a drink."

"Can I come?"

"Oh no, I'm not sponsoring that. You're not old enough, and I know you've got some kind of curfew. What do you want to go to a bar for?"

She looked off into the distance. "That's what people do when they're depressed about love, right? You sit at the bar, ordering shots until the bartender asks you to leave. I mean, they won't serve me alcohol." She shrugged. "But I could get a soda."

He remembered his last breakup during college, a series of vitriolic arguments with his girlfriend, Anna. There were the drunken phone calls, the nights of vomiting on the bus, and the hangovers that left him shuddering in bed for days. "That's not real life. That's just in the movies. Adults deal with heartbreak by just moving on."

"Oh." She shivered. "Well, I'm glad I found you. There's something I wanted to ask. You told me about a sorcerer.

Someone who could raise an army from the ground."

Thomas would have liked to be inside, enjoying a pint with someone his own age, but this would have to do for now. "I told you there was a *legend* about it."

"What if it already happened? My friend—the one from Maremount—said there's a sorcerer leading a supernatural army. They call him Rawhed. Is there anything else you can tell me about the legend?"

He sighed. He wasn't quite sure he wanted to divulge what he'd learned. "I've been reading a bit more about it."

"What did you find?"

He smiled and glanced down for a second. "Well, it's an odd little story actually. Some time in the 1800s, a little boy named Enoch Cosgrove was wandering around the Plymouth forest. He met two beautiful women, and they led him through the woods as the sun set. Little Enoch fell asleep by a tree. When he awoke, he was surrounded by witches holding quahog shells. They told him that an evil sorcerer would appear one day—an Angel of Death. They said that only one thing could kill him. They told the boy to memorize something, but of course he forgot it."

She stepped toward him, pulling her coat tighter. "What did they want him to remember?"

He exhaled a cloud of mist. "A poem about King Philip."

17

Tobias

Tobias's face throbbed from the beating he'd received days before, and he inhaled the steam from his chamomile tea. Despite Munroe's best attempts to spread rumors of his involvement in Sully's death, he felt a sense of calm. Inside the old building, high above the frozen ground, he relished the warmth of his room. The only noise was the gentle clicking of Alan's keyboard.

After finishing his tea, Tobias closed his eyes, lying back and pulling up his blankets. He thought of Maremount as he did every night, and of standing in the long grass with Eden by Athanor Pond, watching the sky turn a hot salmon color while the sun rose. Once, as they'd stood by the bramble bushes, he'd pricked his finger, and Eden had kissed the single drop of blood. He could picture the silent ferryman of Athanor Pond as though he were standing before him. His fingers were long, white talons.

Tobias ran, briers scratching his legs in the thicket. He no longer stood by the water, but in the Tuckomock Forest along a deer trail. He caught a flicker of a bony man stalking him through the old oak trees. Behind him, the hunter snapped twigs, closing in on him. He was desperate for his pike. He looked down to see a child's hat, covered in blood. He tripped and sprawled flat on the path.

Scrambling to get up, his vision went dark, and he struggled for breath. As the air drained from his lungs, a gnawing dread replaced it, as though his body were rotting from within.

He woke and gasped in the dark, quiet room. He tried to sit up, but his muscles wouldn't obey. In the corner of the room, a shadow moved. He tried to push himself up on his elbows, but he was paralyzed. He closed his eyes, and something rustled at the foot of his bed. *Am I still dreaming?*

His eyes snapped open, and he stared at a silhouette hovering by the end of his bed. When it shifted toward him into the faint moonlight, he saw silver hair curled over a withered face. The only sensible thought he could muster was that this old woman must be a teacher's guest who'd lost her bearings. He tried to tell her she shouldn't be here, but his lips wouldn't obey.

The old woman glided closer to his head as he struggled to sit up. She reached a gnarled hand to his shoulder, and then quickly—too quick for such an ancient creature—she pressed on top of him, her knobby knees jabbing into his ribs. With horror, he saw a desiccated face approach his. He closed his eyes as a weight compressed his chest. *How could a withered crone be so heavy?* His body filled with dread as the old woman forced her brittle mouth on his, draining him of breath.

"What's going on?" Alan's voice, thick with sleep, cut through the silence.

The creature jerked upwards, and Tobias opened his eyes again, gasping. The woman crouched above him had transformed, now looking like an aged version of his art teacher, Ms. Bouchard. Her large eyes blinked in bewilderment as her shriveled face rotated toward Alan.

"Ms. Bouchard? Why are you sitting on Tobias? What happened to your face?"

Ms. Bouchard scuttled backwards toward the end of Tobias's bed. Her head swiveled back to look at Tobias, her face contorted with rage. In a panic, Tobias blurted out the childhood rhyme he used to say before bed:

Heigh diddle diddle,
a nighttime riddle
to shield my flesh and bones.
The devils will yell
to hear such spells
and the goblins run off with the crones.

Ms. Bouchard lurched backwards. Her skeletal feet sought out the floor for balance, and she doubled over. She clung to her stomach with skeletal hands. Her head wrenched backwards, and her face grimaced toward the ceiling. She shrieked, joined by screams from Alan. Cracks opened in her skin, and with a sharp report like a ship's cannon, her body ruptured into lumps of flesh, bone, and dust. Particles of the art teacher sprayed all over the room.

Clearly, there was more to his nighttime riddle than he'd been raised to believe. Tobias looked down at his arms. The powdery pieces had turned into droplets of blood on his skin. He gulped in air as if drowning, but then had the horrible thought that he was inhaling bits of Ms. Bouchard.

"What the hell was that?" Alan cried out, staring at his gore-spattered arms.

Tobias gasped for breath, coated in the creature's flesh. It wasn't the first demon he'd fought, but he'd never killed anything before.

"She's all over us. How do we get rid of this?" Alan shouted.

"I don't know." He tried to smear the blood droplets off his arm.

Alan looked at his bloody hands. "Did you kill it with magic? Can you do some kind of magic to get rid of this?"

A cleaning spell wasn't a bad idea. He closed his eyes, chanting a spell for tidying between short breaths. As he spoke, all the dust, bone, and blood swirled off their bodies and beds, depositing itself in the trash. Alan gaped at him, and then stared at the trashcan as though it might birth another monster. After a few moments, with the room in its normal state again, the heaving of their chests returned to normal.

Tobias glanced at the trashcan. "I didn't know that rhyme could kill anything."

"It's a good thing it did. She looked like she was about to suck out your soul. Do you think she's killed anyone before? Do you think she killed *Sully*?"

The sound of footsteps approached on the wooden floorboards outside the door. A key rattled in the lock as they sat in silence. The door creaked open, and Mr. Grunshaw's bearded face poked through. "What in God's name is going on here?"

The boys looked at each other.

Alan's face was serene as he scratched at his stubble. "Tobias had a nightmare."

"Go to sleep, and if I hear another noise out of here, you'll both have a week of detention." His bearded face disappeared again.

"We'll talk about this in the morning," whispered Alan.

Tobias lay back in his bed, his whole body aching. He and Alan remained silent, still shocked. Tobias pulled up his covers, but the room no longer felt quite as safe. After a few minutes, he heard Alan get up and look into the bin. He selected a heavy Civil War textbook from his shelf and placed it atop the lid, hoping to prevent any errant bits of Ms. Bouchard from emerging and reconstituting.

18

Fiona

On the last day before March break, Fiona stood with her hands wrapped around the cold bars of the front gate, watching the morning sky turn a brighter shade of ash. The days were longer, and the temperature had started to warm, but dirty clumps of snow still blighted the Common paths. A world without magic was already beginning to seem intolerable. She turned away from the park. As she walked toward breakfast, she wondered how people coped with the tedium of ordinary life.

In the dining hall, she grabbed two chocolate croissants and some orange juice before sitting down with Tobias and Alan. Tobias's bruise was fading, but the deep circles under his eyes suggested he still wasn't sleeping well. As she approached, the conversation faded to silence. Alan's face looked drawn and tired.

She looked from Tobias to Alan. "What am I interrupting?"

Tobias glanced at his friend. "It's okay. She knows about me."

"I know about what?"

Alan whispered, "Tobias is finally about to fill me in on his background. His *real* background."

Tobias rubbed his eyes. "Fiona can probably summarize it."

She smiled. She thought herself an expert on Maremount. She described everything she could remember: how the language of the gods created reality, that Rawhed controlled the Harvesters, and that Tobias was a Ragman.

Alan's jaw dropped as she spoke, and Tobias jumped in to describe his pike fighting techniques.

Alan clapped his hand over his mouth. "Holy crap." He stared at the table. "I've already seen the monsters, but I was still somehow hoping there would be a rational explanation for them."

Fiona shifted her chair closer. "There's more, though. You know that poem Ann Hibbins recited? It turns out there's a *legend* about a King Philip poem. It's supposed to be able to stop an evil sorcerer. We need to get the whole thing."

Still staring at the table, Alan shook his head slowly. "I knew there was something weird going on with your whole arrival here."

Fiona tapped her hand on the table. "Wait—why is this coming out now? What happened?"

"We were going to talk about who I killed last night," said Tobias in a low voice.

"*What?*"

Alan nodded, listlessly taking a bite of croissant and speaking with his mouth full. "Ms. Bouchard." His eyes had taken on a glazed look.

Fiona gaped. "You're kidding, right?"

In hushed tones, Tobias delved into details of the powder and the gore, and the knobby knees that had pressed into his chest.

Fiona looked down at the table in shocked silence while she digested the information before staring at Tobias again. "I knew there was something weird about her. Was she a witch?"

Tobias rested his chin on his hand. "I think she was a night hag. They're extremely rare. We've eradicated them in Maremount."

Recovering some alertness, Alan nodded. "I've read about them. Succubi. There are beliefs all over the world about them. They're cursed women who sit on your chest and cause nightmares. Lilith was the first one, in the Garden of Eden. Ms. Bouchard was probably a thousand years old before you destroyed her."

Tobias shook his head. "I don't understand why she came here, though. They're only attracted to places of magic."

"Let's look through her desk at lunch," Alan suggested. "It's our last chance before vacation."

Fiona certainly didn't want to miss the excitement of picking through the belongings of a demonic teacher. At 12:30, she wandered into the art room and looked over the old wooden walls. Imitations of Jackson Pollock hung near the door. Above Ms. Bouchard's desk, a black and white image of a frowning Picasso was marked with a comic book font that demanded, "make art!"

She walked toward the desk, and Tobias and Alan soon joined her. She rifled through papers on top of the desk, tossing aside students' pencil sketches. Tobias pulled open the drawers.

Alan peered over his shoulder. "There's hardly anything in these drawers. When Mr. Wormock was here, they were full of candy bars."

Fiona smiled wryly. "And he kept cannoli above one of the ceiling panels. They're probably still there."

Tobias frowned. "Did you say Wormock?"

"The old art teacher." Fiona opened the desk's bottom drawer. "He died of a heart attack."

"*Jeremiah* Wormock?"

"That's it," said Fiona as Tobias's eyes widened. "How do you know his name?"

"I can't believe it. Jeremiah Wormock writes the Danny Marchese books. They're about a detective who solves crimes in Boston. All the literate classes read them." He shook his head. "He's a great writer. Or—he was. The only people from Maremount allowed to live outside the city are a few writers like him. It's never been known how they get to and from Boston, but there's a legend of something called the Darkling Tunnel."

"Wormock was a sorcerer?" Alan's eyes widened as he leaned against a student's desk. "I never would have guessed."

Tobias sighed. "I can't believe he's dead."

"So he would have been practicing magic here?" said Fiona.

Tobias nodded. "He would have been well-trained at the best schools. I wonder if he left any philosopher's guides behind." He scratched the back of his neck. "You said he hid things in the ceiling?"

"He went to Mike's Pastry every day. He had a stash up there." She pointed to a rectangular ceiling panel directly above the desk.

"Hang on." Alan jumped on the desk. He reached over his head, gently pushing the panel aside. He stuck his hand in to fish around the edges of the space. "I think I found a cannoli." He shifted to the other side. "There's paper here." He removed a yellowed card, handing it to Tobias, and carefully replaced the ceiling panel.

Tobias inspected the card. "I can't believe this."

While Alan jumped off the desk, Fiona peered over Tobias's shoulder. In one corner of the card, someone had drawn four symbols. "What are those?"

Tobias took a deep breath. "It's written in the code of the Ragmen. I had no idea he worked with us."

"What do they mean?"

Tobias grabbed a pen from the desktop and turned over one of the drawings to use as scrap paper. On the back, he created a square grid and began inputting symbols and letters into the spaces. Finally, he completed the table.

"These four symbols are the letters *INRI* in our code: Igne Natura Renovatur Integra. It's an alchemical phrase—t*hrough fire, nature is reborn whole.*"

Fiona pulled the card out of Tobias's hand, inspecting the familiar format. "It looks like the cards in the card catalogue, except it's mostly blank. Maybe it's a book in the library—like, a *spell* book."

Tobias stuffed it into his pocket and smiled. "A philosopher's guide."

Fiona led them to the very end of the east wing, where the codes began with I. The shelves stood across from the folklore books, where the painted stars shone from the ceiling. Dusty tomes with faded silver titles lined red oak shelves. Interrupting the I shelves was the tall memorial plaque commemorating the academy's war veterans.

Fiona scanned the shelves around the plaque, searching for the code *INRI*. She glossed over the book titles referencing Boston's history, but where *INRI* should have been, she noticed a green book with no title. She pulled it off the shelf.

Tobias reached for it, but Fiona jerked her hand away and flipped through the pages. "It's blank." She handed it to him.

He turned the book over in his hands. "There's nothing odd about it except that it's blank. Maybe it's invisible ink. There's a spell for that, but I don't know it."

Alan paced back and forth with his hand on his chin, deep in thought, while Fiona crouched down, peering into the space she'd pulled the book from. Something metallic glimmered. Sticking her hand through, she groped around behind the shelf until she felt a lever. She pulled on it, and as she did, the memorial plaque detached from the wall on one side, creaking open on a hinge.

"Holy crap!" Alan nearly shouted. He jumped forward, pulling the plaque open further to reveal an arched oak door set into the wall.

As Tobias and Fiona crammed around him, he turned a black iron knob. When it opened, they were greeted with a musty smell of earth and mildew. There was a stone landing, and a dark stairwell curved both up and down. In the dim light, they could see that the ceiling was low, as though built for a child. The walls glistened with moisture.

Fiona whispered, "What is this?"

Alan turned to them. "Should we go up, or down?"

Fiona exhaled. "Up seems safer. Downstairs might be a dungeon or something."

They stepped onto the landing. Fiona followed Alan up the uneven stairs, running her hands against the damp stone walls. In the darkness, she lost her footing on a crooked step and fell backwards into Tobias, who caught her before she tumbled down. She steadied herself and continued upward. Tobias chanted a spell, and a foxfire orb the size of a basketball appeared in front of Alan.

Alan spun to look at Tobias, his eyes wide. "This spell-casting is going to take some getting used to."

He turned to climb, until they came to a closed door. In the center of the door, a brass snake-haired Fury held a knocker ring in her mouth. Alan glanced back and then pushed the door open as the sphere floated forward, bathing the hexagonal room in a golden glow.

Alan's voice was barely a whisper. "Holy crap."

At the entrance, Fiona's hand covered her mouth as she looked around. Opposite the door, a narrow window interrupted the stone walls. Metal sconces shaped like long hands cradled partially melted red candles in curling fingers. To their right, a stone fireplace contained cinders and blackened wood, and stone gargoyles jutted from its mantle. A rug covered the floor, embroidered with animals and flowers. To the left, wooden shelves held jars of powders, dried plants, and a few leather-bound books.

Fiona took a deep breath. The room smelled like a damp newspaper, and underneath that was a rich aroma of mushrooms. She walked toward a table below the window and gasped. A crystal sphere rested on the table, the size of a cat's head. Beneath it was a wax disc covered in labyrinthine drawings of pentagrams and unfamiliar symbols. Similar wax discs rested under the table legs.

"This is amazing," she said, her voice barely audible.

Tobias joined her, picking up the sphere and turning it around in his hand. "Samael's skeleton!"

She looked up. "Is that really how you swear in Maremount?" Touching the stone in his hand, she asked, "What is it? It's beautiful."

"It's a shew stone—a scrying tool. Some people use mirrors, some use water, and some people use stones like this. They're used to provide answers to questions. I know a little divination spell." He smiled.

"Sweet. This place is incredible." Alan turned to a tapestry that hung on the wall near the door. It depicted a long, curling snake, and astrological signs marked its skin. He crossed the room to the shelves, picking up one of the books and leafing through the pages. "No spells yet. Just some pictures of herbs."

Fiona gazed out the window. A deep mist filled the air outside. It looked as though the tower stood in a cloud. As she tried to work out their location, a scuttling movement behind a gargoyle caught her attention. She shrieked, "What is that?"

Above the fireplace, a tiny, humanoid creature crept along the mantel. Its face looked like a death's-head from a gravestone, but its large eyes shone in the light. It scampered down the side of the fireplace on spindly limbs, darting into a fist-sized hole below the window.

Tobias moved toward her. "It's just a tower imp. It was probably someone's pet at one time. They won't hurt you, but they'll steal your things if you're not careful." He put down the shew stone and turned to inspect the shelves.

Fiona looked over his shoulder as he pulled out another book. Pictures of planets orbiting the sun in concentric circles embossed its leathery brown cover. The pages were yellowed and brittle, each filled with an unfamiliar language on the left side, and Latin translations on the right. Decorating some of the pages were drawings of transformations: plants and vegetables that grew to unusual sizes, a bird changing from white to black, and people transforming into animals.

Fiona pointed to the page. "That must be Angelic on the left? And Latin on the right."

"Yes, this is a philosopher's guide." Tobias's face beamed with excitement. "This one's written in the classic style that starts with the simple spells, and then moves on to more complex incantations. So we've got the easy spells like Dowager Zenobia's Spell for Renewal, Lady Cleo's Cloak, Vicomtesse Dangerosa's Torn Bodice... Ah! Sir Baldrion's Transformation Spell. And this sounds promising—Queen Boudicca's Inferno. The page is a bit burned, but I can still read it." He turned the page, and his jaw dropped. The remaining pages were crumbled brown crisps. "What is this? The rest of the book is burned!"

Alan thumbed through the other books. "None of these have spells. Mostly lots of plant pictures." He turned a page. "And some names. I think they're names. Mishett-Ash? Blodrial? Druloch?"

Tobias closed the spell book, and a small cloud of dust rose from its cover. "A list of gods. Mishett-Ash is the storm god, Druloch is the tree god, and Blodrial's the blood god. He's not worshipped in Maremount, though. His followers hunt philosophers."

Fiona pulled the spell book out of his hands to peruse its fragile pages.

"Tobias, can you ask that shew stone why this room is here?" Alan traced his hands over the tapestry.

"I can try." He bit his lower lip. "There's a very small chance that a demon will appear. They're sometimes attracted by magic. But old philosophers' rooms like this are almost guaranteed to have aura protections. Otherwise no one would've been able to practice spell-casting."

Alan nodded slowly and shrugged. "Sounds fine to me. Plus, you've killed a demon before."

Tobias turned to the table. With his hand on the sphere, he intoned the divination spell. His eyelids fluttered and opened wide again. He began to sway. "Who are these people?"

Fiona tried to peer into the shew stone but could only see the crystal. "What are you seeing?"

After a minute of swaying, he spoke. "I saw the words *Mather Adepti*." His eyes appeared to focus again. "Does anyone know what that is?"

Fiona brought her finger up to her lips. "It sounds familiar. I think it was something Celia mentioned. Someone told her there used to be a secret society here."

"It looked like a coven," said Tobias. "I don't think they're here anymore. They wore old-fashioned clothes. I think the room was unused for a long time—covered in dust—until an overweight, rumpled-looking man started spell-casting here."

"Wormock!" said Fiona. "That sounds just like him. He must have been using this before he died."

"If no one else is using it, we should form a new coven here," said Alan.

"Yes! I want to be a witch." Fiona bit her lip. "I guess you'd be man-witches."

Alan shook his head. "Jesus, Fiona. I didn't get to the ninth level of *Caverns of Chaos* to be called a man-witch."

"We're called philosophers," Tobias interjected.

"The Mather Adepti room," Fiona murmured, touching one of the hand-shaped sconces. "Is it possible to be in love with a room? If it weren't for the tower imp, I'd move in here."

Alan kneeled on the floor, inspecting the bottom shelf. "There's something here." He pulled out a neatly folded letter, sealed with wax, and peeled it open. "It's in that code again."

He handed it to Tobias, who sat down at the table. Pulling out a pen and a piece of paper, he began drawing another grid, filling in the symbols and letters.

"What does it say?" Fiona pressed over Tobias as he worked.

"Just be patient."

Alan stared into the shew stone and Fiona returned to scanning through the philosopher's guide, trying her best to translate the Latin in her head.

After what seemed like ages, Fiona let out a dramatic sigh. "It's too bad you guys don't just have computers with passwords."

"Not that I really care," said Alan, "but we're missing History right now."

"I'm almost done." Tobias copied letters below each symbol. "I can't believe this."

"What is it?" asked Fiona.

"It's a letter from my father."

He leaned back, holding up the letter to read it out loud.

Dear Wormock,

Rawhed and the Harvesters draw near. It is only a matter of time before we retreat to the Tuckomock Forest. This may be my last letter for some time.

Thank you for the papers you sent for the young Ragmen. They may be with you soon, though you haven't yet told me where to find the Darkling Tunnel. Please send me the location as soon as you can. We haven't given the young members much information for their own safety. Please watch over them when they arrive at Mather. Tobias doesn't yet know your identity. He can be rash sometimes and get himself into danger.

I have very important news. Three of the Ragmen were successful in breaking into Sortellian College undetected. They retrieved one of the Mather Adepti journals—an early one. It was written by the philosophers who later helped to create Maremount and contained a clue to stopping Rawhed.

The Adepti wrote that they'd held a séance one night below the Witching Elm. They heard from the spirits of the unjustly persecuted. The spirits told them a great adversary would arise, and there would be a way to stop him—it was a poem about King Philip. We believe it will tell us how to defeat Rawhed.

What's more, the Mather Adepti hid the poem somewhere within the school. It's been kept a secret from the very beginning—the founder of the Mather Adepti had gone mad, and later philosophers concealed things from him. We also believe they enchanted an item, but we do not know what it is. You must begin by searching the school.

—Corvin

Tobias stared up at his friends. "He was looking for the poem in the school before he died. We have to pick up where he left off."

19

Tobias

Tobias finished a final bite of his sugary cereal. Last night, in the Adepti room, they'd tried to call Ann Hibbins' spirit up from the grave again, hoping to hear the full poem, but not a single candle had flickered to suggest a ghostly presence.

He frowned, picking up his tray. With everyone going home on break, he'd be left on his own for a week. At least he could spend the time investigating every inch of the school for the poem. He placed his dishes on a cart and had just rounded the corner to the central hall when Alan jumped in front of him.

"There you are," said Alan. "You really need a cell phone."

"I thought you were going home."

Alan checked his phone. "I've got an hour. Can we go back to the Adepti room? I have an idea."

Tobias walked with him toward the stairwell. "What's your idea?"

"Why don't we ask the shew stone where the poem is?"

Tobias smiled. "Of course. We should've thought of that last night."

They climbed the stairs into the library and snuck into the earthy stone stairwell. In the Adepti room, a frosty morning light glowed through the window.

Tobias picked up the smooth stone. As he intoned the Angelic spell, his eyelids fluttered and opened again. He felt the beginnings of the trance, a tingling sensation that formed in his fingers and toes, and then his consciousness drifted from his body.

He asked the stone to show him where the poem had been hidden all those years ago. As he looked into the smooth surface, it clouded over, and then a muddy swirl coalesced into a blocky shape. The image sharpened into the Mather Academy building.

It faded, and his eyes resumed their focus. "It's in Mather Academy."

Alan opened his hands to the ceiling. "Yeah, we already knew that. Can you ask for more specifics?"

Tobias repeated the spell, entering a trance, but it showed him the same image. "It's not giving us any more specifics." His eyes focused on Alan again.

Alan rested his hand on his chin, looking at the floor. "Maybe just ask about the Mather Adepti. Ask who they were."

When the tingling formed in his body, he saw a group of boys in black clothes and large white collars. They gathered in the Adepti room, chanting together. Some had fair locks and faces pale as dough, while others had brown hair and darker skin—warm skin, like Tobias's. The image faded.

His eyes focused again, and he looked up at Alan. "Their clothes looked like 17th century clothes. Some were English, and some were Algonquian."

"Algonquian students? Here? I never heard that." Alan furrowed his brow. "I bet they died from disease. The Native students at Harvard died from smallpox and the plague. Thank God we got rid of those."

"They haven't in Maremount. My mother and sister died of the plague."

"There's no cure?" He shook his head. "That's awful. I'm sorry."

"It's okay, it was a long time ago. I don't remember them. Philosophers developed a spell to cure the plague in Strasbourg in the 1500s, but its use was so widespread that the aura attracted legions of fairies. They forced the entire city to dance to their deaths. It's been restricted since then." He glanced out the window and sighed. "Enough about diseases. Should we get back to the stone?"

Alan frowned. "Okay. Didn't your dad's letter say the founder of the Mather Adepti went mad, and they had to hide the poem from him?" He nodded toward the stone. "Can you ask who the founder was?"

Tobias returned to staring at the shew stone, and his wide eyes glazed as he swayed. The surface clouded over, and a line of black swirled around, sprouting roots and spikes. It formed into the image of a tree. Was it the Witching Elm? As the image crystallized, he could see it was bushier than an elm and had white flowers.

He snapped out of his trance. "It's a mayflower."

"Mayflower? The ship?"

"The tree. It blooms with white flowers in May. Sometimes it's called a fairy tree. There's always a festival at the beginning of May in a grove of mayflower trees. There's a queen who wears mayflowers in her hair. And once you're fourteen, there's a fertility ceremony."

Alan lowered his chin, staring at Tobias. "You participated in a fertility ceremony?"

"Yes, but I'll miss this year's." He frowned.

"So what does a mayflower mean for our question? The Pilgrims started the Adepti?"

Tobias rested against the wall to think, his hand on his chin. "They were in Plymouth, but maybe they moved here later."

"Ask it again. Maybe it'll give you a better answer."

Tobias turned to the stone. As he chanted the Angelic words, he felt himself drift from his body. He asked the stone to show him a vision of the life of the Mather Adepti founder. Standing above the stone, hands resting on the table, he began to sway. This time the stone turned completely black, like polished obsidian, and gray swirls formed into an image of a shaking woman with a noose around her neck. She climbed a ladder that rested against a tree. Her haunted face looked familiar. Someone below her pulled the ladder away, and she swung beneath the branches, her body convulsing, feet twitching in the air. The swinging stilled; her face withered and rotted before his eyes.

"Tobias!" Alan pulled him out of his trance.

As he came back to the Adepti room, he could see that the shew stone emitted a dark smoke. The disc under it darkened and began to melt, and the room filled with a burning stench. The stone splintered with a loud crack. When Tobias tried to touch it, it burned his fingers.

"What happened?"

He took a deep breath. "It was Ann Hibbins. I recognized her from the séance. It was her execution. They left her hanging to rot after she died."

"Was she the original sorcerer? That doesn't make sense. I mean, I think it was the right time period." Alan stared at the stone. "But since you broke the crystal ball, we'll have to

Google it." He typed into his phone for a minute. "Okay, she was killed in 1656, so she would've been around in the early days of the school, but it doesn't say anything about her having attended here. I mean, they didn't let women into the school until the 1900s." He looked up. "What exactly did you ask?"

"I asked to see a vision of the life of the Mather Adepti founder."

"She was killed nearby. The original sorcerer would've seen her execution and rotting body." After pocketing his phone, Alan stroked his stubble. "Maybe that's what drove him mad."

20

Tobias

In the Adepti room, Tobias sat cross-legged, staring into the tiny flames on the red candles across from him. The room smelled of the scorched shew stone. Beyond perusing the philosopher's guide, he hadn't found much to fill his time after Alan left. He'd spent the past week trapped in the old school building with no one but Mulligan for company.

Of course, he'd picked through the entire school for signs of the poem. He'd combed through the library—the books, the paintings of old war heroes, the frowning busts, the painted ceilings, and the display cases. He'd leafed through every codex in the poetry section on the off chance that it was hidden in an obvious place, and he'd read books about the Mayflower. He'd scoured the Round Chamber and the dining hall.

By Thursday, he'd returned to the Adepti room to see if he'd missed anything, poring through each page of the remaining books and trying to divine hidden meanings in the ornate tapestry. It would have been a considerably better week if Fiona had stayed with him.

As he stared at the melting candle wax, it occurred to him that they hadn't yet gone *down* the stairwell. He jumped up, blew out the candles, and swung open the door. As he descended the stairs, he trailed his hands along the dewy walls. His footsteps echoed down the three flights of curving stairs, and the air became increasingly dank. A dark moss grew on the low ceiling, and an ever-thicker oozing substance made him jerk back his hand from the wall.

At the end of the stairs, he found a door made from rough planks of wood, inset with a small, grate-covered window. He peered through but could see nothing beyond the bars. He turned the iron doorknob, jiggling it from side to side. Locked. He gave it a kick, but it didn't budge. Disappointed, he returned up the stairs toward the library.

Pushing open the memorial plaque, he was startled to see someone scanning the bookshelves on the other side. Celia's blond hair whirled as she started at the creaking of the plaque. Her jaw dropped.

Tobias hovered in the doorway, with only his head poking out. "What are you doing here?"

"I was looking in the folklore section for witch books. What are *you* doing here?" She hurried toward him. "Is that a secret passage?" She pulled the plaque open further.

Studying? A secret library tryst? "Um..."

She pushed past him, looking up the stairwell. "Is it true what I heard about the Mather Adepti? There were, like, *witches* here?"

He sighed. There wasn't much point denying it now, and he might need her help anyway. "Come on," he said, turning back up the stairs.

And so Celia was introduced to the world of the Mather Adepti. She sat across from him on the rug, her blue eyes opened wide as he told her all about the Angelic language, Rawhed, and the bone wardens.

"So during the séance," she said, "that was a bone warden? How did it get out of Maremount?"

He shook his head. "It was a *vision* of a bone warden. The vision must've been sent to stop us from hearing the full poem. I've been searching for it in the school all week."

Celia's cheeks flushed. "This means I called up a poem that could stop Rawhed. Maybe I'm good at magic."

"Before break started, Alan, Fiona and I tried another séance, but nothing happened. Maybe we'd be more powerful as a larger group, like before. We might have to go back to the site of the elm itself."

She shuffled closer to him on the rug. "Mulligan never discovered that the alarm was disabled. Why don't we try it now? Maybe just the two of us can conduct it."

He rubbed his chin. "I guess we could try it with just us." He smiled. "You think you might be a powerful philosopher?"

She shrugged. "Could be." She rose, holding out her hand. "Come on. Mulligan will be asleep by now."

He grabbed it and followed her through the empty library and down the rickety stairwell.

In the vestibule, Celia opened the door to heavy rain, turning back to glance at Tobias. "You still want to go out?"

He nodded. Despite the rain, the air was unusually warm for March. His shirt was soaked through by the time they'd crossed the courtyard. "I thought I was the only one left at school," he said as they walked toward Boylston Street. "Apart from Mulligan."

She shrugged. "I was just hanging out in my room."

"Why didn't you go home?"

"I never go home for break."

He glanced around at the park as they entered. The park lights illuminated very little, but it seemed the Common was empty in the rain. "Why don't you ever go home?"

"Eh, it's not interesting." She waved her hand. "You're the one with the interesting story. You said when you escaped Rawhed, your friends were left behind?"

He nodded. "Oswald and Eden."

"Are they boyfriend and girlfriend?"

Tobias laughed as they walked along one of the Common paths, his clothes now sopping. "They're siblings. Eden's more like my girlfriend. She invited me to the Festival of the Bird King last year."

She looked over at him, strands of drenched hair sticking to her face. "And what happens at the Festival of the Bird King?"

"Someone's anointed King for the day and dosed with magical, intoxicating herbs. He wears a feathered costume. He gets to choose a woman to—well—he gets to choose a woman. After that day, he disappears. It's actually horrible for the birds. They're baked into pies. They tie live geese to the trees." He pushed his wet hair out of his eyes. "Men rub themselves with a salve of wolfsbane and cinquefoil, and they fly on broken tree branches. They fly right into the geese until the birds' necks break. People gamble on who will smash the goose first. Eden knows that I hate seeing it, and she always finds a way to get me away."

Celia grimaced. "Ew. I'm sure they must have more sophisticated activities in Maremount."

Tobias looked around as they reached an intersection of paths and gestured to a spot on the grass. "This is it—where the elm used to be."

Celia stood across from him, rubbing her arms for warmth. "Well, I didn't bring the candles this time. But I guess they wouldn't work in the rain."

"Do you remember what you said last time?"

"I remember. Hold my hands." She held them out, palms up.

He grabbed hold. "I'll try the Angelic words again."

"Ann Hibbins, speak to us and move among us." She held her face upward into the rain. "Ann Hibbins, speak to us and move among us. Answer our questions and tell us our fates."

As she repeated the phrases, Tobias chanted the words for *appear* and *spirit*. Rain dripped into his eyes, and he tried to blink it out. A streak of lightning lit up the sky, touching down on Beacon Hill.

Celia chanted, and thunder boomed, drowning out her voice as it rumbled over the city. What exactly *were* the chances of calling forth a demon? It had happened only a few times with the Ragmen, but the danger was different here. In Maremount, there'd been a whole coven to fight them off. And without a pike to conduct attack spells, he wouldn't know where to begin.

"Ann Hibbins, speak to us and move among us." Celia was nearly shouting now, her face upturned.

Lightning seared the sky above the State House, and a sharp crack of thunder roared through the air. Tobias's hair stood on end.

"Speak to us and move among us!" Celia chanted.

The aura tingled on his skin. "It's working!"

Celia shouted, "Ann Hibbins, speak to us and tell us our fates!"

Rain battered down as they chanted. Lightning flashed again—this time illuminating a craggy face in the gloom behind Celia. Tobias jumped, pulling Celia toward him, and she fell silent.

A sinewy old man hovered in the shadows for a moment before prowling into the dim yellow light. Apart from a loincloth, boots, and a hat, he wore no clothes. A gray beard curled down to his chest, and red eyes shone from his pale face. Iron boots echoed on the pavement as he walked toward them—*clunk clunk clunk*. Instead of fingers, four sharp talons gripped an iron pike. On his head, a pointed felt cap glistened with burgundy streaks of gore.

"Hello, my friends." He spoke in a low voice with a Scottish accent. As he moved closer, he smiled, showing off a set of long, gray teeth as he approached. *Clunk clunk clunk.*

Celia shifted back toward Tobias, whispering, "What do we do?" She clung to his arm, her nails digging into his flesh.

"Don't run," whispered Tobias. "He'll catch us."

Flaring his large nostrils, the man planted his metal boots on the ground just inches from Tobias. Gray eyebrows swooped up his forehead in peaks and curls. "Don't you know that you're playing with things beyond your control?"

"Sorry," Tobias stammered, as though he'd been caught pilfering an apple from someone's orchard.

The man bent toward them, so close that Tobias could discern a bluish sheen to his skin and smell meat on his breath. He raised his eyebrows. "They're coming, you know. The harvest is thin in Maremount now. They'll want a fresh crop here in Boston. Their god is hungry." He grinned. "You're lucky I'm not."

21

Fiona

Fiona took a bite of her mother's homemade pasta al pomodoro. There wasn't much excitement when she stayed at home for breaks, but the cooking nearly made it tolerable. She found an odd comfort in sitting under the kitchen's glass ceiling lamp surrounded by the clutter of books and magazines. Though her mother often bustled around the kitchen, energetically tidying, the results of her efforts to organize rarely made sense. This morning, in the fruit bowl, Fiona had found two apples, a banana, three quarters, unpaid tuition bills, a cork, a broken cell phone, and a Sherlock Holmes novel.

Her mother's cooking efforts always brought with them a certain amount of chaos. Josephine Forzese had learned from her parents to express her frustration in Italian, although neither she nor Fiona spoke the language very well. When she spilled sauce on the floor or burned her fingers, she shouted something that sounded like "va fa Napoli!" By the time she'd finished the sauce and served dinner, Josephine would refocus her attention on her daughter.

As a radio news show crackled in the background, Fiona swallowed a mouthful of garlicky spaghetti. "What's with the tuition bills? Am I gonna get kicked out?"

"Oh, Fiona, don't be ridiculous. You're not going to get kicked out. We're just waiting for the money your father owes us. Anyway, it's not for you to worry about. Did you change your mind about swim classes?"

"Why do I need to learn to swim?"

"Because it's fun, and because we live near the ocean. I've been telling you this for years."

"And I've been telling you that I don't want to step on a jellyfish." Fiona shuddered.

"Well, they don't have jellyfish in swimming pools." Her mother twisted the last of her spaghetti around her fork.

"New topic, please."

"How's your homework coming? You've only got one day left to finish everything. I know you think you don't need to do homework because you remember everything, but it's not working so well for you anymore. You got an F on your Algebra midterm."

"Ugh!" Fiona threw her head back as if pleading with the gods for mercy. "Why can't we talk about anything interesting?"

Josephine shifted back in her chair. "Like what?"

Séances, bone wardens, spell books, Harvesters—she couldn't mention any of these things. "Never mind. I should probably get to work on my linear equations or whatever."

"I'll get the dishes." Her mother stood, wiping her hands on a napkin. "Fiona, I might have to make a trip to New York soon. Your aunt Rose is getting worse."

"Is she going to be okay?"

"It's not looking good."

"Do you have to go?" Fiona hardly knew her great-aunt. She'd had dementia for as long as Fiona could remember.

"She's got no one else." Dinner plates clinked as Josephine piled them up.

She left her mom to the dishes and retreated to her small, messy room. She flopped backward onto her bed next to her teddy bear, Mr. Huggins. Years of love had malformed his face. She glanced around at the familiar walls, decorated with the same floral wallpaper since she was a little girl. Since her childhood, the only additions were the posters of Lord Byron that hung on the walls.

She'd always imagined herself with someone like Lord Byron—someone "mad, bad, and dangerous to know," a wild genius who made heroes out of his nation's enemies and left a trail of broken hearts in his wake. When they'd read *Frankenstein* in class, Fiona couldn't help but seethe with jealousy toward Mary Shelley, a woman whom Byron had counted among his close friends. Fiona had viewed her as a personal rival and had tried to enlist her classmates to her side. "She uses the word 'countenance' in every other sentence. Couldn't she just say 'face'? I mean *come on*," she'd railed. No one else had cared.

And yet now she caught herself thinking about Tobias, who was nothing like Lord Byron. She wished she were still at school, studying spells with him in the magic room. He really had a beautiful mouth. She shook her head, grabbing a hold of Mr. Huggins. Why was she thinking about Tobias's mouth?

For a moment she considered sending him a text, but of course he had no cell phone. Instead, she texted Celia and Mariana to find out what they were doing. After a few minutes, she received a reply from Celia:

> Tobias told me everything. We did another seance. No Ann Hibbins, but a

demon came. He said something about
"they're coming for more bodies." It was
soooo scary!!!

"Oh my god!" Fiona said out loud. She sat up straight in her bed, typing back:

Are you guys OK?!?!

She waited, staring at her phone until the next little blue bubble popped up.

Yeah. But some people have been seeing the elm again in the common. Like a ghost of the elm. And we think something bad might be coming...

Fiona reclined on her pillows, crossing her arms. It was lucky she'd missed meeting the demon, but annoying they'd been practicing magic without her. Before she'd left, Fiona had snapped photos of the spells. Tobias had warned her not to practice them, and then he and Celia gone and held a séance.

She scowled. Surely she should be able to practice a bit, too. Anyway, Mariana had told her that she could protect herself from demons by pouring salt around the room.

She ran back into the kitchen and plucked a canister of salt off the shelf while her mother scrubbed dishes. Returning to her room, she poured it in a circle over the floorboards and grabbed her phone.

While sitting cross-legged in the center of the circle, she scanned through the spells, reading the English titles above the Latin ones. *Vicomtesse Dangerosa's Torn Bodice* had a certain ring to it. It most definitely sounded like a love spell.

She enlarged the text. She was delighted to find that Latin translations were interesting when they had a purpose.

I call my love up from the earth, like an orchid that rises
*   from the soil.*
Uproot yourself from your resting place in the shade,
And seek me through the scorching streets.
Our roots will intertwine, and we will burn in ecstasy.

"This could get interesting."

First, she tried speaking the words in an Ecclesiastical Latin accent. Staring at the posters as she spoke, she imagined that Lord Byron might become animated by her words and leap into three dimensions before her.

After reciting the spell, she glanced around at the floral wallpaper, the white comforter, and the posters on the wall. It didn't feel as though she'd achieved anything, but at least she hadn't created an aura that would attract a demon. She looked at Mr. Huggins's one mournful eye, half expecting a demon to burst from it.

After a few minutes, she tried the spell again, this time changing the pronunciation to her best approximation of a Hebrew accent. After all, the language of the angels probably came from somewhere in the Middle East. With this recitation, she felt a tingling on her skin, like a warm breeze. The wind picked up outside, rattling her windowpanes. She looked at her posters, but Lord Byron remained two-dimensional.

She rose, pulling her curtains aside to look out the window. A dense cloud had descended on her street. Despite the fog, no velvet-coated man materialized out of the mist to stride among Hatch Street's narrow triple-decker homes.

22

Thomas

Thomas sat on the worn leather sofa in his living room, pouring himself a beer and opening his laptop to check the news. He clicked on a story about a teenage boy who was nearly choked to death by cops for taking a picture of them on his cell phone. The law seemed to him less a codified set of rules than an experiment in what the authorities could get away with.

Wind shook his windows, and he stood to look outside. A keening sound pierced the air, and a stocky black cat sauntered through the low-lying fog. He rubbed his arms as cold air seeped through the windowpanes. Even for a Londoner, something seemed particularly bleak about the grayness of the day. Returning to his sofa, he opened another video news story, this one lighter in tone.

A blonde newscaster smirked at the camera as she read the prompt. "Sightings of a bygone landmark in Boston Common are being reported over social media. The old elm tree that marked the meeting spot for the Sons of Liberty died in the 19th century. The story has Bostonians wondering: is this some kind of promotional stunt, mass hysteria, or are we being visited by a ghost from the past? Take a look." Blurry phone footage showed Boston Common at night, though all Thomas could see were a few yellow orbs near the top of the screen—the streetlights lining the paths.

"It's coming back!"

Something blocked out the yellow lights, though it was hard to make out what it was.

"What the—"

A bleeping cut out the rest of his sentence, and the blonde newscaster returned. "Apparently the gentlemen creating the video were alarmed by what they saw. But I have to say, that footage isn't convincing me to call the Ghostbusters just yet."

Thomas closed the video and searched online for the phrase *Boston Elm*, then *Witching Elm*. Thousands of results came up.

In all likelihood, this was just another incidence of mass hysteria. There were plenty of cases of collective psychosis. In the 16th century, residents of Strasbourg had danced uncontrollably for days, in some cases to their deaths. And there were of course the witch trials, and all the imagined torments of spectral visitors and witches' familiars.

He clicked on a link called *Elm Tree Video!!! #CREEPY*. As before, it was shot at night. But this time, a human form shifted into view beneath the dim streetlights. It was a man wearing a tapered, wide-brimmed hat. Light glinted off something. It almost looked like strands of vine leaves around his clothes. His face in shadow, he walked toward the camera and spoke in a low growl. "Druloch will have his feast," was all he said before the footage cut out.

23

Fiona

O n Sunday afternoon, the last day before school resumed, Fiona strolled through the Common. After all the reports of the elm tree's mysterious appearances, she half expected to see ghostly branches flickering in the center of the park.

Instead, as she approached the elm site, she saw a crowd gathered where the tree had once stood. Some kneeled on the ground; others stumbled over the grass, closing their eyes, their lips moving in prayer. A hollow-cheeked old man gripped a sign that said "the King of Truth returns." He pumped it up and down, a glazed look in his eyes.

As Fiona walked past them, a bespectacled woman with snarled brown hair broke free from the crowd and jumped in her path. "Have you been given the words of truth?"

"What words?"

"The King of Terror will return." With a yellow-toothed grin she added, "We're all going to die."

Fiona jerked back, rushing past her toward the Athenæum. She had a few hours to kill before meeting up with her friends in the Adepti room. Tobias had decided that they must form a coven, and tonight would be their first meeting.

She waited to cross Park Street, frowning. Tobias and Celia had called forth a spirit, but she'd failed to perform a spell of her own.

Still, perhaps she'd see some spectral activity at the Athenæum. On a ghost tour, she'd learned that every morning, Nathaniel Hawthorne had sat across from an old clergyman. Since the two were Bostonian gentleman, they'd never spoken directly. As it turned out, this morning ritual of aloofness had continued even after the minister passed away, the author and the ghost eyeing each other but never speaking. It wouldn't do to disturb another man's personal time, even if he was dead.

Once inside the library's red door, she flashed her ID at the desk and began by wandering around the art sections on the lower level, peering out the window at the mossy stones of the Granary Burying Ground. A small part of her still hoped that Lord Byron might emerge bodily from behind a stack of shelves, or that she'd catch a glimpse of him limping through the cemetery on his club foot.

She ambled through one level after another of dusty bookshelves, spotting neither a ghost nor her 19th century paramour. By the fifth floor, impatient with the lack of paranormal activity, she resolved to find something interesting to read. Somewhere in the building lay a book bound by human skin, though she couldn't determine how to ask the librarians about it without sounding like a psychopath.

But the library should have something about Maremount. Setting off to find a reference computer, she glimpsed someone hunched over a desk in an alcove. His hair was brushed forward, and he wore a gray coat, out of which peaked a large open collar.

"Lord Byron?"

He looked up at her with large blue eyes, and she recognized the full lips and perfect cheekbones.

Her hand flew up to her mouth. "Jack. I haven't seen you in a while."

"Did you say *Lord Byron*?"

"No... nope. Did it sound like I said that?" She emitted a short laugh.

"It's the collar, isn't it? Well, sorry to have disappointed you." He smiled and returned to his book.

"Oh no, you're even better." She felt her cheeks flush. *Why can't I say something normal?*

"Thanks, I guess. Are you here to look for a book, or were you hoping to meet dead poets?"

"Oh, you know, either one. There's the book bound with the skin of..." She stopped herself. She didn't want to compound the Hitler thing. "Actually, I was hoping to catch a glimpse of a ghost. They're saying the Witching Elm keeps showing up, and there's a view of the graveyard here. Also Nathaniel Hawthorne used to see a ghost here reading newspapers." She swallowed. "Well, you probably know that story. I mean, you're his great-grandson or whatever." She smiled, shaking her head. "Not that I know everything about you. It's just someone said you were related..." She trailed off, looking out the window.

"I'm related to him, though I didn't inherit his ghost unfortunately. But I do know the King's Chapel cemetery might be better for spotting spirits. It's older."

"Good point." She nodded, and then she could think of nothing else to say. "Well, I might have a look there. Just out of curiosity."

"I'm going there next weekend to make drawings of the grave carvings, if you want to join me. We might see some ghosts."

She smiled. "Yes, I'd like to do that."

"I'll be there Saturday at noon."

"Awesome. Okay, well, I'll meet you there."

She grinned all the way home to Mather, even as she passed the yellow-toothed woman.

The sun began to dip below the horizon as she approached the school. In the courtyard, near the gates, Munroe's copper hair burned in the late afternoon sun. She'd wrapped her manicured hands around the bars, and she pulled the gate open as Fiona approached. As Fiona passed Munroe, she noticed something new: a small tattoo of a chalice on her wrist.

Fiona had always distrusted her—even more after she'd enlisted her friends to beat up Tobias. Yet there was something sad about her, especially since she'd lost Sully. "Everything okay, Munroe?"

She closed the gate, staring toward the Common again. "The Apocalypse is coming. The impure walk among us."

"What are you talking about?"

She glanced at Fiona, shadows beneath her deep gray eyes. "I know what Tobias is."

Fiona's euphoria disappeared as her muscles tensed. "I don't know what you're talking about."

She hurried into the school building, glancing over her shoulder to make sure that no one followed her as she ascended the library stairs. By the time she arrived in the Adepti room, all her friends sat facing Tobias—Celia, Alan, and even Mariana.

Tobias stood before the fireplace, chewing his thumbnail. "There you are."

"Munroe knows about you." Fiona sat on the rug. In front of Tobias was a small pile of goggles, some fireproof blankets from the chemistry room, and a fire extinguisher.

"We've got bigger things to worry about than Munroe." Tobias clutched the philosopher's guide as he paced. "We were all there for the first séance. Celia and I tried to have a second one. We called something up, but it wasn't Ann Hibbins. It was a Redcap, a type of demon. He told us that the Harvesters are coming to Boston."

Mariana gasped. "Coming here? Why?"

"When Rawhed raised the Harvesters from the dead, he may have called on one of the gods to imbue them with power. Celia showed me the moving pictures on the computer. It looked like a Harvester was already here, assessing things. He said something about Druloch. Druloch is the tree god. One who demands sacrifices."

"That doesn't sound good," said Alan.

"The Redcap said that the crop had run thin in Maremount," Tobias continued. "I think it's harder to find people to hang there, now that everyone's scattered. They're going to come here for easy pickings."

Celia arched an eyebrow. "So, what are we supposed to do?"

"We need to find the poem." Tobias joined them on the rug. "If we stop Rawhed, we'll stop his army. And we should form a coven—the new Mather Adepti. We were powerful together when we first raised Ann Hibbins."

"And then what? What if we don't find the poem before they get here?" asked Mariana. "We fight a whole army? Just the five of us?"

Tobias rested his chin on his hand. "Well, no. I think we should hide in the school and hope they don't come in here. But if they do, it wouldn't hurt to know the inferno spell to light them on fire."

Alan smacked his hands together. "Yes! That's what I'm talking about. I like this coven thing."

Fiona nodded. "That explains all the fire safety equipment."

"So what do you all think?" Tobias looked around.

"Well, we're not going to say 'no' to learning magic, are we?" Mariana hugged her knees.

"I've always wanted to learn magic," said Celia. "But might I remind everyone that the last two times we tried anything magical, we called up terrifying monsters? I wasn't scared of the bone warden. But the Redcap had bits of flesh on his hat—possibly human." She shivered.

"She makes a good point," said Mariana.

Fiona could see the concern on Tobias's face as he looked toward the ceiling. He often did that, when he was thinking—looked up and ran his fingers along his jawline. "I'm almost positive that this room has aura protections, like the old philosophers' schools. I don't know how they did it, but I think we're safe."

Celia frowned. "But we don't really know."

"Oh, come on." Fiona jostled her shoulder. "We've always wanted to be witches."

Tobias cleared his throat. "Philosophers."

"Fine." Celia tutted. "I just wanted to make sure that everyone knows we might end up mauled to death by a man with really bad teeth."

Tobias opened the dusty philosopher's guide. "So are we all in agreement?"

They nodded.

"Let's do this," said Alan.

"Good." He smiled. "I guess we're a coven. Soon we'll have an initiation ceremony. But first, we need to do the hard work and memorize some spells." He looked down at the book in his lap, turning the fragile pages. "Queen Boudicca's Inferno. We should maybe clear out some of the flammable things first."

They stood and began clearing out the room, starting with the rug. When the tapestry and wooden table were removed to the stairwell, they sat in a circle on the cold stone floor. Tobias handed out pencils and paper and asked them to phonetically transcribe the fire spell, copying the sounds over and over.

"I hate handwriting," Alan muttered after a while.

Tobias looked up from the book. "This is the first step. If we're going to actually fight with the spells, we must memorize them. We can't refer to a book if somebody's trying to kill us."

They continued copying the sequence until Fiona's hand shot up. "Done! I've got it memorized."

She ran her hands over the chilly stone floor as the others worked, tracing words with her fingers to pass the time. Then she reclined against the wall with a loud sigh. "Can we try it out now? Maybe everyone else can practice at home."

Celia straightened, narrowing her eyes. "Show-off."

"All right," said Tobias. "Has everyone got the fire blankets and goggles ready? I'm not sure how big the inferno will be. I think everyone except Fiona and me should go toward the door. Mariana—you have the fire destroyer, right?"

"The fire extinguisher. Yes."

As the others moved toward the stairwell, Fiona joined Tobias near the fireplace. She wrapped herself in the silvery fire blanket.

"Are you sure you want to do this?" Tobias asked. "We could try it outside, near water at least."

"But this room will shield us from the aura." Fiona secured her goggles. "We'll be fine with the blankets."

"All right. Go on, then."

Fiona chanted the spell. Her muscles tensed, ready to spring backward when the room erupted into a fireball. As she recited the Angelic words, the aura fluttered across her skin like moth wings. She could picture the stone walls growing so hot in the inferno that they melted. As she finished the recitation, she braced herself for an explosion.

There was nothing for a moment. As she held her breath, she could hear only the sound of her thudding heart. Then, a tiny lick of fire emerged in the fireplace, the size of a flame on a birthday cake's candle. She waited, but the little, faltering flame remained the same size.

"Is that it?" Alan called out, pulling up his goggles.

"Was my pronunciation wrong?" said Fiona.

Tobias shook his head. "It sounded right to me. I don't know what happened. Let me try."

They returned to their positions, goggles in place, and Tobias repeated the spell. Fiona braced herself again, but once more only a tiny spark of flame emerged, dwarfed by empty space in the fireplace. In one last attempt, they joined in a circle and chanted the spell together. This time, the flame quadrupled in size.

"I guess the spells are stronger if we work as a group," said Tobias. "But it's hardly an inferno."

Mariana pulled off her goggles. "Who was Queen Boudicca? She sucks."

"She didn't suck," said Alan. "She burned the whole city of London down when it was controlled by the Romans. She must've had something better than this spell."

Mariana rolled her eyes. "Like matches."

"So what do we do now?" said Alan.

"We might as well keep practicing." Fiona unwrapped the silvery blanket. They hadn't created an inferno, but she was pleased to have created anything using just words. "Maybe some of the other spells will be more effective."

"What, like Viscomtess Dangerosa's Torn Bodice?" Tobias tossed down his goggles. "I don't know what sort of person would even use that spell."

Fiona averted her eyes. "At least it would be a way to start to learn Angelic."

"Why don't we try the séance again in here?" said Alan, folding up his fire blanket. "Together we might be able to raise Ann Hibbins."

They agreed to try the séance one more time, joining in a circle. Celia led the chants again, and they held hands under the flickering candles of the Mather Adepti refuge.

"Ann Hibbins—speak to us and move among us!" Celia chanted. She turned her head up toward the ceiling. "Ann Hibbins!"

Nothing rippled over Fiona's skin, and the sound of Celia repeating herself began to annoy her. After a few minutes, she opened her eyes to catch the tower imp peaking out from a small hole below the window. "Guys, I don't think it's working. We've got nothing to fight the Harvesters right now."

24

Fiona

On Saturday morning, the day she'd arranged to meet Jack, Fiona woke in her usual tangle of bed sheets. She slipped into Celia's jeans, green sweater, and gold ballet slippers. The only thing she wore of her own was a silver pendant containing an old photo of her grandmother.

After spending all her free time in the musty old building, she found the fresh spring air a relief. Boston winters were brutal, but when life began to bleed back into the earth, it smelled glorious. Under the dappled light of the Common trees, Fiona forgot about the Harvesters. As she entered the cemetery, she spotted Jack crouching before a gravestone, drawing in a notebook.

He rose as he saw her approach, gazing at her from beneath his dark eyelashes. "There you are!"

"Hi, Jack." She glanced at the illuminated tree leaves above her as she stood by his side. "It's a beautiful day." She took a deep breath.

"It is. Have you been here before?"

"We came here when we were reading *The Scarlet Letter*. I remember there was a grave with a fancy A on it, like the A in the book." It was a relief to have something factual to talk about.

"You mean Elizabeth Pain. She's buried right over there." He pointed to a gravestone to the right. "She was arrested right after the Salem Witch Trials. They said she killed her baby."

They strolled toward the grave, and his arm brushed against hers.

She bit her lip. It was hard not to ask him about his famous relatives. "When we read *The Scarlet Letter*, they told us Nathaniel Hawthorne was a descendant of one of the witch trial judges. So that means you're related to the judge, too."

"Oh. *That*." He brushed his black curls back with a faint smile. "Not one of the high points in our family history."

"Kind of cool, though, in a creepy way."

They stopped, crouching in front of Elizabeth's grave. The stone featured a stark image of a winged skull. Above the death's-head stood an hourglass with angel wings. Two pillars on the sides were marked with leaves and corn, and what appeared to be drooping pairs of breasts. In the corner, the ornate letter A decorated a stately shield along with two lions.

"That's the one," she said. "I remember thinking the carvings on the side looked like, you know, like boobs." *Boobs*—what an awkward word. But her tongue always tripped over the S's in *breasts*, and she couldn't very well say *tits*.

Jack laughed, throwing back his head. "They *are* boobs, but they're supposed to represent the spiritual nourishment provided by ministers."

She smiled, staring into his pale blue eyes. His cheeks were beautifully flushed today. "You seem like you know a lot about cemeteries."

He held out his hand as he rose. "I just like history, and there's not much left from the past here except the gravestones. Plus, they're good for drawing."

She grasped his hand, standing. "What have you been working on?"

He showed her a sketch. It was a beautifully rendered image of a skull-and-hourglass engraving—chilling and delicate at the same time. "They were Puritan favorites. At funerals, they'd give out gloves or flasks decorated with skulls and hourglasses."

"Like goth party favors?"

"Pretty much. Skulls and skeletons were really the only pictures anyone saw. Besides the boobs. *Fugit hora; memento mori.*"

She glanced at the hourglass on the stone. "Time flies; remember death."

He smiled. "Right. Your mother's the Latin teacher. What's it like having a parent at the school?"

They began walking in the shade of the trees.

"It's okay. Sometimes people complain to me about their grades. But she gets the summers off, and we stay at my aunt's house in Nantucket. Last summer Mariana visited the island from New York, and we rode bikes the whole time. Also, with my mom in the school, I get to hear some of the teacher gossip."

"Does your mom know what happened to Ms. Bouchard?" He linked his arm into hers as they walked the winding path.

"That one's a mystery. I think she might have just run off." She looked toward the street. "There are a lot of strange things going on."

"Teachers disappearing, the elm tree reappearing—those sorts of strange things?" He sighed. "And now Munroe has been talking about witches."

"Has she? Do people believe her?"

"She's very convincing. She says your friend Tobias is a witch."

Fiona was surprised that Jack had been paying enough attention to know who her friends were. "Boys can't be witches." It was the best she could come up with. "But it does feel like something... *dangerous* is coming, doesn't it?"

He glanced at her. "Like we're all going to die?"

"I hope not quite that bad." She frowned. "But you know if anything bad happens, just stay in the school. Or come find me." She turned, touching his arm with her free hand.

He grinned. "Really? Will you protect me?"

She gazed at him solemnly. "I would do my best."

"I feel safer already from whatever monsters might be after us."

"You should feel safer. My mom used to sweep the monsters out from under my bed before I went to sleep. I learned her technique, so I'm perfectly capable of sweeping the monsters away from you."

He arched an eyebrow. "Does that work for real monsters? Or only imagined ones?"

She nodded. "I believe it's a fool-proof, all-purpose monster remedy."

His face became serious. "Well, you must come over before I go to sleep and sweep the monsters out."

Her heart raced when she thought about going to his room.

He glanced at his watch. "Damn, I have to go already. I have some reading to do. Will you be around next weekend?"

"Yeah. Assuming the monsters haven't gotten us first." She smiled.

25

Tobias

Tobias rolled over in his bed. Someone was shaking his arm.

"I'm sleeping," he mumbled into his pillow. He pulled the blankets up around him.

"Tobias, wake up." It was Alan's voice.

Tobias rolled over, opening his eyes to find his roommate standing over him. Moonlight streamed through their window.

"Something's happening outside."

Tobias sat up, rubbing his eyes. A ragged, high-pitched noise wound through the streets outside.

Alan darted to the window. "Did you hear that? It sounded like someone screaming. But it didn't sound like the usual college drunks."

Tobias threw off his blankets and followed Alan to the window. He pressed his hand on the cool glass as he looked out toward the park. A group of young people ran out of the Common and across Boylston Street. One of the women was screaming, "Oh my God!"

Tobias's breath caught in his lungs. They watched as two more people fled the park.

Alan turned to him. "Should we call the police?"

As he spoke the words, police sirens howled in the distance, and red and blue lights flashed near Park Street. Two large, tan-colored armored vehicles rolled down Boylston and cut left into the park. A flat voice announced through a loudspeaker, *"Please disperse. This is a crime scene. Please disperse for your own safety."*

As Tobias watched the pulsing police lights, he heard only the wail of sirens, until the school intercom crackled in the hallway. "Hello?" It was Mulligan. "Is this on? I don't know how to..." There was a shuffling noise. "Students, please stay in your rooms. This is a lockdown procedure. Please lock your doors and remain in your rooms with the lights off. This is not a drill."

A droning sound throbbed overhead—a rapid-fire beating of the air. A large white circle of light danced around in the streets.

"Helicopters," Alan murmured, staring out the window. The light swerved into the Common and back to Boylston. "They're searching for someone."

A burgundy hat flashed through the searchlight in front of the school gates and disappeared again.

"It's the Redcap." Tobias felt sick. He'd brought him here.

The white circle hovered on the pavement near where the Redcap had been, and after a few seconds, a severed head rolled into the light. It was a man with close-cropped black hair. Alan jumped back from the window and covered his mouth, muttering something into his hand. Tobias could hardly breathe.

"Was that a policeman?" Alan asked, just as the Redcap darted into the searchlight again. Grinning, he took the gore-streaked cap off his head and dipped it into the policeman's puddled blood before disappearing into the dark again.

A short burst of automatic gunfire drew the light further into the park, illuminating a large oak tree at the border of the Common. A group of men in tapered hats stood beneath it, pulling on a rope. A writhing body bathed in white light rose above them.

Tobias's stomach dropped. "It's the Harvesters." He stepped away from the window. "They're here."

26

Fiona

Fiona leaned against a yew tree in the courtyard beside Jack, toying with the locket around her neck. Across the street, the sunset filtered through the trees in the Common, flecking the ground with sparks of light. The bodies had been cut down, but a thick red smear marred the pavement in front of the school, and armored police vehicles still rumbled through the streets. The police had erected temporary metal fences around the park, and yellow tape zigzagged between them.

Fourteen people had been hanged, two beheaded, and six shot—possibly by friendly fire.

"Were you awake when it happened?" asked Jack.

"Mulligan's announcement woke us. Celia and I had to lean out the window to see what was happening. I saw the head." She took a shuddering breath. As much as they'd talked about Harvesters and demons, she'd never seen the slackened jaw of a corpse before, or the rapid exsanguination of a severed jugular. She swallowed. "And then the guy was jerking around when they hung him. And they could have come into the school."

"If Grunshaw hadn't been enforcing the lockdown, I would've found you." He stuck his hands in his pockets, turning to look at her. His eyes looked almost green in the golden light. "Or at least I could have swept the monsters away for you."

"I never really got any sleep, even after the Har—" She stopped herself. "Even after the terrorists disappeared. My mom was on the phone with me forever. It feels like after the marathon bombings, except I didn't see those up close." She shivered. "Everyone stayed up to watch the news, waiting to see if the police would catch the guys. But they never did."

"What does everyone think happened?" He rested his arm on the tree.

"Munroe says it was witchcraft because the terrorists disappeared so quickly. And because there's a tiny tree growing in the spot where the elm once stood. I saw a picture. It doesn't look like it's made of bark. It looks like bone."

He frowned, running his fingers through his hair. "Witchcraft accusations don't seem like they belong in this century, but the events don't seem natural."

Fiona took another shaky breath. The lack of sleep had a dulling effect on her senses, making her calmer than she would have been otherwise. "Munroe keeps saying her father's on a witchcraft task force. Everyone seems to believe her." She turned to him. "Were your parents worried?"

He shook his head. "I don't imagine so."

"Why not?"

"I don't hear much from them."

"Why? Where do they live?"

"They're from Salem originally. Home of the witch trials."

She shuddered. "I don't understand how people in Salem used to watch public hangings for entertainment."

"Maybe in the old days, it felt like a sacrifice to a destructive god. Maybe people thought *better her than me*. Anyway, you don't need to be scared." He pulled at a ringlet next to her cheek. "If anything else happens, I promise to keep you safe, even if I have to throw Grunshaw out the window. And maybe you need a break from staring at the hanging tree. There's more to being from Salem than just witches. I could take you sailing, so you could forget about all this."

"Sailing sounds nice." She blinked, gazing into his eyes. She was only half awake.

He twirled her ringlet around his index finger. "Next weekend—we'll go out into the harbor."

As she looked up at him, he leaned down to kiss her on the mouth. She felt her whole body light up with euphoria. And then he was off again strolling back toward the school building. She was dizzy with excitement for a moment, until the red stain on the pavement called her back to reality.

She turned, heading back into the main entrance and climbing the creaky stairs. After stopping by her room for a pillow and blankets, she dragged them to the library. She unlatched the memorial plaque, sneaking into the Adepti room. The silence of the hidden room would provide some respite after her sleepless night.

She threw her bedding down and pulled off her locket, hanging it from one of the sconce's long fingers. Still in her clothes, she snuggled into her pillow against the wall.

When she awoke, the room was dark except for a bluish glow from the window. She sat up and looked around, rubbing her eyes. She was starting to like the idea of staying here. None of the teachers were on the lookout for students spending too much time in the library, so she could come and go unnoticed. She rose, stretching her arms over her head. Maybe she could make the tower imp her friend, the way prisoners befriended rats.

When she walked over to the window and peered out, she could see very little. In the gloaming, a hint of coral light tinged a deep gray mist. She returned to her pillow and pulled her scratchy wool blanket around her. In the dim light, an embroidered goat's head on the rug leered at her.

Maybe she should rethink this idea. What if demons haunted this tower—spirits who would drag her to a grisly death as she slept? She bit her thumbnail, thinking of a sharp-toothed spirit with flaming eyes. A creaking noise sounded outside the door, and something like footfalls echoed in the stairwell. She held her breath—probably only the wind troubling an old building. The footsteps stopped.

She'd just started to breathe again, when she heard knocking, like knuckles rapping a coffin lid. She threw off her blanket and rushed to the philosopher's guide, flipping the pages in a panicked scramble for the transformation spell. The sound of her own name interrupted her search.

"Fiona?"

She exhaled, closing the book. It was Tobias's voice. "Thank God. I thought you were a monster." She crossed the room, yanking open the door.

"That's only sort of true." Tobias stood in the dark, holding two paper bags. "I didn't see you at dinner. Celia thought you might've come here. I thought you must be hungry." He walked into the room, sitting down on the rug near the tapestry. "And I wanted to see if you were okay after last night."

She hadn't eaten all day, and she grabbed a paper bag, sitting next to him on the floor. "Thank you so much. I don't think I've ever forgotten to eat before." She pulled open a bag and began chomping through a bagel. "What do you mean, you're sort of a monster?"

Tobias looked down, rubbing his face with his hands. "Celia and I brought the Redcap here."

Fiona swallowed. "Oh yeah. Well, maybe it wasn't your fault. Maybe he was drawn in by the aura from the Harvesters." She was suddenly aware that she'd sat very close to him. Heat from his arm radiated against hers.

He nodded, unconvinced. "What are you doing in here?"

"It's quiet. Celia's always on the phone to Lucas, and I haven't been able to nap. And we're safe from the Harvesters here. I'm thinking of moving in."

"I like it here, too. I might stay for a bit."

"Nice. We could practice more magic." She brushed some crumbs off her lap. "I guess I shouldn't worry so much about the Harvesters since the police are all over it now."

He stretched his legs out on the rug, looking up at the ceiling. "But they don't know what's really going on. They don't know this was only the beginning."

27

Fiona

Lying on the floor in the Adepti room, her chin propped up in her hands, Fiona scrolled through pictures on her laptop. Police tape still blocked off most of the park, but a photographer had snapped the burgeoning elm tree from a distance. It looked about five feet high, with curling alabaster branches. *The Witching Elm.* Was it some kind of monument to Druloch?

While she waited for her friends to arrive for their coven meeting, she stood and pulled the philosopher's guide off the shelf. A cloaking spell could prove useful in another Harvester attack, and she wanted to try out Lady Cleo's Cloak. Based on Tobias's earlier phonetic instruction, she was able to piece together the pronunciation. After stumbling through it a few times, she finally felt her skin prickle as she recited it.

As she completed the spell, her body and clothing shimmered away to transparency. It was a disorienting feeling, to look down and see only the floor below. A dizzying moment of panic overtook her. *Have I transformed myself out of existence? Is that even possible?* She stomped the floor just to hear the sound of her feet, and she sang a few lines from

Cats, reassured by her tuneless voice. A few minutes later, when her skin began to glimmer back into view, she breathed easier. Fully visible, she reclined against the wall as she waited for her friends.

Celia and Mariana were the first to trudge up the stone stairs. Mariana had draped herself in a long black wizard robe and a necklace that looked like a spider web. Stuffed under her arm was a box of Damon's Doughnuts. They joined Fiona on the floor and waited for the guys, tucking into the doughnuts.

Celia picked at her glazed treat. "It's kind of weird how we're going to classes like nothing happened. I mean, they keep saying we can go to a counselor, but then we're just supposed to go to class and do math."

Fiona sighed. "They think it's another isolated terrorist attack. Like the marathon bombings. They don't know it's a full-scale invasion."

Mariana's purple lipstick was now covered in a white powder. "Not that I think we should just run away, but if the Harvesters are coming back—are we safe?"

"This room feels safe." Fiona glanced around at the tapestry and the hand-like sconces dripping with red wax. "I know it's creepy, but I don't think the Harvesters could get in here. If they come back, we should hide in here."

Celia sat up straight. "And we need to keep practicing magic and looking for the poem. You guys were right. I mean, *someone* needs to find it, right? Or they'll just keep killing people."

"I've been trying to learn the spells in my free time," said Fiona. "I've practically moved in here now."

Celia played with a strand of her blond hair, staring at the window. "It's lonely in our room now. I wish I could have Lucas in your place."

"Ew. That's my brother you're talking about." Mariana grimaced. "Have you told him anything about the Mather Adepti?"

Celia shook her head. "He doesn't know anything. But if the Harvesters come back, we should take him in here with us for safety, right?"

"So are we going to choose who gets to live and die?" As Fiona took a bite of her jelly doughnut, she paused to stare at its glistening red center.

"Let's not think about that." Mariana's skull ring gleamed as she waved her hands dismissively. "Celia's right. We should just focus on doing what we can—looking for the poem, and trying to learn the spells."

As Fiona took another bite, she heard a gentle scraping sound behind her. She turned to find the tower imp dragging her locket across the floor toward the windowed wall.

"He's got your necklace!" Celia shrieked, her blue eyes snapping open as she jumped up.

Fiona leapt up. "Oh my God! Can you catch him?"

Celia recoiled. "I don't want to touch him. What if he bites?"

While he dragged the necklace closer to the wall, he looked up at the girls with large, mournful eyes. He pulled the necklace into his small hole below the window.

Mariana tilted her head as she watched him. "How odd. He's like a sad magpie."

"What else do you think he has in there?" asked Celia.

"I don't know. I'm not sticking my hand in. But Tobias said he's harmless." Fiona shrugged. "So I'll just ask him to fish it out."

The girls crept toward the hole and peered in, but could see only darkness. Celia flashed her phone light, eliciting a hiss from the creature.

Just then, Alan and Tobias pushed open the door, covered in mud.

Fiona pointed at the imp's hiding place. "That thing stole my necklace! Can you get it?"

Tobias brushed dirt off his hands. "Can we do it after the meeting? I'm sorry we're late. We were digging in the courtyard. There was some uneven ground, and we thought maybe the poem was buried."

"Sure, whatever," said Fiona.

They formed a circle on the rug. Tobias began the lesson by asking everyone to recite fragments of Angelic spells.

After the drills, they practiced the spells individually. While Alan mastered the fire spell, Fiona read through Frater Basilus's Spell for Wind. Mariana smiled as she practiced Sir Isaac's Spell for Growth, magnifying the size of a half-eaten chocolate doughnut.

A slight mishap occurred when Fiona's wind spell collided with Alan's fire spell, casting a flame onto Mariana's long robes. Tobias stomped out the fire with his foot as Mariana shrieked.

"Next time," Tobias declared as they finished their lesson, "after the language drills, we can do an initiation ceremony. In a vision, you'll learn how to transform into your familiar. The invisibility and transformation spells are probably the only ones that might be useful if the Harvesters attack. As much as it's important to study Angelic, I don't think growing cakes will help."

Everyone rose. While Celia and Mariana left for their rooms, Tobias lingered behind to retrieve Fiona's necklace from the tower imp, and Alan stuck around to see if he could catch a glimpse of the creature. Tobias got down on his knees in front of the hole and reached in. Fiona heard a distant whimpering noise and some scuffling, and then Tobias pulled out his arm. In his hand were two paperclips and a brass button.

"Let me try again. There was more in there." He reached in and grasped around, finally pulling his hand out—this time with a skeleton key. An attached note read: *Don't Upset Bess.* He handed Fiona the key, and after he reached back in, he pulled out Fiona's necklace.

"Thank you so much!" She crossed to the bookshelf, secreting the necklace into her large, floral-printed cloth handbag.

The imp's gray face emerged from his hole, and he looked out at the three humans with dolorous eyes. Alan gave him two quarters and a nickel, which he dragged into his sanctuary, though his sad expression remained fixed.

"They always look that way." Tobias plucked the key out of Fiona's hand, examining it before looking up with a faint smile. "We need to try this on the door downstairs."

28

Tobias

Tobias led Fiona and Alan down the stairwell, illuminating it with a glowing orb. At the bottom of the stairs, he stopped at the wooden door and slid the key into the lock. There was a sharp intake of breath as it clicked open into a dark space with a thick, moldy spell.

Tobias directed the light forward. It cast a dull glow on a low passage made of arched, earthen walls. Particles of dirt caught in his lungs. They walked forward, huddled together, until Tobias noticed some white flecks embedded in the dirt. He bent down, brushing aside some of the soil to reveal a smooth, ivory surface.

"What is it?" asked Alan.

"Bones." He jerked upwards, almost smacking his head on the low ceiling.

As they continued walking, more bones became visible in the walls and floor, with a few distinctly human skulls embedded in the dirt.

Fiona whispered, "Do you think we should turn around?"

"I think we're okay," said Tobias, his shoulders tensed.

"Yeah, I mean they're just bones." Alan laughed nervously.

Tobias felt Fiona's nails dig into his arm as the tunnel opened into a large earthen room. The foxfire illuminated uneven rows of dark shelves arranged haphazardly around the room. Jars of fetuses, syphilitic skulls, and desiccated human limbs lay on the shelves, and a misshapen wooden stool rested on the floor.

They froze as a wavering, high-pitched voice filled the room with a song. Tobias pulled Fiona closer.

Girls and boys are come out to play,
I have not seen the light of day;
Shut your windows and shut your door,
And hide with your playfellows under the floor.

A hunched crone tottered into the dim light. A gray cap hung over her scraggly white hair and wrinkled skin, shielding her eyes. Her dark dress draped over an emaciated figure.

"Are you Bess?" Tobias asked, his voice barely audible.

The woman replied with a shriek:

Bessie Pain, whipped in vain,
Wicked sinner, once again!

"Bessie Pain?" Fiona whispered. "Elizabeth Pain? Are you the ghost of Elizabeth Pain? The lady with the gravestone?"

"Not a ghost. I never died."

"I thought I saw your grave. With the A on it." Fiona's voice faltered.

"The city is filled with liars. Under the earth, you find the truth. What do you see when you walk about upstairs?"

Fiona stammered, "I don't know."

"Paintings of heroes, gilded and gleaming. But I live with the bones they buried to build their city upon a hill." Bess chanted:

Eggs, cheese, butter, bread,
Stick, stock, stone, dead,
Hang them up, lay them down,
On corrupted frozen ground.

"Corrupted frozen ground..." Tobias recognized the line from the poem. "We're looking for the whole poem. Do you know it? The King Philip poem—about the corrupted frozen ground?"

"I have no need for it." She stepped closer to Tobias, lifting her chin to peer at him through bloodshot eyes. She roared, "Where's Wormock?"

"You knew him?" If she knew Wormock, maybe she was friendly to the Ragmen, despite her terrifying appearance.

"He brought me cakes." She smacked her lips. "Some with honey and some with flowers made of sugar and cream."

Tobias attempted a smile. "He was a friend of my father's."

"Where is Wormock?" She shuffled closer. One eye was half-closed, while the other bulged.

Tobias glanced at Fiona. He wasn't sure how to deliver the news. "He's not around anymore, I'm afraid. A succubus killed him."

Bess sighed, and with a groan she lowered herself onto the stool. "I feared it would be him. Terrible business. But everyone's got to go sometime, except me." She snorted. "I guess he won't be coming through here anymore."

"What do you mean, coming through here?" asked Tobias.

She spat on the ground and then rubbed her mouth with the back of her hand. "To get to Maremount. I used to let him through, since he brought me the treats."

Tobias's heart raced. *Is this the Darkling Tunnel?* "You let him through? This goes to Maremount?"

"If I say the right words, yes." Grasping her back, she rose again. "But you'll need to bring me something."

"What would you like me to bring you?" he asked.

She folded her arms, rubbing them with her hands as she stared at the ground. She kicked at a stone near the stool. "Cakes."

"Cakes?" He repeated. "You'd like cakes? To get me home?"

She nodded. So this was the route home, if he wanted to take it.

Fiona squeezed his arm, leaning into him. "You can't go back yet. The poem is in Boston. And we need you to lead our coven, or we'll get our heads hacked off." She turned to Bess. "Ms. Pain, you don't know anything about the King Philip poem?"

She coughed. "Right. Wormock asked me about that, too."

"Do you know where it is?" asked Fiona, but the woman shambled back into the shadows again. Her voice rang out:

Search in the cupboards, search under stairs,
Search in the pantry behind the chairs,
High and low and everywhere—
You're searching for what is not there!

This seemed to be the end of the conversation.

Fiona whispered, "Are we supposed to go?"

"Wait!" Suddenly agile, the old woman darted into the dim light and pointed her gnarled finger into Fiona's face. "Are you Fiona?"

Fiona took a small step backward. "Yes?"

Wheezing as she gripped Fiona's shoulders, Bess raised her filmy blue eyes into the light. Her irises clouded over to a milky gray. Her jaw detached, elongating her face. She emitted a deep howl that half sounded like screaming, and half like a choir of angels singing. Fiona shrieked.

Alan grabbed Fiona's arm, yanking her away from Bess, and they sprinted back through the earthen tunnel, followed by Tobias. When they were all through the basement door, Fiona scrambled to lock it behind her with the key. They bolted back up the stairs and into the Adepti room.

Fiona slammed the door shut, gasping for breath. "What *was* that?"

Tobias put a hand on her shoulder. "It's okay. She won't hurt you."

She shook her head. "How do you know?"

He swallowed. "It was just a—just a banshee."

As Alan caught his breath, he slid down the wall to a sitting position. "Don't they kill you by screaming at you?

"No, it's nothing like that." Tobias inhaled slowly, looking at the floor. "They just predict death. But it's probably not Fiona's. It could be a loved one or a family member." *It couldn't be Fiona.*

Fiona frowned. "A family member?" she asked in a small voice.

Tobias nodded.

"My great-aunt is very sick." She crossed to the darkened window. "I don't even really know her. She's been sick for a while."

"Do you want to call your mom?" said Tobias.

She pulled out her phone, punched a few numbers, and

held it to her ear, biting her thumbnail. "Mom? Everything okay?" She began pacing from the window to the door. "Everything is fine here... What do you mean? I just wanted to see if everything was okay... When are you leaving?" She bit her thumbnail. "Okay. I'll see you when you get back... Yeah, I'm studying... I will! Love you. Bye." She disconnected and stuffed the phone back in her pocket. "It's my great-aunt. She's at death's door. My mom's going to the hospital in New York."

"That's too bad about your aunt, but thank God it's not you." Alan looked up at Fiona. "Or your mom."

She joined him on the floor, closing her eyes as she slumped against the wall. "You don't know how much time Celia, Mariana and I spent trying to call up spirits. Now I just want all the spirits to stop. I feel like I need to go watch football or shop in a supermarket to cleanse my mind with something totally mundane."

"Pretty soon the supermarkets will be full of Harvesters," muttered Alan.

Tobias sat cross-legged across from Fiona. "You said you'd heard Bess's name before?"

"Her gravestone is at King's Chapel. They say it might've been the inspiration for *The Scarlet Letter*."

Tobias frowned. "Well, I guess the poem isn't in the school anymore. What did she say? We're looking for something that's not there."

Alan threw back his head, covering his face with his hands. "This is a disaster."

They stayed up as long as they could, trying to come up with a new plan, until Alan and Fiona fell asleep on the floor. Tobias lay down near them on the beast-embroidered rug, tucking himself into Fiona's blanket, but sleep wouldn't come.

He understood what Fiona meant about wanting it all to stop. But with Rawhed's Harvesters serving their god just a few hundred feet away, it wasn't about to get any more mundane.

29

Fiona

For over a week, students languished within Mather's gates as heavily armed police scoured the city for the terrorists. The Boston Police Commissioner assured the public that his best analysts were reviewing video footage and asked for a few more days of lockdown. As the days passed, residents and shop owners grew restless, and the Commissioner announced that the terrorists had fled the area. In a national address, the President promised the criminals would be hunted to the ends of the earth.

Fiona wondered how much, exactly, the government knew. Was it true what Munroe had said—that a secret task force hunted witches?

Late Saturday afternoon, she left the school gates for the first time since the attacks. Jack had texted her that morning, asking her to meet him by the waterfront for the promised sailing trip. An excursion into the harbor, he'd said, would grant her some respite from the bloody images in her head.

In the Common, memorials had blossomed around trees— bouquets, candles, and American flags. From the news, Fiona had learned that the man she'd watched strangled to death had been a Swedish designer named Karl. Among the flowers, people had left pictures from his life: swing dancing with his girlfriend, snuggling his cats, and posing in colorful porkpie hats.

As she walked north through the park, she peered over at the smooth, white branches that grew ever higher, now twelve feet at least. No one could explain the tree's presence. When work crews had failed to remove its impenetrable roots and branches, people had begun to murmur about magic. They whispered that sorcerers had summoned a cursed plant— maybe even a weed sprouting from Hell itself.

All the park rangers could do was erect metal fencing around the tree, though its boughs had soon cleared it. As the tree grew, so did the crowd around it, a swarm of red-eyed wanderers raving about "the truth." Around them, FBI agents in black jackets lingered, staring at passersby through dark sunglasses.

Walking past the Common, Fiona quickened her pace, planning exit strategies through the doorways and alleys around her. She clung to the keys in her pocket, allowing one to protrude from her fist. The Harvesters could reappear at any time.

She breathed easier as she approached the waterfront. Jack waited by the dock, wearing a navy-blue pea coat and a gray scarf. He stood by a medium-sized sailboat. She smiled, hugging her coat around her against the salty wind.

"Have you ever sailed in the harbor?" he asked.

"Not yet. Your parents have a boat and everything. That's awesome."

He looked into the clear blue sky. "The weather's supposed to be good for it."

For someone who'd grown up in South Boston so close to

the harbor, she had very little experience with water, despite her mother's best efforts to enroll her in swimming lessons.

Jack took her hand to help her into the boat. "I think this is the only real way to see the city." He guided her toward the cockpit. "And it'll be nice to get away from the Common after everything that happened."

She sat on a cushion, and he gave her a bottle of sparkling cider to open while he hoisted the sails. She struggled with the corkscrew, and after a few minutes she placed it to one side. She gazed out into the harbor and at the distant islands dotting the horizon.

"Does anyone live on the harbor islands?" She held onto a gunnel for stability as the boat bobbed over waves.

"On some of them, yes. Not as many as there used to be. There were once Native populations, but diseases wiped them from the islands in the early 1600s. And then there was Deer Island."

"People lived there?"

"A long time ago, the Christian Indians were sequestered there during King Philip's War. Most of them died from starvation. Later, it was a stopping point for refugees from the potato famine."

As he spoke, the waves swelled. She hoped she wouldn't be nauseated. He turned the boat into the wind and reefed in the sails.

"Did anything good happen in the harbor islands?" she shouted.

"They used to hang pirates over there. Does that count as good? They left their bodies in the gibbet as a warning on Nix's Mate." Jack pointed to a nearby island. "It was named after Captain Nix. He killed and buried his first mate there to protect their treasure."

"Was the treasure ever found?" she asked.

"No, why? Are you looking for some more adventure in your life?"

"Actually, for the first time, I'm looking for less."

"You want a quiet life?" He smiled, shouting over the wind. "A cup of tea and some books in the evening?"

"That sounds nice. Or watching reality shows about cheerleaders competing to get plastic surgery before prom night." She should have said something more sophisticated. She should have said shows about English aristocrats during World War I.

Jack tacked into the wind. He called out a warning to Fiona to watch out for the boom. She looked up as it swung over the cockpit and then stared out over the ocean again.

Elizabeth Pain must have spent time in the old Boston Gaol with some of those pirates, in a freezing dungeon with iron-spiked doors. In her history class, she'd read about Captain Kidd, the Scottish privateer commissioned by the government to attack French ships. He'd lost control of his crew and slipped across the subtle dividing line between government-sanctioned privateer and outlaw pirate. The rumor was that he'd buried treasure in a number of places. Before Kidd was sent to London to be hanged, he was placed in the Boston Gaol, alongside Quakers, witches, murderers—and perhaps a banshee.

As she looked out onto the harbor, it seemed to her that she gazed into the very foundations of the city; that it formed a sort of gateway between the Old World and the New.

Jack tacked again, and spray blew over the side as the bow crested a wave. She could imagine him on a pirate ship, his sober clothes replaced with flounces, red scarves, and jewelry.

Her vision was cut short by a violent downward lurch of the boat. This was how Percy Bysshe Shelley had died—flung from a sailboat while thoughts of beauty distracted him. The wind picked up speed, and the boat smashed the waves again as it hurtled forward. Fiona curled up in the driest corner of the cockpit and did her best to suppress her urge to spew.

He shouted, "We should turn around."

Dark clouds gathered on the horizon. For a moment, though most of the sky was the color of iron, a few buttery sunrays lit up the sailboat. Then, Fiona felt the air go colder as roiling storm clouds totally hid the sun. Jack brought the boat about, aiming the bow toward Boston. The ship heeled sharply, and she clung on, looking into the churning water near the lower gunnel. What if she were thrown into the dark ocean? She envisioned an unholy legion of jellyfish ushering her to her final resting place amongst the pirate skeletons.

"Are you okay?" He shouted over the howl of the wind.

"Is this normal?"

"Sorry. It's a bit rough. The weatherman promised clear skies."

"I never learned how to swim," she yelled.

"What?"

"I don't know how to swim!"

He glanced at her as he struggled to steer the boat. "It won't come to that."

The boat heaved in the waves, and she held tight to a cleat. Lightning seared the sky.

He called out, "The gods must be angry about someth—"

A boom of thunder drowned him out. Rain started to batter the sailboat. She closed her eyes, and then a large wave buffeted the boat. *So much for a quieter life.* As the boat plunged downward, she lost her grip on the cleat and felt herself tossed out of her seat. In the next moment, Jack held on to her, and she was steadily seated again.

As they sailed back to shore through the squall, she held on with a death grip until they reached the dock. She exhaled with relief, stepping out and shivering in her sodden coat while Jack moored the boat.

He guided her through the rain toward the street, his arm around her shoulders as they walked. Soon, she snuggled against him in the back of a yellow taxi, her teeth chattering.

"They need to get that fireplace going in the dining hall again," she said.

"We should sneak in to light it at night. I don't think Mulligan knows what's going on since the terror attacks. He won't notice."

She smiled. "That would be nice. We could have tea and read books."

"What would you read first?"

"Lord Byron."

"Oh, right. You like his poetry."

She shook her head with a faint smile. "More his life, honestly. I mean, he lived in Venice with a monkey." She looked out the window as the cab drove past Quincy Market. Armored police vehicles patrolled the streets.

Jack pulled her closer to him. "You seem to spend a lot of time with that new kid, Tobias."

"I guess so." She sat up a little. "You haven't really met him, have you?"

There were little shards of gold in his blue eyes. "I've seen him. How much do you know about him?"

Now there was a question she didn't want to answer. "What do you mean? Is this to do with Munroe calling him a witch?"

He sighed, looking away. "I didn't believe in that stuff, but then the apparition of the tree started appearing, and now it's growing there. And it's not a normal tree. The police tried doing some kind of controlled explosion, and they can't get rid of it."

She narrowed her eyes. "And you think Tobias has something to do with the tree?"

"I don't know. He says he's from England, but he doesn't sound English to me. He showed up at our school, got into a fight with Munroe's boyfriend, and then the boyfriend died looking like a mummy. Then a teacher disappeared. We still don't know what happened to her. And there's a video clip of one of the terrorists from before the attacks. He said something in a weird accent that sounded vaguely English, but not exactly. It sounded a lot like Tobias's."

When he put it all together that way, it didn't sound good. She frowned, looking out at the Common as they passed it. "He's from a rural part of England."

"I think maybe you should reconsider your friendship with him."

She glanced at him, his black curls falling over his forehead as he frowned. She felt her cheeks flush with irritation as they approached the school. "You don't know what you're talking about." The cab slowed, pulling over outside the gates.

Jack smiled wryly as he pulled out his wallet. "*I* don't know what I'm talking about?" He pulled out a fifty-dollar bill and handed it to the driver. "Keep the change." He opened the door, climbing out, and Fiona followed him.

She scowled as they walked through the courtyard.

"Maybe you should trust that I'm capable of picking my own friends."

He sighed, opening the front door and looking into her eyes. "I'm just telling you this because I'm worried about you. I think you could be naïve about what you're getting into."

Her cheeks burned hotter. Why was it that guys always thought they knew everything?

"Thanks for your concern," she said as they went inside. "But I really don't enjoy being patronized, so I'm going to be naïve somewhere else."

She stormed off toward the library. It could have been such a nice afternoon, or at least reasonably nice considering the recent supernatural terror. Why did he have to bring up witchcraft? She would have been better off talking about reality TV or comparing herself to Hitler.

30

Thomas

Voices echoed off the tiles in the Harvard Square T station as Thomas Malcolm stepped off the subway car. Tucked into his wallet were a Harvard ID and a key that he'd managed to procure from another grad student. Over drinks in South Boston, he'd convinced his friend that accessing Harvard's Widener Library was crucial to his King Philip research.

Of course, he hadn't told Emil the real reason he wanted to visit Widener's stacks: the library had the most extensive documentation on Maremount in the world, including alleged firsthand accounts. He'd been there years ago with a collaborator when they researched his first book.

He only hoped that the door monitors wouldn't notice that the photo ID in his wallet belonged to a white person.

He walked through the iron-and-brick gateway onto the Harvard campus, following one of the old paths toward the center of Harvard Yard. Until recently, he'd dismissed the Maremount Treatise as a hoax, but with all the weirdness of the past two weeks, maybe the original sources warranted a reexamination. He squeezed past the tourists photographing the statue of the old Puritan, John Harvard, and strolled toward the giant columns of the Widener Library that loomed over the campus.

He rubbed his chin as he climbed the great stone steps. Was using someone else's student ID actually illegal, or just frowned upon? As he entered the library doors, he found a student slouched over a book. Thomas pulled out the ID, planting his thumb over Emil's photo. The student gave him a cursory nod, returning to his chemistry book.

Thomas exhaled, shoving the card back in his wallet. He continued through the main atrium and climbed the marble staircase into the enormous library. Winding through the library's ten levels were almost sixty miles of bookshelves. A student could get lost within the cavernous honeycomb of books, but Thomas knew exactly where he was going. As he reached the top of the stairwell, he turned left, continuing down a long hall until he stopped at an oak door. He fumbled with the lock and opened the door to reveal a much smaller library.

At the far wall, three tall windows illuminated a large wooden table surrounded by chairs. Oak bookshelves lined the walls, reaching all the way to the ceiling. He crouched toward the bottom of a bookshelf near the windows, scanning the spines for the Maremount Treatise. He glanced over the W's until he found the author he was looking for: Edgar Waldron. He pulled the old leather-bound book off the shelf, brought it to the table and began leafing through the yellowed pages.

The narrative began in the Old World. Queen Elizabeth's successor, King James, had a particular interest in witch-hunting. Thomas knew this story. As a young man, the King's ship had sailed into a squall, and the terrified monarch blamed the incident on magic. James became paranoid that sorcerers planned a violent death for him, and he personally oversaw the torture of scores of accused witches until they confessed.

Thomas turned a brittle page to an illustration showing the young King sitting in judgment before cowering women.

Under Charles I, the persecution of witches had become more intense, and philosophers began immigrating to the New World. Bostonians strolling along the Charles might be surprised to learn that the river was named for someone who'd ordered the torture of suspects by dunking them under water for hours at a time and then burned them alive if they survived.

When he turned the page, he found a piece of paper tucked into the book. As he unfolded it, he found a hand-drawn family tree of the Maremount royal family. The Throcknell dynasty had begun with King Malchior in 1693, and continued to the current monarch, Balthazar. Below Balthazar's name, someone had scrawled "*Princess—b. 1998?*" Thomas folded the paper again, returning it to the book.

He studied an ink illustration of the King's famous Witchfinder, Matthew Hopkins. Around his neck hung a pendant. It wasn't a cross, as Thomas would have expected. It was a chalice. He turned back to the image of James I, who wore the same pendant affixed to the side of a velvet hat. He wasn't familiar with the iconography. Was it supposed to represent the Holy Grail?

As he turned another page, a white-haired man in a black suit entered the room. Thomas cleared his throat and tried not to look up. Hadn't Emil said that no one ever used this room? He stared at the book, trying to feign natural behavior as he listened to the man's footsteps approach. He didn't want an embarrassing scene. He was a respectable doctoral student, after all.

The stranger pulled out a chair, sitting directly across from him. Neatly trimmed nails tapped on the tabletop. "Thomas Malcolm."

Thomas jerked his head up as the ruddy-faced man stared at him. "How do you know my name?"

The man reached into his coat pocket and pulled out an issue of the *Journal of American Folklore*—the very issue that had published Thomas's Maremount paper.

The man licked his finger and turned the pages, as though reading a story to a child. "'Alleged exiles from Maremount report that the first king, Malchior, was a descendant of Merlin. He was chosen in an endurance ritual conducted in the wilderness by a group of aristocratic sorcerers.'" He closed the journal and placed it on the table. His mouth spread into a thin, crooked-toothed grin. "You know a lot about magic, don't you, Thomas Malcolm?"

He shook his head. "I'm sorry—who are you?"

The man leaned forward, his voice suddenly intense. "We are those who watch. We are those who protect. We shed light into the darkness. We have always been here. And do you know who we've been watching recently, Thomas Malcolm?" He pressed forward even further and pointed directly into Thomas's face, mouthing the word you.

Thomas reeled back. "*What?*"

"Maremount, the Angelic language, the history of anti-witchcraft organizations—it's quite the search history you've got. Most people don't believe in these things."

The man stood and reached into his pocket, pulling out a card. "I have a feeling you might know some people we'd be interested in speaking to. When you feel like talking, give us a call." He laid the card in front of Thomas before striding out of the room.

Thomas picked it up. There was a phone number, and an arc of words read *lux in tenebris lucet*: light shines through the darkness. Below the words was an emblem. It was a chalice, in fact—exactly the shape of the one he'd just seen in the illustrations.

31

Fiona

On a Sunday night, the full coven joined to celebrate Fiona's birthday in the Adepti room. Though Fiona's mother was still in New York, she'd sent Mariana money to buy Fiona a chocolate mousse cake. That morning, outside Fiona's room, two new books about Lord Byron arrived—along with a note asking her to remedy her D average in Algebra.

Soon, Fiona's great-aunt would be taken off life support. This evening's candlelit celebration was a welcome distraction from thoughts of dying relatives and tumbling heads, and watching Tobias try to muddle his way through "Happy Birthday" brought a smile to Fiona's face. She took a bite of the dark chocolate cake, savoring the rich flavor, while Alan described the banshee's horrible scream to Celia and Mariana.

When they finished scraping up the last crumbs, Tobias held up the philosopher's guide. "It's your birthday, Fiona. I don't suppose you want to spend it practicing Angelic?"

She sighed. "We probably should."

As they sat on the floor, he repeated Angelic phrases from the book. By nine o'clock, Alan had begun to fiddle with his pencil, and Celia yawned, tracing her finger along the beast designs on the rug. Mariana checked her phone every thirty seconds for news stories about the terrorists. Only Fiona maintained eye contact.

"When do we get to transform?" Alan interrupted Frater Basilus's Spell for Wind. "I think I've got the wind spell down."

Tobias closed the book and rose. "All right. Here's how it works. Everyone has a familiar spirit. A familiar is an animal who aids you in your alchemical quest. With the right spell, you can take its shape. It begins when you're initiated into a coven." He paced in front of the fireplace. "While in a trance, you'll transform into your familiar. After that, you'll be able to transform with the right spell. In a few weeks or months, your familiar animal will come to you, and you'll name it. Mine's a crow called Ottomie."

"I hope I get a snake." Mariana smiled.

"But you need to be prepared." Tobias raised his index finger. "It takes a toll, physically and mentally. Your mind won't work in quite the same way when you're an animal. If you don't get control, you're at risk of losing yourself to the bestial side. It's harder when you first start. You have to remember that you're still you, even if you're in an animal's body."

"Got it," said Celia, twirling her fair hair around her finger. "Can we start now?"

He instructed everyone to sit in a circle and placed a small white candle in front of each person. In the center, he burned musky incense in a brazier. He asked everyone to repeat after him and began chanting in Angelic.

As she repeated the words, Fiona grew lightheaded. She

closed her eyes and felt herself rise out of her body. She wasn't quite sure where her limbs were until she felt wet gravel beneath her hands and knees. She was kneeling in the dark. By the sound of trickling water, she thought she might be in a streambed. A dripping noise echoed through the space. Reaching out, she touched slippery granite to her right, covered in a thin sludge. She stood, bumping her head on a low ceiling.

"Please. Don't let my familiar be some sort of troglodyte or inbred cave person." Her voice echoed off the walls.

After she rose, her skin started to feel tighter on her body, and then it hardened. With a nauseating lurch of her stomach, she bent over as her muscles contracted. A sharp pain ripped through her elongating fingers, and they ruptured into leathery wings. Disoriented, she lost her balance as her legs shortened, but within moments, her wings beat the dank air. The pain and nausea subsided, and a squeak rose from her throat.

She gasped as she discovered that not only could she see in the dark, she could also see sound. The squeak molded the cave like mercury, giving shape to its bumps and crevices. Stalactites dripped water onto the cave floor, and rivulets of liquid damped the walls.

She emitted another squeak. The noise echoed off something fluttering toward her through the caves. Another bat? As it flew closer, she discovered that it was a creature with delicate, papery wings, like an old man's skin. It circled her, and every contour of its body pressed into her mind. It was a moth, but not an ordinary one. It was larger than it should be, and from its back, an image of a human skull stared out. Entranced, she followed the moth as it flew through the cave's tunnels, as if she were drawn by the creature's gravitational pull.

A scream ripped her out of her trance. Her body began its rapid expansion, her skeleton swelling within her flesh. Her eyes snapped open, and there she was, back in the Adepti room. She dry-heaved on her hands and knees. Her muscles burned, and her blood felt acidic in her veins.

She glanced toward the fireplace to find Celia lying on the floor, moaning. Nearby, Alan slumped against the wall, gaping at a gash on his arm. Tobias had taken off his shirt in an attempt to staunch the bleeding. Her face pale, Mariana rested against the tapestry with her hand over her mouth, black bangs hanging in front of her face.

"What happened?" Fiona panted, eyeing Alan's bloodied arm. Her head throbbed, and every muscle resisted as she tried to move back into a sitting position.

"Celia attacked Alan," said Mariana.

"Why?" Fiona gave up, lying flat on the ground.

"I said I was sorry," mumbled Celia from the floor.

Tobias finished binding Alan's arm, tying his shirt in a knot. "Celia transformed into a mountain lion. Alan was a wolverine. Celia got a little lost in the beast." He frowned at Celia. "I did warn you."

"I hope it doesn't hurt too much, Alan," said Fiona, forcing herself upright. "I was a bat. What were you, Mariana?"

"Snapping turtle," she said, closing her eyes and swallowing. "Ugh, I feel rough."

"I almost lost my damn arm." Alan glared at Celia.

"You probably antagonized me." Celia sat up. Her face had a greenish tinge, and she rested her head in her hand. "I'll get you some bandages or whatever in a minute."

Tobias looked around the room. "Is everyone okay? I mean, besides Alan?"

"I'm fine." Mariana clutched her stomach. "So at some point, I'm going to meet my snapping turtle friend? What is it—like a Native spirit animal thing?"

Tobias shrugged. "It's just a philosopher thing."

"But is any of it Native magic? Like the original Mather Adepti—they were English and Algonquian," said Alan listlessly, staring at his wounded arm.

Fiona sat up and stretched. She tried not to stare at Tobias's shirtless chest. "What do you mean they were *Algonquian*? Here? At Mather?"

"We learned that from the shew stone," said Tobias.

Mariana listlessly fiddled with the pentagram around her neck. "But you don't see them recognized anywhere. They're not in any paintings. Just white people." She opened her brown eyes long enough to roll them. "As usual."

"They aren't listed in the colonial wars on the war memorial." Fiona's muscles slowly relaxed. She avoided looking at Tobias.

The room was quiet as the coven members rubbed their sore muscles and skin. Celia's face gradually returned to its normal hue, and she worked to smooth out her hair.

Mariana rose to stretch. "What did the banshee say, about not finding what you're looking for?"

"*You're searching for what is not there,*" Fiona recited.

Mariana paused mid-stretch, staring down at her friend. "Maybe she didn't mean the poem isn't there. Maybe it meant that you should be searching for things that are missing. Like the names of the Algonquian students on the memorial."

"In order to get into the library, we pulled the blank book." Tobias rubbed his chin, pacing. "And we went through the memorial that left off the Algonquian names."

Alan grasped at the white shirt wrapped around his arm

as a deep red stain spread within the fabric. "The card in the catalogue that led us here was blank. No titles."

"That's not a bad idea," said Fiona.

"We need to look around the rest of the building." Alan shut his eyes again. "But Celia needs to get me some ointment first. Or sew up my arm."

"We could look around in a couple of hours, after we rest up and everyone else is asleep. Fiona faltered as she rose, resting her hand on the wall. "We can use Lady Cleo's Cloak."

Celia rubbed her shoulder. "We should revisit the Round Chamber."

As Fiona rested against the wall, she thought of the hours she'd spent in the Round Chamber, tuning out the droning voices of her teachers while she stared at the names engraved in the wooden walls. "Celia's right. There are names there. All English names, like the memorial plaque."

Mariana checked her watch. "Should we meet up again at midnight?"

"Sounds like a plan," said Fiona.

Celia stood, offering her hand to Alan. She pulled him up, and he rested on her shoulder, hobbling toward the door. Mariana shuffled after them, while Tobias lingered behind.

"I don't want to walk around without a shirt," he said. "Mind if I wait here?"

Fiona glanced at his strong shoulders. Feeling a blush rise in her cheeks, she forced herself to look up at his face. "That's fine. I mean—what?"

He sat down against the wall and looked up at her. "Are you feeling okay? You seem distracted."

She sat across the room from him and stared at the tapestry. "Guess I'm lightheaded. From the transformation, obviously."

She emitted a short, awkward laugh and tried to change the subject. "So this would just be like an ordinary day to someone from Maremount—transforming into an animal."

"There are a lot of things there that you'd find strange, but beautiful things too."

"Like what?"

"I can think of a few things that I'd show you. If Rawhed were gone." He leaned forward, resting his elbows on his knees. "There's the pond where you could see the gemstones from the water spirits' garden. In the North End—what you call Copp's Hill—there's a night garden for observing the moon. It's right near Fishgate."

"That sounds lovely." She sighed. "Here it's just a cemetery."

"There's a burial ground there too, and a soul-mill where you can hear the voices of the tormented spirits who power the machine."

She shuddered, and an image flashed in her mind of the death's-head moth. "Speaking of death, what's the deal with the other creature I saw? There was a moth with me. With a skull on its back."

He stared at her. "What do you mean, a *moth*?"

"It was flying around me, and I followed it."

His frown deepened. "Are you sure?"

"Yeah. Why? What does it mean?"

"I don't know. It must be another philosopher, but it's no one from our coven. It makes me think..." He touched the smooth skin under his jawline. "It makes me think someone might be watching us."

32
Tobias

At midnight, they regrouped in the Adepti room. Tobias had borrowed one of Fiona's sweaters. His broad shoulders stretched the green wool.

With the full coven gathered, he handed Fiona the tattered spell book. "Do you want to lead us in Lady Cleo's Cloak?"

With everyone standing in a circle, Fiona intoned the spell, and the others repeated after her for additional power. When they finished the recitation, Tobias watched as everyone glimmered out of view.

So this was what it felt like. He'd never had the chance to try a cloaking spell, though he'd seen them before. Father used to use them to smuggle books from the bookstores forbidden to Tatters.

They tiptoed down the stairwell into the darkened library. He smiled faintly. Could he be on the verge of discovering the key to Rawhed's destruction? He could be home soon, eating his father's bread pudding by the fireplace—a hero to the Tatters. Not that he was in it for the glory, of course.

They crept through the abandoned hallways toward the Round Chamber. The auditorium door creaked as someone pushed it forward and flicked on a light switch, and they slipped into the hall. Tobias felt an elbow brush against him as he walked around the curving wall to the right, examining the names engraved in the red oak.

"Gardiner, Cary, Webster, Woodward..." he read. On the right side of the room, a large portrait of the colonial Governor John Winthrop interrupted the names. "These are the same names as those on the plaque."

"This one looks different, though," Mariana's voice echoed from the other side of the Round Chamber. "Philalethes."

Tobias turned to see the carving on the opposite side of the room.

"Philalethes," Fiona repeated. She was right by his shoulder. "I think that's ancient Greek for *lover of...* something. *Lethes*, whatever that is. It seems like a pseudonym."

"So maybe his real name is missing. Maybe that's the missing thing we're looking for," said Celia from near the entrance.

"There's a smaller carving in the first letter of his name," said Mariana. "It's deep. Hang on—I think it's an upside-down triangle with a line through it."

"That's the alchemical symbol for earth." Tobias's heart beat faster. "Philalethes might have been one of the Mather Adepti who hid the poem."

"So what do we do now?" asked Fiona.

"The earth symbol usually goes along with three other symbols, all placed across from each other like points of a compass." Tobias spoke quickly in his excitement. "So air would be somewhere near me, water would be in the back of the hall, and fire would be near the back of the stage."

Celia and Alan hunted for the symbol for water, which they located near the entrance doors. Mariana searched the brick fireplace on the stage, while Fiona and Tobias inspected the wall next to them. They found the air sign on a brass plaque below John Winthrop's long, folded fingers.

Tobias smiled, absentmindedly rubbing at the soft sweater that stretched over his arms. "We've got air. That just leaves fire. You find anything yet, Mariana?"

"Not yet. I mean, it's a fireplace, but I don't see the symbol. Either it's not here, and that's a clue, or I'm just failing at finding it."

"If it's the same height as our symbols, it should be near the mantel," said Alan.

"Guys?" Celia said. "I can push on the symbol, like a button. It goes into the wood when you press it."

Tobias jabbed his index finger into the air symbol, and it sunk into the brass. "Ours does, too."

"Maybe we're supposed to push them all at the same time," said Alan. "I'm heading over to the earth symbol."

When Alan was in place, they counted to three. As they pressed the signs, a brick edged out from the fireplace. Mariana's invisible hand pulled it out, and from behind it, a piece of paper wrapped around a thin, cylindrical object.

"I've got it, guys," Mariana called out, unfurling the paper. "It's the poem. And a wand or something." A piece of paper and a thin wooden stick floated in the air.

The others rushed over to join her. This was it—they had the key to stopping Rawhed. The hangings, the torture, the imprisoning of Tatters—it could all end now. Tobias was going to fulfill the Ragmen's mission.

"It's got a picture of a snake," said Mariana breathlessly. "Someone take a photo."

Tobias crossed the stage, bumping into someone's shoulder. They crowded around the poem. At the top, a drawing of a snake twisted into an infinity symbol. Its tail rested in its mouth—the ouroboros. Around the drawing's border, someone had written, "*the beginning and the end.*" Mariana turned the drawing back to herself, and read:

We wait beneath corrupted frozen ground.
Unconsecrated, tangled roots enshroud
our crumpled necks and long-smothered embers,
where the hours fly, and death is remembered.

In nameless hollows, Philip's men await—
the unlamented...

The hovering poem lowered for a moment. "This is the new part," said Mariana.

The unlamented clawing back their fates
from those who fanned the flames with pious breath—
those sanguine, celebrated gentlemen.

The King, his voice extinguished after death,
awaits in buried ash to speak again,
made whole above the one who made him mute—
The burned, the chopped, the choked rise from the roots.

Mariana took a deep breath. "So... what do we do?"

Tobias pulled the poem toward him, running his fingertips along his jaw. These didn't seem like instructions. "I recognize the snake," he said. "It represents the power created by the union of opposites, the beginning and the end of the universe, just like it says. It's the cyclical nature of the world—the past will be repeated. But I don't know what the poem means."

The wand hovered higher. "What about this?" said Mariana.

Tobias grabbed the rough hickory wand. He tried to remember what he'd learned of wands, but they rarely did anything interesting. "I think they can be used on enchanted items. You can trace it around an object to enchant it, or to un-enchant it."

"I can run the poem by Thomas Malcolm," said Fiona from his side. "He knows all about poems." Her eyes were beginning to appear, hovering near the mantel.

"We should get back." Tobias clutched the wand as they crept back through the Round Chamber. They'd found the poem, though he didn't yet know what it meant. It seemed he had some serious research to undertake before he could get back to his own fireplace.

33

Fiona

In the Western wing of the library, near the tall windows that overlooked the courtyard, books of New England history spanned most of the lower level. Warm lights gleamed off metallic titles, and a few deep blue tomes interrupted the rows of deep maroon and brown spines. Paul Revere claimed two entire shelves, and William Dawes commandeered a respectable row of books.

Fiona yawned, rubbing her eyes as she surveyed a dusty bookshelf. A few disruptions had delayed her research into the poem's hidden meanings. Last night, she'd stayed up late trying to rush through three months of Algebra homework in one evening. And this morning, Celia had burst into her room with a new crisis: she'd discovered Lucas locked in an unsportsmanlike clinch with Sadie on the blue gym mats.

Fiona crouched down to the "colonial wars" shelves. The phrase *the one who made him mute* replayed in her mind. Did it describe the person who'd killed King Philip? Thomas hadn't been much help recently, explaining only that he'd been "working on something."

On the bottom shelf, two books comprised the entire King Philip section. She pulled out a slim volume the color of dried blood: *King Philip's War.* She paged to the index, scanning for the word "Death," and then flipped to page 234. After skimming through, she learned that two men had killed the King in Connecticut's Miery Swamp. Caleb Cook and John Alderman shot him as he wandered alone in the wilderness.

As Fiona skimmed the chapter, the sound of footfalls turned her head. Jack approached through the Western wing, dressed in a fresh white shirt and gray pants.

Her cheeks reddened as he neared. "Jack."

He smiled. "Late night studying?"

"Something like that." She rose, gripping the book.

He nodded toward her hand. "What's that?"

"Something about King Philip. It's for class."

Gazing at her, he took a deep, shaking breath. "For class?"

Is he nervous? "History." She swallowed. She was starting to feel bad about lying to him.

With a half-smile, he gave a little nod. "I've been meaning to get in touch with you. I'm sorry about the other day. About being patronizing." He glanced at the floor, rubbing the back of his neck. "I can be overbearing sometimes."

She shrugged. "I guess you thought you were doing the right thing." It was a relief to talk to him. "Apology accepted."

"I'm going to something Friday evening. It's a fundraising party at the Athenæum. Do you want to come with me?"

"Sounds sophisticated. What time?"

"Seven. It has a nature theme. Herbal drinks, that kind of thing. They're raising money for the restoration of a reading room."

"I'll wear my finest fig leaves."

She smiled. Surely the world could grant her one night off from both the battle against Rawhed *and* her plummeting grades.

34
Tobias

Tobias and Celia walked outside in the spring air as the sun set behind the buildings. He'd been disappointed to learn that Fiona was desperately cramming for a math test that night. It would have been nice to huddle up in the Adepti room to puzzle over the poem. She couldn't really expect to save the city from a supernatural army *and* pull up her grades.

He found, instead, that the newly single Celia was free. After telling him about the details of her breakup with Lucas, she wanted to know what everything looked like in Maremount. They strolled through the North End—one of the neighborhoods that he knew best in its Maremount incarnation. Many of the streets followed the same patterns, and Tobias pointed out the location of his favorite pub, the Burning Serpent. But what she really wanted to know about was the royal family. Arm-in-arm, they walked back toward the Common in the gathering dark.

Entranced, Celia gazed at him, blue eyes opened wide. "So the King used to be married to a different queen?"

He nodded. "Exactly. Until he had her hanged in Lullaby Square."

"Why did he kill her?" She twisted a strand of her blond hair.

"He married a younger queen, Bathsheba. She was prettier. Bathsheba didn't want any rivals. So she accused the old queen of treason. And King Balthazar was in love with Bathsheba, so he did what she wanted."

"So the new queen is, like, evil."

He shrugged, looking into the King's Chapel cemetery as they passed. "They're all evil, if you ask me."

"Because they won't let Tatters like you into schools?"

"Exactly."

She crinkled her forehead as they came closer to the Common. "You don't sound like I'd expect a Tatter to sound. I mean, you can read, and you sound educated."

"I guess I'm not normal." He smiled. "My dad used to steal books to teach me to read and to speak properly. No one else in our neighborhood talks like we do—not even the Ragmen. But he thought it wasn't fair that only the rich children could learn anything."

"So what happened to the rest of the royal family? What happened to the King's daughter? From the old queen?"

He frowned and shook his head. "I don't know. She was either exiled or killed. No one heard from her again."

"And what about the old queen's other royal relatives?"

"You seem awfully interested in the aristocrats."

She tilted her head. "No offense, but rich people are more interesting than poor people."

He laughed. "Is that so? Well, I don't know what they're up to, and I don't really care. No one's heard from any of them in the past year, since Rawhed took over the fortress."

They were at the edge of the Common when a high-pitched scream pierced the air.

Tobias pulled Celia toward him, standing in place as he listened. The shrieking grew louder. The image of a child's blood-soaked hat flashed through his mind. A woman sprinted toward them, fleeing the park.

Celia clung to his arm. "Should we see what's happening, or run?"

"I'll go see what it is. Maybe you should go back to the school."

"I'm not going back by myself." She narrowed her eyes. "I'm staying with you."

They edged into the park as military vehicles sped along Tremont Street and screeched to a halt near the edge of the park. Armed guards stormed out of their Humvees and ran into the Common.

A voice blared from a loudspeaker, *"Everyone must vacate the Common at this time. I repeat: all people on Boston Common must vacate the area. Please disperse."*

"It's too dark to see what's happening in the middle of the Common." She dug her fingers into his forearm. "I wish you could do your light spell without people noticing."

"I want to go in further." It was his duty to fight Rawhed's tyranny, even if he didn't have his pike with him.

She looked over at him, nodding. As they moved toward the center of the park, he saw that the white elm's spiky boughs now towered over the other trees.

A hail of gunfire rang out. Tobias ran behind a bench, pulling Celia down with him. The Common went silent again. As they crouched, he intoned a simple protection spell. After a few minutes of silence, they slowly stood.

"Let's go back to Mather," said Celia.

He rose, glancing toward the tree. Just a hundred feet from them stood the ivory elm. Its branches curved like antlers, and a bright, silvery light emanated from its trunk and boughs.

He squinted his eyes. Silhouettes swung below the tree's limbs. With a sharp intake of breath, he realized they were bodies, swaying in a lolling motion like the tongues of sick dogs. "The Harvesters are killing again."

He watched as a Harvester stepped away from the tree toward a police officer and fell backward as he was caught in the spray of bullets. But within the elm's silvery light, the Harvesters seemed protected from the gunfire. They stood tall as soldiers crept toward them, firing machine guns.

Celia pulled Tobias's arm, but he stood transfixed. They weren't in the line of fire.

"Go back, Celia," he hissed.

He stepped closer, watching as one of the Harvesters grabbed a tall, blond soldier by his shoulders and pulled him into the tree's light. The Harvesters threw a noose around his neck. He grasped at his throat as they strung the rope over a branch, hoisting him up. The man's face reddened at first, and he gripped the noose before his whole body succumbed to jerking motions. His face turned from red to purple.

"I need to do something." Tobias moved toward the tree, but Celia gripped his arm.

"Are you crazy? You can't just go fight them. There are at least ten of them. And I'm not walking home by myself."

Tobias watched the twitching soldier. She was right. He couldn't let his emotions overwhelm him.

"Let's go," she whispered as Tobias looked back at her.

The look of fear in her eyes made the decision for him, and they ran back within the school's gates. Ms. Ellsworth stood in the courtyard, trying to see into the park. As they pulled open the front door, Mulligan was announcing over the loudspeaker that everyone *must stay in the building*. Instead of locking themselves in their rooms as instructed, students swarmed the hallways. Some cried, and many were on their cell phones. They'd heard the gunshots, and the news of another terrorist attack had spread quickly through the school.

Celia followed Tobias to his room, where they found their friends huddled around a laptop on the floor.

"Thank God you guys are back," Fiona said, lowering her phone. "Did you see what's going on?"

Alan rose. "They're back, aren't they?"

"What did you see?" Mariana's face was flushed. She sat against Tobias's bed.

"The Harvesters are in the park," said Tobias. "The elm is full size now. They're hanging people from it."

Mariana leapt up, moving toward the window. "Did they look like they might come here? We're only a few hundred feet away!"

Tobias's heart raced as he sat on the bed. "They might, but they were mostly staying near the tree."

Celia hugged her knees. "We could hide in the Adepti room."

"Or even the cellar," said Fiona.

A burst of shouts from the other side of the door interrupted them. "They're outside the gate!" "They're here!"

Peering out the window, Tobias saw Ms. Ellsworth sticking her head out of the gate to view the flashing lights in the park. Her brown ponytail hung down her back in a straight line. She seemed not to see the two Harvesters in tapered hats approaching her across Boylston Street in the dark. Vines coiled around their black clothes.

Tobias opened his window to shout at her. "Ms. Ellsworth! Get inside!"

She turned to look up at his window, her mouth opened in shock. By then, the Harvesters were upon her.

He couldn't stand there and watch while they dragged a teacher to her death. He flung open the door. His heart hammered as he ran through the hallways. A Ragman couldn't hide in his room while Harvesters dragged women around. A Ragman's duty was to fight tyranny. He barreled down the stairs into the vestibule.

Wrenching open the door to the courtyard, he saw a lanky Harvester dragging Ms. Ellsworth away from the school gates by her ponytail. Her legs flailed on the pavement, and a flat, tan shoe flew into the air.

Gunshots rang out from the park as he sprinted across the courtyard, calling out to his teacher. Across the street, the Harvester yanked Ms. Ellsworth over the grass by her hair. Tobias sprinted through the gate toward them, dodging a car that skidded past.

Ms. Ellsworth screamed, kicking her legs toward the man's shins. She grunted, trying to wrench free as he pulled her.

What had he learned with the Ragmen? Land your pike blows when the enemy gets ready to swing. Use an overhead swing as a first attack. Use a thrust for the kill. He was the best pike-fighter in the coven.

Only, he didn't have a pike. He glanced down at his empty hands as he ran across the grass.

He caught up to them as they dragged Ms. Ellsworth past the Central Burying Ground. *A Ragman's hands don't tremble when he's scared.*

Tobias grabbed Ms. Ellsworth's rangy abductor by his shoulder. The man turned, scowling and clinging to the English teacher's hair. The Harvester had a close-cropped brown beard and a long, bony nose. His thin lips were clamped together.

"You can't take her. She's our teacher." Tobias found himself unable to come up with anything better.

The second Harvester, a blond man with a doughy, beardless face, lurched toward Tobias, grabbing his shirt collar. Gritting his teeth, Tobias shoved him off as adrenalin coursed through his veins.

Someone grabbed Tobias's arm from behind, and he turned to see Fiona pulling him back toward the school. "You can't be here, Tobias! There are more coming!"

"Get back in the gates." As he looked at Fiona's terrified amber eyes, he felt rough hands grip his throat. While he struggled to free himself, he gazed into the blond Harvester's face. The grip tightened. All he could think was that the man's eyes didn't glow like he'd remembered. They looked like ordinary human eyes, sagging and tired. Tobias felt a sharp pain in his chest. His lungs were going to burst.

He could hear Fiona's shrill scream over the rushing blood in his ears. He kicked out his leg. Fiona broke the chokehold by smashing her elbow into the Harvester's pale face. She grabbed Tobias's arm, pulling him back to the school in an all-out sprint. Tobias coughed and gasped as the school gates came into view.

Munroe stood before the gate, a fierce look on her face. She held a large knife in her hand. As Tobias picked up speed across Boylston Street, he could hear a Harvester shouting behind him, "Submit to the King of Terror!"

"Get inside, Munroe!" yelled Fiona.

In their panic, Ms. Ellsworth had been left behind.

As they neared the gate, Munroe rolled up the sleeve of her shirt and held the knife over the veins in her arm. What was she doing?

"Get inside!" Tobias yelled as he slipped through the gate after Fiona.

The gate slammed shut as soon as he entered, and he turned to see a Harvester stopping short in front of Munroe. Tobias wrapped his hands around the iron rails, watching as Munroe sliced into her arm with the knife. The Harvester gaped at her as her scarlet blood dripped onto the pavement.

Color rose in her face as she screamed. "Your false god will not protect you. The impure will not enter these gates. I claim this place for Blodrial!"

Tobias gasped as recognition finally dawned on him. The chalice—it belonged to Blodrial, the ancient god of blood. He'd seen it in an old book about magic.

The Harvester stumbled back. Munroe turned toward the school and rubbed her bleeding arm against the school gates, leaving a crimson smudge across the Mather Academy insignia.

"What the hell is going on?" shouted Fiona.

Munroe remained before the gate, her arm dripping. The Harvester shuffled further back, a look of confusion on his face.

"There's magic in her blood," said Tobias. "She drinks Blodrial's blood. It's keeping the Harvesters out."

"What?" Fiona shook her head. "Munroe? She drinks—what?"

"One of the old gods," said Tobias, catching his breath as he hung onto the iron fence.

The Harvester edged back into the park.

Fiona looked at Munroe. "So are we safe now? With her blood on the gate?"

"I think so." He wheezed. "Let's get back inside." He leaned on Fiona as they crossed the courtyard.

He rested his head against her neck. She had a nice vernal smell, like grass and lilacs. It was calming after his fight with the Harvester—if he could call it a fight.

The sirens blared on, and a pre-recorded voice droned over a loudspeaker: *"This is an emergency message. Please remain indoors."*

When they entered the vestibule, Mulligan's office door was shut as he continued to make announcements.

"Should we go to the Adepti room?" asked Fiona, supporting Tobias. "I want everyone to memorize the cloaking spell."

Tobias nodded as they walked up the stairs.

"What's up with Munroe? Is she on our side or what?" asked Fiona.

"The Blodrial cult is from the Old World. The *ancient* world, in fact. They use magic, but not our kind; not Angelic. They've never been in Maremount. I don't remember much about them. I'm not as keen on history as Alan is." They climbed the steps to the library. His throat throbbed where the Harvester had throttled him. "But I know they're not fond of philosophers. In fact, they want us all dead."

35

Thomas

Thomas sat in the empty café drinking a large cup of coffee and staring out the window toward the Common. Like most Bostonians, glued to their internet feeds and televisions, he hadn't slept at all during the previous night's attacks. He'd watched in horror as dozens of people were dragged to their deaths at the elm. Once again, the invaders had disappeared as quickly as they'd arrived. After hours of searching, the police had failed to find them. With growing hysteria, the authorities had once again sealed off the city center. No one would be allowed in or out until every terrorist was captured.

It had become clear to everyone that these were no ordinary terrorists. No one had been able to remove the corpses from the trees, not with saws or blades. Something stopped them from getting close enough, and the bodies continued their forlorn swaying.

Thomas swallowed, staring into the park from his café table. He couldn't argue it away anymore. All signs pointed to something supernatural. A magical tree materializing, killers who disappeared into thin air—this was the work of something otherworldly.

The world as he'd thought he understood it no longer existed. He took a deep, shaky breath. It wasn't just the Harvesters. He'd been researching that phrase—*lux in tenebris lucet*. What he'd found had unnerved him. The coffee probably wasn't helping his jitters, but he needed it after all the sleepless nights.

He took a long sip of his strong brew and looked up just as Tobias and Fiona walked in. Like Thomas, they both had dark circles under their eyes, and deep purple bruises marred Tobias's neck.

"What happened to you?" Thomas asked when they sat down.

Tobias sighed and touched his neck. "Harvester."

"Jesus Christ." Thomas looked from Tobias to Fiona and back. "They're real, aren't they? I mean, the tree..." He shook his head. "You're lucky to be alive."

"I know," said Fiona. "But we know a cloaking spell that we can use if we need it. It makes us invisible. We can teach it to you."

"A cloaking spell. That's a real thing now..." He tapped on the table and then hunched toward them. "Where did they go? How did they just disappear?"

Tobias rubbed his eyes. "You said the legend was that a sorcerer raises an army from the grave, right? So they were already dead. The dead have the ability to travel between worlds. It's how we see ghosts from the other side."

Thomas frowned. "You really confronted them, up close?"

Fiona nodded. "But don't tell my mom. She'd freak out. She won't stop calling me. She's coming back from New York, but they won't let anyone through the police barrier."

"You two need to be more careful, you know that?"

Fiona touched his arm. "So you believe me now about Maremount?"

"Witches, ghosts, demon séances, whatever messed-up magical stuff you're talking about, I'm on board. What do we need to do to stop this? There's a poem, right?" Thomas tried to keep the hysteria out of his voice.

"We have the whole thing now." Fiona pulled out her phone and showed Thomas a snapshot of the old handwritten text.

He read it to himself a few times, and then pointed to the top. "What's this about the beginning and the end?"

"It's the moment of death and rebirth of the universe, I think," said Tobias. "There's a wand, too. We don't know what it does yet. It might be used to remove an enchantment from something."

"Do you get what the poem means?" Fiona pressed toward him over the table. "What are the instructions?"

"The King, his voice extinguished after death, awaits in buried ash to speak again, made whole above the one who made him mute—the burned, the chopped, the choked rise from the roots." He shook his head. "I don't know. I was hoping I'd just know." He took another sip of coffee. Under the table, his leg bobbed up and down. He looked up. "There's a whole other thing, too."

Tobias frowned. "A whole other what?"

Jesus. He was making even less sense than them. He pulled the chalice card out of his wallet. "A man gave me this. Said he'd been watching me."

Fiona squinted at it. "That's Munroe's symbol. The symbol of Blodrial."

Thomas nodded. "You've seen this?" He'd been reading about them for days in old conspiracy theorist journals. "The

Blodrial cult is called the Purgators. They're a cult of witch hunters. They started in ancient Rome. The witch-hunting Kings, James and Charles the First, were both members. The Purgators led the witch hunts in England. You know, the *Malleus Maleficarum?*"

"*The hammer of the witches,*" said Tobias. "The witch-finding guide."

"The Purgators drove the sorcerers out of Boston," Thomas continued. "Led to the creation of Maremount. And I think the witch hunters are still here. There are some of them in the government." He whispered, "and they might be watching us." He knew how he sounded. He sounded like a complete nutter, like the ranting woman in the park who wore pink tube socks over her trousers. He took a deep breath, shaking his head. "Anyway, I don't want to sound paranoid, but somebody gave me this card and said to call him." He shoved it back in his pocket.

"Munroe has that tattoo. Her dad is a senator," said Fiona. "And he must be a—what did you call it?"

"Purgator," said Thomas. "It means something like purifier."

"Her family has been at the school forever," said Fiona.

"So you don't know what the poem means?" said Tobias.

"Have patience. I'm going to think about it some more," said Thomas. "I'm a bit sleep-deprived at the moment. This is all madness." He rubbed his eyes. "Send me that photo. I'll keep working on it, but you two should get back to school."

Fiona texted him the picture, and they said their goodbyes. Gripping his hot paper cup, he stepped out into the spring air. Wandering into the Common, he saw, for the first time, the new elm tree and its ivory boughs curling into the air. The dead hung from its branches, and police labored to cut them down, surrounded by yellow tape. Every time a policeman approached the bodies, he seemed to be repelled backwards, like there was an invisible barrier. For a few minutes, Thomas watched the police moving forward and back in in a macabre quadrille.

This was a place of death long ago. It wasn't just hanging—there were severed heads in this celebrated spot of liberty. His students were always fascinated to learn how the Thanksgiving alliance had turned deadly in the decades after the *Mayflower's* landing.

He walked along one of the Common's old cow paths. He always got an interesting reaction from his students when he talked about Matoonas, the Nipmuc leader. Matoonas's son was falsely accused of murder, and the Puritans displayed the son's head on a pike in this very park. Years later, during King Philip's War, Matoonas himself was captured along with a second son. The Puritans decapitated them both, jamming their heads onto pikes that faced each other. The idea was that since the soul resides in the skull, father and son would be forced to stare into each other's moldering eye sockets in the afterlife. It wasn't enough to kill them in one world. You had to destroy them after death, too.

He rubbed his forehead and looked down at the poem as he walked. Something flickered in his mind. *His voice extinguished after death... made whole above the one who made him mute.*

He put his hand over his mouth. He understood what the spirits wanted. They wanted the King to speak again.

36

Fiona

As she rifled through Celia's closet, Fiona had a brief respite from thinking about terrorist attacks. Earlier in the day, she'd run into Jack and was surprised to learn that the Athenæum would go forward with its fundraiser, despite the bodies that rotted nearby—including Ms. Ellsworth's. Though students and faculty mourned her loss at Mather Academy, something of a blitz spirit had arisen within the lockdown area, defiance tinged with hysteria. No one wanted to "let the terrorists win."

That afternoon, Celia had appraised the jeans and T-shirt Fiona planned to wear and instructed her to select a dress from her closet. A black sheath dress hung next to a yellow chiffon sundress and a long, emerald silk gown. She didn't know much about clothing, but the green dress's low backline reminded her of a 1930s movie star. She cast off her uniform and slipped into the gown. It draped over her as though someone had designed it for her. She grabbed a belted black coat to wear over it.

When she stepped out into the courtyard, she caught a faint scent of putrefaction. The parents of Mather students were unhappy that their children were once again trapped within police barriers, but no one wanted to complain too loudly. Standing in the way of law enforcement officials was the same thing as helping the terrorists—though now, with the supernatural tree dominating the park, people were slowly starting to replace the word "terrorist" with the word "witch."

As Fiona passed the elm, she noticed that the work crews had given up trying to remove the bodies. Instead, they labored to erect a giant metal scaffold around it. Someone would likely drape it with cloth to shield the eyes of passersby from the grim sight. But not, unfortunately, from the stench.

She pulled her coat tighter as she crossed the center of the park. Her mother would have wanted to see her in the gown. She would have tried to fix Fiona's hair, too, but she was locked outside the perimeter.

When Fiona opened the red door to the Athenæum, a woman dressed in black directed her to the coat check. Leaving her coat with a young man, she wandered up to the second floor. Many of the women had dressed up for the event's nature theme. A long-haired woman wore a garland of leaves around her head, and her companion wore a wreath of flowers. The women in the room sported an array of colors—green dresses, flowers, and a white Grecian style, while most of the men wore sedate suits, some dressed up with colorful bowties. Many guests held glasses filled with brown drinks and herbs.

She strolled into a large room draped with floral garlands. She didn't quite belong here, among all these elegant adults. She turned back toward the stairs, relieved to see Jack standing by a doorway, dressed in a dark gray suit. As she touched his shoulder, he turned and smiled. He kissed her on the cheek and handed her a glass of cold herbal tea before they set off to wander the first floor.

"I guess people weren't put off by the prospect of another attack," she said.

He smiled and raised his glass. "We can't let a little terrorism get in the way of our parties." A look of concern crossed his face. "You were safe, though? I tried to find you. Grunshaw hid in his room this time. But you weren't in *your* room. I was worried."

"I ran outside after someone." She didn't really want to get into another discussion about Tobias. It was obviously a sore point.

The color drained from his cheeks, and something flashed in his eyes—anger? "You went *outside*? During the attack?"

She nodded and sipped her drink. She wasn't going to get off this topic easily.

"Let me guess: You went after Tobias."

"He was trying to save Ms. Ellsworth."

"Was he now? Well, he didn't." He turned away, frowning. "I told you he was bad news. He invites chaos everywhere he goes." He glanced at her again, touching her collarbone with the tip of his fingers. "I know there's something you're not telling me about him."

Oh, you know, just that he's a sorcerer from another world who's teaching me magic in a secret coven. Nothing big.

She felt bad about lying to him, but there was too much to tell at this point. She sighed. "Can we talk about something else?"

He tilted his head. "Well, I guess I don't want to anger the best friend of a witch. I might end up a newt."

She rolled her eyes.

He smiled faintly, brushing her cheek with the backs of his fingers. "I don't like the idea of you running into the Common while people are being murdered. But I guess I understand that you can take care of yourself."

"Thank you." She put her arm through his, and they started walking. "So, what made you decide to come here? You don't seem like the social butterfly type. Is it some kind of Hawthorne family thing?"

He looked around. "You're right, actually. I really have no interest in talking to anyone here. I came early to get a preview of their temporary exhibit—the Voynich Manuscript. I spent some time studying it before you arrived. Do you want to see?"

He led her to the exhibit room, the same room where Tobias had first confessed about Maremount. The stained glass was replaced by enlarged images of yellowed drawings and inscrutable script. In the center of the room stood a glass-encased stand containing the Voynich Manuscript itself. Walking over for a closer look, Fiona stared at the crooked chunks of handwriting in a language she'd never seen.

"What is this?" She gazed around the room at drawings of women in baths of green water.

"No one is quite sure. It surfaced in the early 20th century, and it was carbon dated to the early 15th century. It seems like it might be an alchemical text, but no one has deciphered the language."

Fiona looked closer at the brown ink and small looped letters. It looked a bit like Angelic, but it wasn't. There were no Latin translations to help her.

"It was probably some sort of code." Jack waved his drink around as he spoke, and the pink had returned to his cheeks. "There are rumors that the great alchemist John Dee once owned it in the 1500s. Now that everyone's talking about witchcraft again, it suddenly seems more interesting."

"So the witchy talk sparked your interest?"

"I just like a mystery, really." He smiled and took a sip of his drink.

"Do you have any particular theory about what it means?"

He looked into the air, chewing his lower lip, and then said, "It could be a coded magic book, or 15th century science, or it could be—"

His words were cut off as the library's lights blinked out. Jack hugged her to him. In the darkness, someone shrieked, and a glass shattered. She could feel Jack's breath on her neck.

She whispered into his ear, "What's going on?"

In the nearby rooms, people chattered. A man began to shout, "Nobody panic!" over and over, his voice rising in pitch.

"Where's the exit?" a female voice called out, and then a banging noise rang through the room.

A man shouted, "The entrance is locked!"

Fiona held tighter to Jack. He had a musky smell, like myrrh.

"Wait here," he said, and she reluctantly released him.

The guests' voices grew louder, discussing alternate routes out. She almost thought she could make out the sounds of Angelic in the din. As she fumbled toward the main hall, a single flame punctuated the darkness, followed by screams. Her heart thrummed hard in her chest. Someone was on fire, burning from the chest outward. Flames erupted toward the ceiling. Fire illuminated the man's face from below, and agony contorted his features. Another flame followed from someone else's chest. As shrieks rang through the room, Jack stood by her again.

"We should get out of here." He grabbed her hand, leading her away from the smell of burning flesh.

Disoriented by the darkness and smoke, she didn't know where he led her. Clinging to his arm, she stumbled after him down a stairwell. "Where are we going?" She tried to stop herself from crying, but she let out a sob.

"I know a way out."

"Do you know what happened back there?" Her breathing wasn't normal. She was nearly hyperventilating.

He hugged her shoulders. "Take it easy. I'm getting us out of here."

"People were burning." With shaking hands, she pulled her phone out of her bag to dial 911, but there was no reception. "Is your phone working?"

He opened a low door into what seemed to be an earthy-smelling tunnel. "Someone else is calling for help now, I'm sure. There were a lot of people there."

She held his hand as they walked underground, and she traced her other hand along the damp walls for balance in the dark.

"It must have been something to do with the terrorists," he said. "Or witches, or whatever they are. I don't know why they'd come to the Athenæum. Maybe they were after the book. We're going up stairs in just a moment."

Her heart hammering, she tripped on a loose stone as she climbed, but Jack steadied her. They halted, and he pushed on something above them until a small door swung open to the fresh night air. Police sirens whined in the streets around them. He helped her out, following after her. As she stood and took in her surroundings, she recognized the crooked tombstones and obelisks of the Granary cemetery abutting the Athenæum. They had just crawled out of what appeared to be a crypt.

She took a shaky breath. "How did you know about that exit?"

"It's an old Hawthorne family secret." He wiped a tear off her cheek. She hadn't even been aware that she was crying. "You need to get home. I'd like to walk you, but I'm going to have to go back and help. I just wanted to get you away from the witches as quickly as I could. It was so hard to tell what was happening. Take this." He reached into his pocket and pulled out a small glass bottle on a silver necklace strand. "It's a good luck charm for your way home. Trust me—it'll work. "

Before she could protest, he pulled the collar up on his coat and disappeared back into the crypt. She looked down at the charm. In the streetlights, she could just make out that some kind of dried plant filled the glass. She fixed the clasp around her neck and let herself out of the cemetery, eager to secure herself behind the school gates. She crossed the park in a jog.

When she arrived in her room, she pulled out her phone and found a text from Thomas:

> Field trip to America's hometown tomorrow. Meet in the park. Bring your friends and the wand.

37
Thomas

Apart of Thomas had hoped that it wouldn't work—that they would intone the spell and remain completely visible, that maybe there was still a rational explanation for it all. He'd hoped that he could go back to his cocktails and cigarettes and let the police do their job. But he'd watched as his hands and body disappeared in front of him after they'd chanted the spell. It was a dizzying feeling, like vertigo—when everything you thought you knew about the world was thrown upside down.

Thomas wondered, not for the first time today, if he'd lost his mind. He was in the middle of a group of teenagers on a skull-hunting mission to a Plymouth cemetery. They'd used the invisibility spell to sneak through the police barriers that morning.

In his right hand, he gripped a thin wand made of hickory wood. Now fully visible, Celia sat across from him on the train, flipping through a fashion magazine. Alan hung on to the baggage racks above his head, swinging his legs below him. In many ways, they seemed like ordinary kids.

At least, until they began an excited discussion of the Purgators' blood magic and Fiona's traumatic date the night before. On top of that, Mariana's skull-adorned ensemble suggested that she was only too happy to spend her free time in a cemetery.

"So their chests just burst into flame?" Mariana toyed with her skull ring, asking for the same details for the third time.

"Yeah, and I could smell the burning, and then Jack whisked me through an underground passage."

Tobias looked away from the window. "How did he know about the tunnel?"

"I don't know. He said it was a Hawthorne family thing."

"That doesn't make any sense." Tobias crossed his arms and resumed staring at the backs of buildings whirring past. "He's peculiar."

"Well, he thinks you're a witch," muttered Fiona.

"Philosopher," Tobias corrected with a note of irritation.

Mariana turned to Thomas and tapped his knee. "So you said you were going to tell us on the train. About why we're going digging in a cemetery." The excited look on her face was a little unnerving.

"You're quite morbid, you know that? Shouldn't you be into shopping and pop music or something?"

"Don't patronize me." Her voice was scathing as she narrowed her black-rimmed eyes.

Thomas held up his hands in a gesture of surrender. The last thing he needed was goth rage on top of the terrorist threat. "Sorry. All right, the poem says 'the King, his voice extinguished after death.' I figured out what that means. See, King Philip—"

Celia looked up from her fashion magazine. "Wait, who is King Philip again?"

He sighed. Something about this part of history was hard for Americans to remember. "You know the first Thanksgiving, yeah?"

She sneered. "I'm not an idiot."

"Right. The Native leader who helped the Pilgrims in the 1620s—his name was Massasoit Ousamequin, leader of the Wampanoag. Massasoit was his title, like *king*, but it stuck as his name. There's a giant statue of him in Plymouth. He saved the Pilgrims from starvation. That was King Philip's father."

Mariana stared at him. "So if his dad saved the English, why did they cut off his son's head?"

"It was fifty years later. During that time, the English and the Natives clashed over land rights and hunting. And the English panicked about losing their Englishness. Being hanged, drawn and quartered—one of the worst executions the Puritans could think of—was reserved for those who'd gone native."

"Rough. I didn't know the colonists pulled people apart with horses." Alan grimaced as he took his seat across the aisle.

"Massasoit had made a strategic alliance with the English," continued Thomas. "The Wampanoag had been ravaged by disease. But the English numbers kept increasing, and the Wampanoag numbers kept decreasing."

"So did the war start over resources?" asked Mariana.

Thomas nodded. "The English started demanding that the Native population give up their weapons. They wanted more land, so they provoked a war." The teenagers were leaning toward him now, listening intently. "Things really got started when they hanged three of King Philip's closest advisors. The war raged for several years after that."

"How does this relate to the poem?" Alan rested his hand on his chin.

"When King Philip was captured at the end of the war, the Puritans cut off his head and mounted it on a stake. They quartered his body and scattered the limbs."

"Brutal." Alan rubbed his hand over his mouth.

"The Puritans were dreadful," added Tobias. He seemed to be in a bit of a mood today.

"The Natives in the area believed that the soul resided in the head, so beheading someone meant their soul was doomed to endless wandering," Thomas continued. "And the English believed that remaining unburied would achieve the same purpose. The King's head still rotted outside Plymouth decades later, when a Puritan named Cotton Mather came along."

"His grandfather founded our school," said Mariana.

"Cotton Mather was a cranky old bastard, and he wasn't overly fond of King Philip," continued Thomas. "He ripped the jawbone off the skull in a fit of pious rage."

Tobias turned to stare at him. "So what does the poem mean?"

"Your magic works through language, right? It was like Mather was scared that the old King still had some power, some magic to fight with. So he silenced him. The poem said *the King, his voice extinguished after death*. They're talking about Cotton Mather stealing the jawbone. *Made whole above the one who made him mute*—this part is the instruction. The spirits want us to make King Philip's skull whole over the corpse of Cotton Mather."

"And Cotton Mather is in Plymouth?" asked Fiona.

Thomas shook his head. "No. But we've got to find King Philip's skull. We're supposed to give him back his voice by reuniting him with his jawbone."

"Wow," said Fiona. "Maybe that mending spell will be useful after all."

"And I think we need to give Metacomet a proper burial." Thomas rested his forearms on his knees. "*The chopped, the burned, the choked rise from the roots.* An army will be raised somehow. Maybe another army of the dead, I don't know. The spirits of the wrongfully killed. Anyway, whatever the spell does, it needs to happen in Maremount. That's where Rawhed is, right?" He shifted back in his seat, rubbing his chin. "That's where Tobias's people are fighting him, too."

The students' eyes were wide with fascination. Thomas was quiet as he let them digest this information.

"Whoa..." said Alan.

"And you think we'll find King Philip's skull in Plymouth?" asked Tobias. "Where his head was left on the pike?"

He glanced out the window. They were close to Plymouth now. "It said 'the beginning and the end' at the top of the poem. What if it literally means the beginning and the end of the war? The war started in Plymouth. And there's a good chance King Philip's head ended up here after it rotted off the pike. I think we need to look for his skull where the gallows once stood that started the war, and where the pike once speared his head. Both of those things were on the old Gallows Hill, where the cemetery is now."

"Cool." Mariana smiled.

Thomas rubbed his eyes. He declined to tell them that he'd stayed up all night alternating coffee with whiskey, picking through all the contradictory mentions of gallows locations in old books. He'd begun to neglect his classes in the past few weeks, and unmarked papers towered above a dozen half-eaten bowls of cereal on his kitchen table.

Tobias frowned. "When we get everything we need, Cotton Mather and the King's skull, I'll go back to Maremount to perform the spell with the Ragmen."

"On your own?" said Mariana.

"The Tatters and the other Ragmen have been fighting him all along," said Tobias. "It's too dangerous for anyone else to come."

"But you'll need us," said Fiona. "What if you can't find the Ragmen? You said they're in hiding."

Tobias shook his head. "You don't understand what it's like there."

Fiona crossed her arms.

The train pulled in by a red brick building at the Plymouth station. When it ground to a halt, Thomas stretched his legs and put on a pair of sunglasses against the glaring afternoon sun. Followed closely by his new teenage posse, he walked along South Street and through Plymouth center. He became lost in his thoughts again. If he was correct, the locals had at one time called this Gallows Lane in recognition of the journey some would take to their deaths. In England, at least, convicts were allowed to hop off the cart for one last drink before their demise, thus going *off the wagon*. He didn't believe they were afforded any such comforts in the New World.

He glanced over at the neat colonial houses that lined Leyden Street as they wandered up a small hill, past the old courthouse. Alan sung to himself, drumming on his thighs as they climbed the brick walkway onto Burial Hill.

Trees lined either side of a path leading up the shady hill, and the ground became more densely packed with graves the further they climbed. When they reached the peak, Thomas looked around, clutching the hickory wand. Apart from its large size, the cemetery looked like many other colonial burying grounds, though the view was particularly beautiful. From his vantage point, he could see out to the clear blue harbor where the Pilgrims first arrived. Philip's head once rotted here, not far from where Plymouth honored his father with a statue.

After a brief discussion, Alan and Tobias turned to investigate the graves closer to the ocean, while the girls headed down the hill in the opposite direction, spreading out amongst a few tourists. Thomas stood atop the hill with the sunlight warming his skin for a few moments before the shrill sound of a wren recalled him to his mission.

Looking around, he saw that the graves all seemed to face the same direction. Most of the older ones lined the main path. A sign caught his eye. As he approached, he read that two forts had been built on this hill: one in 1621, and the other in 1675 in the heat of King Philip's War. He could picture a bleak, weather-worn and windowless building on this very spot.

Celia's shout interrupted his thoughts: "There's a skull here with no jawbone!"

He rushed down the hill to where she stood in front of a gravestone engraved with a jawless skull and crossbones.

Celia pointed to the stone. "Do you think the missing jawbone could mean something?"

"It's a good guess, but I've seen this design before. They have them in Boston too. It was some kind of template, I think."

She frowned and wandered off. There were thousands of graves on Burial Hill, many of them unmarked. The newer stones displayed weeping willows or angels. The Plymouth colonists didn't favor the grotesque imagery so beloved of their north shore cousins, though a few death's-heads and anguished skeletons glared out from the older headstones.

Thomas walked from grave to grave as the shadows grew longer. Occasionally, Fiona's friends distracted him.

"It's a timber rattlesnake!" Mariana shouted after a long period of fruitless searching.

Celia jumped backward. "Are they poisonous?"

"No," Mariana replied. "They're *venomous*."

Alan cupped his hands around his mouth and yelled, "Are we still looking for what's absent? Because it's pretty hard to look for what's absent."

The air began to cool as the sun dipped lower over the horizon, and the gravestones' shadows crept down the hill toward the water like long fingers.

"We might have to catch the train soon," Thomas called out. "I'm sorry. I don't know how to find an unmarked site."

He watched as the rattlesnake slithered through the tall grass, sliding over the graves down the hill. He glanced at the stone to his left. A crude carving of a skull stared out, hollow-socketed, from the curved top of the gravestone. Beneath its vacant eyes was an inverted-triangle nasal cavity, and— oddly—a heart-shaped mouth.

"Caleb Cook." He read the name aloud, and his mind sparked with recognition. "This is the grave of one of King Philip's killers! It's a connection, at least. This could be the unmarked gallows spot." Thomas held up the wand as Tobias jogged over to join him. "So what do I do with this? Do I flick it or something?" He almost thought he should be wearing a large, pointed hat and holding a broom.

Tobias looked over the stone as the others joined around. He pulled the wand from Thomas's hand and began tracing the engraved skull. "If it's enchanted, this wand will transform the aura. It will remove the enchantment."

When he finished tracing, the skull glowed with a pearly light, and white flames flickered for a moment before dying out. Tobias stood back to watch.

"Holy crap," Alan whispered.

After the flames sputtered out, the clumsy skull carving bulged near the forehead. There was a collective intake of breath as it protruded further, its rough granite surface smoothing over into bone.

"Oh my God." Celia gripped Thomas's arm.

Before them, the triangular nasal cavity shrunk, and a few yellowed teeth sprouted from the upper jaw. Thomas held his hand below the skull, now almost fully detached from the gravestone. With a final pop, a fully formed human skull— minus a jawbone— separated from the gravestone, dropping into his hand.

"We've got it," said Alan in awe.

Thomas brushed the fissures on the top of the skull with his fingers. "I can't believe this is it. King Philip."

He looked at the ancient object before him, its ivory surface covered in a delicate web of mold. He stared into the dark eye sockets. This man—this potential relative—had once struck the Puritans with a terror so deep, some said the memory had led to the mass psychosis of the Salem Witch Trials.

"We've got the beginning," said Fiona. "Now we just need the end."

38

Tobias

I t was cold cereal for dinner in the dining hall again. Not only were students' parents unable to get through the police perimeter, but the school cooks were shut out as well. Tobias didn't eat until 8 o'clock, long after the dining hall normally shut its doors, but there was no one to close them anymore. Only a few teachers remained at the school—those who lived near the Common or within Mather itself. Tobias tried to remember the last hot meal he'd eaten.

He cleared his tray and trudged up the stairwell. The boys' hallway was dark, though a light at the far end flickered on and off. As he walked down the corridor, something under his feet caught his eye. He glanced down to see small squares of paper littering the floor. He picked up a piece for a closer look, and found an image of a demon cowering before a chalice— Blodrial's chalice. Printed on the other side in a gothic font were two words: "The Protectors."

He stuffed the paper in his pocket and continued toward his room, pausing at Connor's open door. Connor—the cherub— sat on the floor in front of his computer, his knees curled up into his chest. Tobias watched from the doorway as a news story played from Connor's laptop.

A sleek-haired woman spoke solemnly into the camera. "From guns to prayer groups, local organizations are taking matters into their own hands in the fight against terror. *Spiritual* terror some are calling it, and they're promising to reclaim the city."

Connor glanced back at Tobias, who could see the dark shadows beneath his eyes and that his cheeks were no longer quite as round as they once had been.

"Munroe's going to help us." Connor stared at him, his face expressionless. "Did you hear? She stopped the witches with her blood. It's because she's pure. She said there's a Mather witch." He turned back to his computer screen, and Tobias continued to his room.

When he opened the door, he found Alan sitting at his laptop. Alan pulled off his headphones. "Have you seen Munroe's new cult?"

"The Purgators." Tobias pulled the crumpled paper out of his pocket. "I guess they're going public, now that everyone's scared of witches."

Alan shuddered. "Witch hunters. Fricking creepy."

"I told you that Thomas got a visit from one of them, right?" Tobias sat on the floor, leaning against his bed. "Did we ever hear from him about finding the jawbone?"

"He emailed earlier." Alan pulled out a small bag filled with a dried herb from under his bed. "He thought the ending we're looking for could be where King Philip was shot in the Miery Swamp. So he went to Rhode Island by himself and spent all day digging there, but he didn't find anything." Alan broke up small pieces of the herb as he spoke. "I'm sort of getting burnt out on thinking about this stuff now. I want to relax for a night."

Tobias nodded, and over the next hour, as they reclined against their beds, Alan played recordings by a musician called Brian Eno. Alan shoved a chunk of the dried herb into a clay pipe he'd bought in Lexington—a replica of the type they'd used in colonial days. They smoked as they listened to the music, and it made Tobias double over and cough when he inhaled.

After they passed the pipe back and forth a few times, Tobias found himself entranced by the music. He realized that neither of them had spoken in some time.

"What were we talking about before?" he asked, his mouth dry. "Did someone say something about..." He trailed off, unable to remember how he had started his sentence.

Alan's eyes were red, and he handed Tobias the clay pipe again. Tobias's fingers grew hot as he drew smoke into his lungs.

"How weird was that thing with the skull yesterday?" Alan asked. "Like, it came out of the gravestone. And then we were holding a King's *skull*. Wait—was that even real?"

"I know! What?" Tobias replied, and they both burst into laughter.

Alan's eyes were half-closed. "Everything is messed up. The whole tree thing. It's like, I mean, there's dead bodies near where they sell fried dough. And the skull. The skull guy used to be a whole King, and now he's just bones."

Tobias blew out a cloud of smoke. "It's odd to think that someday, we'll all be dead bodies."

"That's messed up."

The conversation died out again, and Tobias listened to the sounds of a piano over what sounded like distant ghosts shrieking. He felt overcome with fatigue, and he crawled off the floor onto his soft bed. His eyelids shut as he rested his head on his pillow.

It seemed as though his bed floated in a large lake, drifting along on the waves of the music. The sky was a vault of stars, and since his father had taught him, he knew which was the North Star and which was Venus.

His bed reached the shore, and the sky grew pink as his feet touched the sand. He walked in the field outside Scorpiongate, and his fingers brushed the long grass. Tobias could see a man approaching, wheeling something along. As he drew closer, he saw that it was Father pushing a large wicker cart. There were people in the cart—his mother and his sister. Their heads knocked together as the basket rolled.

"They're getting sicker." His father's eyes darted all around—looking at Tobias, and the grass, and the sky, and back to Tobias, but he wouldn't look at the basket. "I must ask the philosophers to heal them."

But when Tobias looked at his mother and sister, he could see that their lips were blue, their skin was gray, and their chests no longer heaved with breath.

"Tobias!"

His eyes opened, and Alan stood over him. He lay in his room again, and he exhaled. His chest was hollow with sadness.

"Tobias, something's happening in the dining hall."

"What?" The image of the knocking heads faded from his mind.

"Munroe is stirring something up."

Tobias struggled to get up, feeling drawn back to his bed as if it were quicksand, but after a few moments he stumbled to his feet and followed Alan out the door. He ran his hands along the walls as they shuffled through the halls and down the stairwell to the dining hall. As they entered, he saw Munroe standing on a long wooden table. She was in a tight red dress instead of her uniform, and her arm was bandaged. Dozens of students gathered around her.

"I think we all know what's going on now." Her voice was a low hiss. "The tree that won't come down, the terrorists who disappear into thin air. This isn't ordinary terrorism. This is witchcraft!" She held up her bandaged arm as she prowled back and forth on the table, her feet bare. "You all saw what I did. I have the power to repel them."

"Go Munroe!" someone shouted appreciatively.

She stopped pacing. "But there's one here among us. What happened to Sully? What happened to Ms. Bouchard?" She turned to look at Tobias, folding her arms. "Maybe Tobias can tell us." She bent forward, addressing him as if he were a child. "Tobias, can you tell us what happened to Sully after you punched him?"

Everyone stared at him, and some students edged closer.

"Where are you supposed to be from?" Connor stepped toward him. "My dad is English. You don't sound like him."

"Where is the principal?" Tobias whispered to Alan.

"He hasn't left his office since the last attack," Alan whispered back. "Let's get back to our room."

With bags under his eyes, Mr. Grunshaw trudged into the dining hall, ordering Munroe off the table. But as Tobias and Alan hurried back to their rooms, Tobias could still hear the excited shouts about the *Mather Witch* echoing through the corridors.

39

Thomas

Surrounded by crooked stacks of papers, Thomas shoveled another forkful of chicken tikka masala into his mouth. As he chewed his cold dinner, he glanced at the mud he'd tracked into his kitchen the day before. Under the gray Rhode Island sky, he'd spent six hours digging through the dirt for the jawbone. It was the spot where King Philip had been killed—where the war had ended. Yet for his efforts, he was no wiser as to the location of the jawbone.

He'd just taken another bite of chicken when the phone rang, and Fiona's name appeared on the screen. "Hello?"

"So you didn't find anything?"

"I pretty much just flung earth around for six hours. The wand did nothing. I'm just glad there was no one to see me waving it around. Anyway, the location didn't fit our pattern."

"Why?"

"There was a little stone memorial there. It ruins the whole pattern of unmarked sites. The things you found were based on clues of what was *missing*. The gallows was unmarked. This one had a sign."

"So maybe that wasn't the end of the war that we're supposed to look for?" said Fiona.

"People usually refer to King Philip's death as the end. After his body was dismembered, the Puritans sold off his wife and children as slaves in Bermuda. The Wampanoag still live in New England, but he was the last King."

"So what are we missing?"

"Some sources place the end two years later, in 1678. I'm not quite sure why." He took another bite of his dinner.

"How do wars get officially ended?"

"There was a treaty. I guess the end location could be where they signed the treaty. I really don't relish the idea of an earth-flinging trip in Maine, though."

Fiona went silent for a moment.

"Are you still there?" he said.

"You know that war in Iraq?"

He sighed. "I'm familiar with it, yes."

"They hung Saddam Hussein after they invaded, right? I was just thinking, maybe the Puritans hung some people at the end, too. After the treaty, to get rid of any last enemies."

Thomas dropped his fork on his plate, spattering bits of fluorescent-orange masala sauce on his shirt. "Fiona, you're a genius." He dropped his phone on the table, hit the speaker button, and began rifling through a stack of papers.

"What's happening?"

"When I was looking for the execution spot of the three men at the start of the war, I found a book that chronicled all the executions around Boston Common." He shuffled through the papers around him as he spoke. "I found it!" He held up a page photocopied from a book called *Boston Common: A Diary of Notable Events*. "The diary stopped naming the Natives they killed after a while. There were just too many of them. After Matoonas had his head cut off, more were killed every few years. The descriptions get more and more vague—*some Indians captured were hanged*. At least forty were killed after King Philip's capture."

"So the last execution could be the ending point?"

"Two years after King Philip died," said Thomas, "there were nine random executions I couldn't figure out. It just said *nine Indians shot on Windmill Hill*. It was in 1678. They must have been captives of the war, maybe high-ranking Pokanoket Wampanoag members."

"That must be it! The ending point. The whole thing started and ended with executions."

"Any idea what Windmill Hill is?" he asked.

"Tobias said there was a mill in the North End in Maremount, one that runs on imprisoned spirits. There are parallels between both worlds left over from the old days. Maybe that's Windmill Hill."

He paced around his apartment, excited now. "What part of Boston would that be?"

"Copp's Hill, I think."

Thomas straightened. "Copp's Hill? Cotton Mather is buried there. In fact, Cotton Mather is probably buried *with* the jawbone he ripped off. I should have thought of that to begin with. We'll get everything we need in one place. The minister and the jawbone."

"It's within the police perimeter. When are we going?"

"Get your worst clothes ready. We're going grave-robbing tonight."

Close to midnight, Tobias and Fiona met Thomas near Windmill Hill. They joined Thomas to cast their shovels into the earth in the old burial ground. Thomas brought a duffel bag for transporting the King's jawbone and minister's bones, and Tobias dragged along a few shovels.

When they arrived at the cemetery, an iron fence blocked their entry. Thomas stood guard while Fiona and Tobias clambered over the spiky gates before he followed them in. On the hill's peak, the cemetery overlooked the Charles River on the northern side, while narrow triple-decker houses loomed over a cramped street at the southern edge. Crooked graves jutted from the grass in meandering patterns interspersed with a few maple trees, just beginning to bud. At one time, a gallows must have stood here near the windmill, and at the base of the hill, a ferry would have taken passengers across the river to Charlestown.

They searched through the cemetery while Tobias illuminated the graves with a sphere of light. After a few minutes, they found the Mather family tomb near where they'd entered. A few drops of rain fell as Thomas appraised the stout brick memorial. Lightning speared the sky over the river.

"It's not just a grave. Cotton is below several feet of cement." The rain fell harder in heavy drops.

"We'll have to dig through the side." Tobias handed him and Fiona shovels.

Thomas's clothes were already damp in the rain, and the wind chilled him, but he thrust his shovel into the hill along with Tobias and Fiona, who argued over Tobias's determination to return to Maremount by himself.

"I'll go with him," Thomas said when they'd dug several feet into the earth. "I'm the only adult. Plus, I know how to fight even without magic."

Arms throbbing with fatigue, they worked into the night, piling up mounds of mud beside the pit. They shoveled as the storm battered them with rain, and they continued after it passed. At last, in the very early hours of morning, Fiona's shovel hit something hard: a collapsed wooden casket. When Thomas pulled the splintering pieces apart, he found a skeleton clutching a jawbone.

"It's here." Thomas reached down for the jaw. He handed it to Fiona, and then placed Cotton's muddy bones into his bag, one by one.

"Careful," said Fiona.

"I got it." He fed pieces of the ancient minister into his duffel bag.

When he finished, he helped the two teenagers climb out of the slippery pit. Hoisting himself out, he saw Tobias's body tense as he stared into the heart of the cemetery. Thomas followed his gaze. In the night sky, three pale green moths with long, curving tails flew toward them through the moonlight.

Fiona rested on her shovel. "What are those?"

The moths fluttered to a tomb below a tree, and Thomas's breath caught in his throat as he watched them rupture into human forms. It was that vertigo feeling again—only this time, his heart thudded in his ribs.

Standing before him, all three men had close-cropped beards, wearing somber clothes with wide, white collars, tapered hats, and vines coiled around their limbs. In the front, a robust blond man with a bulbous nose stood taller than the other two. Behind him were two dark-haired men whose similarly slender frames and piercing blue eyes suggested they were brothers.

Thomas fanned out his arms. Tobias stepped forward in line with him.

The blond spoke a word in Angelic, and a torch ignited in his hand, illuminating his golden beard from below. The three Harvesters stepped closer, stopping only a few feet from Thomas's face.

"We seek the blasphemous Leviathan's skull," said the man with the torch.

Thomas could hear Fiona's panicked breathing behind him. He gripped the duffel bag in both hands, suddenly wishing he'd trained to fight three men at once. Would Tobias be any good in a fight?

The Harvesters chanted in Angelic. It sounded like separate spells, and the flame grew larger. The blond held his hand into the flame, pulling out a ball of fire.

"Run!" Thomas jumped forward, punching the blond in the jaw. The man fell backward, unconscious. Though the brothers continued chanting, the fireball sputtered out.

Thomas turned, rushing after Tobias and Fiona, who scrambled over the cemetery gate. They sprinted toward the main road, hurtling down the hill toward sparse early-morning traffic.

At the intersection, Thomas hurled himself in front of a car that screeched to a halt inches before him. He shouted to Tobias and Fiona to get in and wrenched the passenger door open. The driver, a middle-aged white woman, screamed in terror as he jumped in. Behind him, the back door slammed.

"Drive!" Fiona yelled, but the woman kept screaming, staring at Thomas as she cowered against the driver door.

He looked out the window and could see the three Harvesters coming toward them as the morning sky lightened. The blond hurled a fireball. It thudded against the rear window, and the woman's screaming intensified.

"Drive!" Thomas shouted.

The car lurched forward as the woman slammed her foot on the gas.

"It's okay," he said over her wails. One of the kids should have been in the front seat. "We're not trying to hurt you. There were some terror—"

"Was that a gunshot? Is this a gang thing?" the woman sobbed, swerving back and forth over the double yellow line. "Can I just give you the car? I have money."

He put up his hands in a gesture of peace. "We don't want the car. We'll get out soon. It was the terrorists."

She gasped for breath, sobbing.

Fiona leaned forward from the back seat. "We're only seventeen. We go to private school. He's getting a Ph.D. We're not in a gang."

The woman glanced in her rearview mirror at Fiona's face, and her breath began to slow. "Terrorists were after you? The witches?"

"They were in the cemetery."

After a minute of crying, she said, "You should call 911."

"We did already," Thomas lied.

She sniffled. "Oh my God. They're everywhere."

As the sun rose, the woman dropped them off near Mather Academy, and the three of them snuck into the Adepti room. They sat on the floor. Thomas slumped against the wall.

"Nice punch," said Tobias. "They have a much better fire spell than we do, but it seemed like the punch interrupted it quite well."

"Thanks. Nice running."

Tobias rubbed his eyes and smiled faintly. "I thought I ran away quite manfully."

"I guess Rawhed knows about the bones," said Fiona. "Do you think he can find us here?"

"I think I should bring them to Maremount right away," Tobias said. "I just want a few hours of sleep."

Fiona yawned. "We're coming with you. You need the whole coven."

"I need to talk to Bess," said Tobias. "She wanted cake. Do you have any here?"

"You think I would hoard cake in my room?" she asked, but even as she spoke Tobias was rifling through her stash of junk food. He produced a plastic-wrapped marshmallow snack, dyed green for St. Patrick's Day, and a few chocolate cupcakes.

"These will do," he said. "I'm going to talk to her now, then I'll rest for a few hours before I go."

"I'm going with you," said Thomas. He wasn't fond of the idea of encountering more Harvesters, but he couldn't let Tobias go into danger on his own, even if it was his home.

With the cakes in hand, the three of them walked down the stairwell to the tunnel. Thomas's chest tightened at the sight of the bones and the faltering sounds of children's rhymes floating through the air. This was like a nightmare.

A bent crone stumbled toward them through the darkness.

One for sorrow,
Two for mirth,
Three for a secret,
Four for death.

"Hello, Bess. I don't think I ever told you my name. I'm Tobias, and this is Thomas and Fiona. We brought you cakes, like you asked." He deposited the treats in Bess's gnarled, quivering hands. "I'll need to get to Maremount in a few hours."

A toothless grin spread on her face. "Lovely," she said from beneath her tangle of gray hair. "I've got a Thomas here too, bless him." She pointed to a skull resting at his head level. Ashy fungus grew in the sockets. "Killed for buggering his farm animals."

Thomas nodded and gave a half smile. "I see. That's..." He cleared his throat, letting the sentence die out.

She sat down on a stool and chewed, gazing into the remainder of the cupcake as though it were a crystal ball. "This one's got cream," she said after a moment. "I take much pleasure in cakes with cream. You want to get home, crow-boy?"

"I need to bring something back to Maremount," he replied. "We're trying to finish what Wormock started. Thomas will come with me."

"I'll need more of these." She mumbled something unintelligible and ripped open the green cupcakes.

"We have more," said Fiona.

They thanked her and turned to leave. As they walked out of the tunnel, Thomas heard her wavering voice filtering through the tunnel's dank miasma.

Little Tobias crow-boy had a fine skull,
A bag full of bones, one man full.
Here come the moths to scare the boy away,
But Little Tobias crow-boy will die another day!

When Thomas reached the tower room, he collapsed against the wall. A pink morning light filtered in from the window, but his eyes closed against it. In a couple of hours, he would join Tobias in the Darkling Tunnel. He didn't know what awaited him on the other side, but it couldn't be much worse than what was happening here. Couldn't be much worse than a night bus full of London teenagers, come to think of it, and he'd survived those.

On the rug beneath him, a three-headed dragon unfurled a triad of curling red tongues. He stared at the image until his eyes began to close, thinking of the red tongues of fire that sometimes rose from the alley behind his apartment in East London. When he'd first moved there, a small house had stood on stilts over train tracks, and below the tracks was the place for burning cars. As soon as one burnt car was removed, another would take its place. Sometimes, other things were burnt—an old sofa, or a refrigerator full of blackened eggs—and he'd have to shut his windows against the acrid smell. Before he fell asleep, he tried to call up soothing images: the deer in the tall grass of Richmond Park and the burbling garden fountain near the Temple Church.

40

Tobias

Tobias peered over at Fiona lying next to him on the rug. By the slow rise and fall of her chest, she'd fallen asleep. With her tangle of golden-brown ringlets, she reminded him of the wild-haired spirits who grew from sea foam and lured men to their deaths in the wintry Atlantic. She turned toward him in her sleep, and he clamped his eyes shut, suddenly afraid she would awake to find him staring at her face.

This was it. In a few hours, he'd leave for Maremount with a sack of bones. He'd reunite with his old coven, and together they'd make the King's skull whole with the mending spell. He sighed, rolling over. The idea of going back to Maremount wasn't as exciting as it should have been. Here, he lived like a real philosopher, practicing spells in a protected tower room, with all the food he wanted. And there were his new friends here, and Fiona...

He fiddled with the locket of Eden's hair at his neck. With a twinge of guilt, he realized that he hadn't been thinking about her as much. Maybe she'd moved on, too. After a few minutes, he opened his eyes to peek at Fiona one last time before sinking into a dreamless sleep.

Screeching from within Mather Academy startled Tobias. Alarmed, he looked over at Fiona to find her already awake and upright, her hair snaking around her head.

"What the hell is that noise?" Across the room, Thomas rubbed his eyes.

Fiona blinked. "I think it's the fire alarm."

A faint smell of smoke filled the room. Tobias sat up, trying to clear the fatigue from his head.

"I'm going to see what's happening." Thomas sprang up.

They followed him down the stone stairwell into the Caldwell Library, and the smell of smoke grew stronger. Screaming pierced through the walls. As Tobias reached the library exit, Connor knocked into him, falling backward on the landing. His lower lip quivered as he stared up at Tobias from the floor.

"What's happening?" asked Tobias.

"As if you didn't know!" A few drops of spit erupted from his mouth as he spoke, scrambling to his feet again. His eyes blazed. "Witch! Witch!"

Tobias shook his head. "What?"

"Calm down." Thomas stepped forward. "What's going on?"

Tears sprung into Connor's eyes and his cheeks reddened as he shouted. "Calm down? Are you crazy? The witches are outside. They killed all the police and lit the school on fire." His eyes darted around the stairwell. "I'm not going outside. I don't care if the school burns to the ground. I'm not getting my head cut off."

Tobias turned to Thomas and Fiona. "Can you two get the other girls? We'll meet up back in the Adepti room."

"Will you be all right on your own?" said Thomas.

"I'll be fine," said Tobias, already hurrying toward the boys' wing. A few students ran up and down the stairs in a panic, many on their phones with their parents. Connor screamed for Munroe over and over in the stairwell.

In the hallway, Tobias covered his nose with his shirt as the smell of smoke grew thicker, stinging his eyes. He rushed to his room as a couple of straggling students bumped into him.

"There you are!" Alan shouted as he pushed the door open. "The building is on fire, but the Harvesters are killing people as they come out."

Tobias glanced out the window and saw the tapered hats and vined clothing of Harvesters on the other side of the gate. Some hurled fireballs toward the school, while others shot students with muskets as they escaped the flames. Tobias could see one of his classmates—Jared—lying on the ground. He writhed, clutching his bleeding stomach. Mulligan's sagging body hung from the gates in a noose next to Grunshaw's.

Tobias's heart hammered in his chest. "They must be after the jawbone. It's up in the tower room. We have everything we need for the spell now. Bess can get me to Maremount through the tunnel."

"Get us to Maremount," said Alan, leaping up.

"It's too dangerous for us all to go."

Alan threw his hands up. "Are you *kidding* me? We're about two minutes away from death by supernatural army. My parents have been calling me nonstop convinced that I'm about to die, which I probably am. Have you seen our teachers?"

He had a point. "Fine. Let's go."

He opened the door and coughed as smoke swirled into the room from the hallway, but he stalled in the entryway. Coming toward him were Munroe, Connor, Sadie, and a dozen other students. Connor clutched a baseball bat, while Munroe gripped a knife in her right hand, her fiery hair streaming behind her as they approached.

"Tell them to call off the attack!" Munroe screamed at Tobias, breaking into a run.

He edged backward. "I'm not on their—"

Before he could finish, Munroe yanked him out of the doorway and pushed him against the wall, pressing the knife to his throat. He felt a sliver of pain where the blade jabbed his skin.

Her gray eyes were inches from his face. "Tell them to call off the attack," she said in a low voice.

For a second, he considered transforming, but he balked at using a spell in front of an angry mob of witch hunters.

"He's not a witch!" Alan shouted, pulling on Munroe's arm.

Munroe ripped the chalice off her neck with her left hand and pressed it against Tobias's cheek. "I know someone killed Sully with magic," she hissed. "Was it you?"

He held her eyes with a steady gaze. "No."

She stared at his cheek, and her lower lip trembled. "Are you in league with the witches outside?"

"No. I'm not with them."

Her brow crinkled in confusion, and she pulled the pendant away from his face, lowering the knife. "He's telling the truth." She raised the necklace in her hand. "This would've burned him if he'd lied. He's not with them. Someone else killed Sully." Tobias saw the fear in her eyes as she stepped away.

"If it's not him, then who killed Sully?" Connor screamed.

"I don't know," she stammered.

Tobias wasn't with the Harvesters, but he knew what they wanted. What would happen to Munroe and the others if he left them there to be slaughtered?

"What's going on?" Thomas approached them through the hall, followed by the girls.

Celia covered her mouth with her arm. Mariana doubled over, coughing in the acrid smoke.

Fiona pulled her shirt up over her nose, her eyes streaming. "We need to get out of here! The building's going to collapse around us."

Sadie rushed toward Munroe, gripping her arm. "Are you sure Tobias's not with the witches outside? He can't stop them?"

"He's not the Mather Witch," barked Munroe.

Sadie shouted, "What about *Celia*?" As Celia approached, Sadie's freckled cheeks flushed. "Lucas said you refused to talk about your family. No one even knows where you come from."

Celia's nostrils flared, and she crossed her arms, muttering something under her breath.

Tobias held out his hands. "Everyone, stop. I have an idea. Just let me get up to the library."

As Munroe looked on, Sadie prowled toward Celia, narrowing her eyes. "Did you curse Sully? Did you bring the witches—" She blanched, suddenly stumbling back.

Golden hair sprouted from Celia's limbs as feline features transformed her face. Her back lurched forward over muscular, leonine legs. As the transformation spell was completed, light glinted off her sharp teeth. She growled at Sadie.

The witch hunters shrieked, and Connor readied his baseball bat, tears in his eyes. They'd found their witch.

Tobias's fists clenched. "What are you doing?"

"Celia's the witch!" Munroe pointed her knife toward the mountain lion. "She never liked Sully."

The ceiling heaved and cracked above them. It was now unbearably hot in the hallway.

"We need to get out," said Thomas. His voice was muffled as he shielded his nose with his shirt. "Let's go. *Now.*"

A beam crashed at the end of the hall with a great boom, and a cloud of cinder and sparks erupted into the air. Someone pulled on Tobias's arm—it was Thomas, dragging him toward the stairwell with the rest of the coven. Mariana coughed uncontrollably, trying to use the walls to steady herself, but they were too hot to touch. Fiona wrapped Mariana's arm around her shoulder and dragged her along toward the library.

Smoke stung Tobias's eyes as they descended the stairs. What in the gods' names was Celia up to? He pulled his shirt up over his face as they hurried through the smoldering library. There was a yelp as they reached the memorial plaque. It had burned Mariana's hands as she opened it.

Behind the rest of the coven, Tobias climbed the stairs into the Adepti room. The air was a little clearer, and Tobias caught his breath. The duffel bag of minister's bones lay in the corner, the King's skull resting on top.

Mariana gasped for breath between coughs. "What happened to Celia?"

"I don't know what she was doing," said Tobias, running his hand through his hair. "I think we should just give them the skull. We're condemning people to death if we don't."

Fiona grabbed him by the shoulders. "Tobias—think about the big picture here. I know you don't want our schoolmates to die, but if we can destroy the Harvesters, we'll prevent a lot more deaths. Right? Otherwise they'll just keep killing."

"You think that's what we should do?" He rubbed his forehead with his palms, staring at the floor. "Fine. Maybe the other students will find a way out safely. We need more cakes for Bess."

"And the preacher's bones." Thomas held up the duffel bag.

Mariana pulled out her phone. "Oh, thank God. Lucas made it out past the Harvesters. My family keeps calling me."

Tobias dove into Fiona's stash of treats on one of the shelves. It felt like he hadn't slept in a week. He filled the crook of his arm with half a dozen packaged cupcakes.

As he stood, the door swung open. Celia tumbled in, covered in soot.

"Thank God you're okay," said Mariana. "What happened to everyone else?"

Clutched in Celia's hands was a small plastic knife-block containing four kitchen knives. "This was all I could find in the kitchen. We might need weapons in Maremount, right?" She picked up Fiona's backpack and shoved it in.

Tobias shook his head. "Why did you have to transform just then?"

"Let's get going." Celia frowned. "We can talk in the tunnel."

Thomas stepped forward, holding out his hand. "I'll feel better at least if you let me carry the weapons."

"Fine." She handed over the backpack, picking up the skull and jawbone. "I'll take these." She picked up Fiona's large, cloth handbag, placing them inside.

Laden with cake, bones, and kitchen knives, they stumbled down the hot-walled stairwell. Parts of the building cracked around them as they descended. Despite the musty air, Tobias breathed easier as they entered the cool passage below ground, marching toward Bess.

The crone eyed them over the remains of a chocolate cupcake. "Back so soon?"

"We need to get to Maremount," said Tobias.

"Also, you should probably know that the building's burning down," added Thomas.

"What a muddle young people get themselves into." Bess sighed.

"We brought more cake for you." Tobias unloaded an armful of cupcakes into her eager hands. "Can you say the Angelic spell for us?"

"Not Angelic. Just English. I guess you'll need it done now. Always in a hurry." Bess tutted as she stood, rubbing the small of her back with her hand. "Follow me."

As they moved among the rows of bone-lined shelves, Tobias could hear Mariana's labored breathing behind him.

"What's wrong with her breathing?" Bess asked. "Has she got the consumption?"

"There was a lot of smoke," said Mariana. "There are people trying to kill us upstairs."

"Well, don't worry." Bess fought with the plastic packaging of a cupcake as she walked. "There's not much to fear down here, except old Claw-fingered Jack, of course." She ripped the package open and shoved a pink cupcake in her mouth.

Claw-fingered Jack. Hopefully that was just Bess's sense of humor. Finally, they arrived at a wall at the end of the passage. A high dirt ceiling curved over their heads, and artfully arranged bones were embedded in the walls. Lines of skulls formed columns and crosses. In the center of it all, ribs and femurs created a rounded door shape.

Bess turned to face them. "You're sure you want to go?" She had a smear of pink frosting across her chin.

"We're sure. We'll die if we don't," said Tobias.

"You'll die no matter what!" She let out a wheezy laugh. When no one returned the laughter, she cleared her throat and faced the bone-wall. She recited:

See saw, sacradown, sacradown,
Which is the way to Maremount Town?
One foot up, the other foot down.
That is the way to Maremount Town.
And just the same, over dale and hill,
Is also the way to wherever you will.

Within the door, the femurs and ribs trembled. A few popped out onto the ground before each row of bones rattled down in a cloud of dirt, exposing an opening over six feet high. Coughing, Tobias stepped back from the heap of bones, staring into the doorway. Though it was large enough to climb through, it was difficult to see where it led.

Tobias turned to her. "Will we be able to come back?"

"Just say it again, but with *Boston*." She turned, hobbling away.

"Thank you," he said, and he stepped over the pile of bones and through the entrance, followed closely by the others.

"Tobias?" Bess croaked.

He turned to see her striding toward him. "Yes?"

She stood just inches from his face now, and she dropped her cake. A gnarled hand grasped his shoulder, and her filmy eyes opened wide, clouding over. Her jaw unhinged, and she screamed her piercing and melodious scream. Tobias's stomach clenched at the sound.

"Who?" Tobias demanded, as she unlatched her hand from his shoulder. "Who is going to die?"

Bess glanced around for her cake, and she brushed off the dirt as she picked it up off the ground. "I don't know that, dear."

Tobias stared at her as she took a deep breath and shuffled off, seemingly exhausted from her work.

"Maybe it's just a grandmother or something," Alan offered.

"I don't have a grandmother," said Tobias.

"Probably Munroe," Mariana said. "Or Connor, or Sadie, or any of the others."

"They were trying to climb down the vines outside when I left them," said Celia. "They might've made it out with Munroe's magic blood. Let's go."

"Maybe we should have taken them to Maremount," said Fiona as they began trudging through the tunnel.

"I don't think you understand." Tobias called up an orb to guide them through the darkness, and it cast a faint light on glistening mud walls. "Maremount won't be any safer."

41
Tobias

There were no bones in this tunnel, just the dirt and the damp. Tobias envisioned the earthen ceiling crumbling and caving in on them, burying them in between worlds. He swallowed. He had a terrible feeling that he would be the one to die.

Fiona walked beside him. "You don't think it's going to be one of us, do you?"

He took a deep breath. "We just need to stick together when we get there. You'll be okay. We've got the invisibility spell."

She pulled her phone out of her pocket, frowning at it. "I don't know what happened to Jack."

Tobias bit his lip. "Well, at least you know he escaped the Harvesters once before. He seems to know how to take care of himself."

"I guess so." She sighed, shoving her phone back in her pocket.

They walked through the dank tunnel air, and the ceiling got lower as they pressed on.

"Celia," Tobias began. "Are you going to tell us why you decided to transform into a lion in front of our schoolmates?"

Celia sighed. "Sadie made me angry, for one thing. Going on about Lucas."

"And for another?" Tobias frowned.

"You said you had a plan to end the attack and needed to get to the library. I didn't want you to give up the skull." She sounded annoyed.

"Because you wanted to get the Harvesters out of Boston for good?" said Fiona. "I agree."

"It's not just that. I want Rawhed out of Maremount."

Tobias found it hard to breathe in the soggy tunnel air. "Why do you care so much about Maremount?"

Celia spoke in a small voice. "Because it's my home."

Tobias stopped walking, and Celia bumped into his back. He pivoted to face her.

"Wait—*what*?" Fiona turned to her friend.

Tobias's mind reeled. *From Maremount?* "What are you doing here?" He stepped toward her. "Why didn't you tell us before?"

She took a step back, almost as if scared. "I was sent to Boston when I was five. When my father executed my mom." She trailed her fingers over the handbag containing the skull. "Boston is where exiled members of the royal family have always been sent. To Mather Academy."

Tobias's mouth hung open. *Is she joking?*

"There used to be a man who'd come to check on me," she continued. "I called him Uncle Perkins. But he stopped coming after Rawhed took over. And you said the royal family have been imprisoned."

"Who are you?" His voice was a harsh whisper.

"Lady Celestine Throcknell. But I used to be a princess," she said with a note of sadness.

"*You're* the missing princess?" Thomas's asked incredulously. "I saw your family tree."

Tobias couldn't believe what he was hearing. So this was why she'd been so interested in all the royal gossip.

Celia lifted the handbag and sighed. "Can we go now? I still want to kill Rawhed. My father may have exiled me, but my cousins are in Maremount. They're the only family I have."

As Mariana and Alan looked on, open-mouthed with shock, Tobias shook his head. "You've been lying to us. How do I know we can we trust you?"

Celia looked down at the ground in frustration. "Look, I couldn't tell anyone. Perkins told me Rawhed was rounding up royals. And I know Tobias was here in secret, but it's different for him. He's just a Tatter." She looked over at him. "No offense. I mean, you speak very well and everything. But it's not like anyone will really care what happens to you."

"Celia!" cried Fiona.

"That came out wrong." Celia's eyes welled up. "I just meant he's not a political target or whatever."

"I get what you mean," said Tobias.

"Okay. Can we *go* now? We're all on the same side. We all want to kill Rawhed and to get back to our families. I've been living without mine for most of my life. Everyone else gets to go home on Christmas or Thanksgiving." Tears spilled down her cheeks and she wiped them off with the back of her hand, smudging dirt across her face. "And during the summers I never had anyone to talk to, and there's no one at all now that Uncle Perkins is gone."

Alan awkwardly patted her back.

"I had no idea how to get home," she continued. "I never knew there was a tunnel here. I could have gone home as soon as you told me about it. But I didn't, because I wanted to see this through. We're a coven now, even if it means I'm in a coven led by a Tatter." She sobbed.

"Okay, okay." Tobias rubbed her shoulder. Maybe he was only a Tatter, but he didn't like sobbing. "We all want the same thing."

"Should we go then?" Celia sniffled.

Tobias turned, and they trudged on in silence, funneling into a single file as the tunnel narrowed. In the cramped space, Tobias's arms brushed the sludgy walls. Only a few inches separated the top of his head from the muddy ceiling. The dirt that pressed around them had a sulfurous smell.

He took a deep breath, particles of earth catching in his throat. Maybe he wouldn't be the one to die. Maybe the banshee had howled for the schoolmates he'd left behind.

Behind him, Mariana coughed.

"What are we heading into?" Thomas wheezed. "When we get to Maremount—you said it was dangerous. Is that because of the bone wardens?"

Mud coated Tobias's arms, and he held his elbows out to the side, trying to make more room as they shuffled through. "The wardens will come after us immediately if we use magic within the city walls. We should use Lady Cleo's Cloak before we leave the tunnel. I'm hoping we'll be near the south of the city. I want to find my old coven. But they might be outside the southern gates, in the wilderness. If so, hopefully the cloak will last long enough for us to get out of the city again."

He could see a stream of light ahead. "We're almost there." As he continued toward it, the tunnel came to an abrupt end. The blue morning sky shone through a hole the size of a dinner plate, just a couple of inches above Tobias's head.

"It's a narrow exit," he said. "Fiona, can you lead us in the cloaking spell? I can never remember that one."

When they finished chanting it together through Mariana's coughs, he reached his hands up into the fresh air. Something scratched his arms as he pushed the earth apart above him and dug his fingers into the dirt. He pulled himself into the light, wriggling to free his shoulders and then his legs. He found himself in a large thicket of blackberry bushes. Thorns tore the bottom of his shirt. As he looked over the brambles, he found himself outside the city gates on one of the northern shores. They were outside Scorpiongate—not far from his home, but perhaps too far from the Ragmen's new hideout.

"Tobias!" Fiona's voice called from below.

He was confused for a moment, as he could see clods of dirt moving around on the ground, until he remembered that they were invisible. He felt around for Fiona's arms and then pulled her out into the briary shrubs. She coughed, gasping for breath as she got her bearings above ground.

One by one, each coven member slithered out of the narrow opening, bodies covered in sludge. Once everyone was birthed from earthy canal, Tobias led them out of the thicket and over the rocky ground toward the glistening Charles River. He caught a glimpse of an elegant figure slithering in the spumy brine, a flash of oily green and gold skin, white hair and blue eyes, before it disappeared again below the froth.

"What was that?" asked Fiona.

"A nippexie," he said. "A water spirit."

She exhaled. "Amazing."

He inhaled the clean waterside air. He knew this water well, full of eels and mummichogs.

Thomas's voice interrupted his thoughts. "We need to find your friends, right, Tobias? I've got the preacher. Celia, you've got the skull?"

"Got it," she said.

"We'll have to pass all the way through the city to the other side," said Tobias.

Unable to see each other, they held onto hands and arms as they walked toward the city gate. As the large stone arch of the gate came into view, Tobias could see the golden cage that hung from a sculpted scorpion at the top of the gate.

"What is that?" said Alan.

"It's a gibbet. A punishment."

The criminal's grimacing face became clear as they drew closer. Within the cage, glass encased her, filled with a pale gold liquid. Red hair undulated around her face, and pain contorted her features. Two pale scorpions speared her neck on either side. Everything was deathly still within the cage, except her eyes, which shifted from the sky to the ground and back again.

"Is she alive?" Mariana whispered.

"Yes. She'll stay like that for the remainder of her sentence," said Tobias in a hushed tone.

"What did she do?" asked Alan.

"Probably treason," said Celia. "Maybe treason against Rawhed and not the proper sovereign."

"Sounds about right." Before they entered the gate, Tobias gripped Fiona's hand on one side and Alan's on the other. "No one can speak when we enter the city. The bone wardens stand on either side. We don't want them to sense us."

They walked through the entrance into the narrow city streets. Tobias glanced back after they entered. High on the wall hung the hollow-eyed bone wardens, frozen in guard over Maremount. He'd always avoided Scorpiongate; a glimpse of the wardens' large antlers from a distance had satisfied his curiosity. Up close, he could see they were shaped like men but with longer arms and legs. A thin, almost translucent layer of skin covered their skeletons and tendons. For a moment, he was almost certain they'd be able to hear his blood rushing as he stared at them, but they remained still. Under each warden lay a large pile of bones, like scraps in the roost of a large carnivorous bird.

Turning his back on the wardens, he continued into the city. They were in his neighborhood—Crutched Square. After living in Boston, he'd forgotten how cramped the city streets were, and how the uneven buildings always looked like they might topple onto the cobblestones. He'd also forgotten about the sludgy sewage that ran down the centers of the alleys in his neighborhood.

On the lower levels were the shops, and crammed into the bulging upper stories were tiny homes, with chimneys poking out of the roofs at odd angles. The city looked even worse than when he'd left, and as they walked down Loblolly Row, he saw that many of the buildings were abandoned. Where Anequs's Pudding Shop had once stood lay a burnt shell of blackened stone and wood. Broken glass littered the floor throughout the Sign of Golden Crucible, and two dead cats lay in the rubble across the street. It would have been nice if he could've shown Fiona his neighborhood before it had been torched.

He quickened his pace as they neared his home, and they rounded the corner to Black Bread Lane. In place of his narrow house and the bakery below it, he found only a pile of char and twisted metal. He broke free from the group and kicked over a burnt plank of wood, hoping to find a remnant of his former life—maybe part of a book or at least one of his father's pie tins. But there was only ash.

He couldn't picture what had happened after he'd left. The fire must have spread quickly. Maybe Oswald and Eden had become lost in the smoke. His father must have fled south, into the wilderness outside the city. The raven had said they were still alive, hadn't he?

Fiona's voice whispered, "Tobias!"

He swallowed and walked back toward the center of the street, groping around in the air until he found her hand again. They climbed the steep slope of Curtzan Hill. Planks of wood were nailed over the windows of the Swan Ladies' Tavern.

Hurrying down the other side of the hill, they approached the center of the city, passing only one shop front that remained intact: the Worshipful Company of Theurgeons. The velvet-robed philosophers had set up shops in the Tatter neighborhoods, charging the poor to divine changes in their fortunes.

Though most of the city had been silent, a crowd roared as they approached Lullaby Square at the bottom of the hill. When they turned the corner to the large open marketplace, the first thing Tobias saw was a throng of people milling around in the square in agitated swirls. The towering Throcknell Fortress and the watchtower loomed over the crowd, casting them in shadow.

In front of the fortress stood the Lilitu Fountain, a stone structure about six feet high and twelve feet wide. From the side of the fountain, the petrified head of the last succubus killed in Maremount spewed the town's drinking water.

Above the crowd's din, a clopping noise echoed off the stone walls. With a lurch of his stomach, Tobias recognized the sound. An execution would take place here today. He looked back at his friends to find that their outlines had already begun to appear. His mouth went dry.

"We need to go," he whispered.

Celia replied, "I want to see what's happening."

"There's not much time left," Tobias said. "The spell is wearing off, and we're only halfway through the city."

"No. I want to see what's happening."

His breathing quickened and he could feel his face flush with irritation. "You said you were on our side. Stay here if you want, but give me the skull."

"I can see you now." Fiona stared at Tobias. Her body was now translucent, and her amber eyes hovered in the air.

"We have to leave." He started walking, pulling Fiona with him, and the others followed.

But Celia remained rooted in place with the skull. He turned for her, and as he did, the towering Tricephalus came into view. The crowd fell silent. The three-headed monster was Maremount's living gallows. A flat triangle, parallel to the ground, formed its gray body. A grotesque and vaguely equine head jutted from each of the triangle's corners, and black nooses hung from the sides. Three spindly legs propped up the corners and moved the creature into the town square with a jerky gait.

The Tricephelus halted its march behind the Lilitu Fountain. One of the heads grimaced and snorted, lashing the air with a pallid tongue.

"Celia! We need to go now!" In his panic, Tobias shouted.

Their bodies had become fully visible now, and Celia stood on her tiptoes, clutching the handbag with the skull. She strained to see over the crowd as a Harvester guard in an embroidered red and blue outfit ascended the fountain's platform.

"We bring before you today a man convicted of the most heinous crime of treason against the Champion. Today, the

Champion shall be avenged!" His palm thrust into the air, the guard smiled, looking from one side to another as though expecting applause. The crowd remained silent. He nodded to someone on the platform below him. "Bring him up."

The Champion. Tobias had forgotten that was what the Harvesters called Rawhed.

Two more guards hauled up a young man, no older than Tobias. But the man wasn't a Tatter like he was. He wore a ripped jacket, and his shoes were muddied, but his clothes were laced with pearls and ribbons. He trembled as a guard fixed a noose around his neck.

A scream pierced the air. "Stop! Stop!"

It was Celia. The grim-faced crowd turned to stare at her, murmuring. She rushed forward into the throng, clinging to the handbag. Panicking, Tobias rushed after her.

Her voice echoed off the stones of the watchtower. "I'm Lady Celestine Throcknell, daughter of King Balthazar. You must release my cousin! I have something the Champion will want."

Tobias was right behind her now, and he grabbed the back of her sweater. As she spun around, he tore the bag from her grasp and turned to sprint back to the rest of the group.

"Run!"

With Thomas leading the way, they left Celia in the square and fled toward a long and narrow alley that led south. Tobias gripped the bag as he sprinted. Behind them, the guards' ceremonial swords clanked. Their best chance at this point was to go invisible and hope the bone wardens wouldn't find them.

Tobias gasped, "Fiona, can you say the cloaking spell again?"

As they ran, Fiona led them in the spell, and their bodies faded to invisibility. But when they finished intoning the words, the sonorous bells of the watchtower began to toll, calling forth the bone wardens.

"Where are we going?" said Thomas.

"We're coming to a canal at the end of this alley," yelled Tobias. "Take a right at the water, and it will take us out of the southern gate."

He tried to run faster, but he bumped into someone in front of him, nearly tripping over a pair of legs. The end of the alley came into view, and the putrid scent of the Shoremuck Canal hung in the air. As he neared the alley's mouth, he heard a scream, and an invisible body stopped short in front of him.

"There's a bone warden coming!" Mariana shrieked. "Go back!"

He was pushed backward as his friends crammed back into the alley. He stumbled, falling onto someone. Fiona yelped beneath him and pushed him up, and his heart pounded as he scrambled to stand again. They would need a spell to get out of this, but his magical knowledge was useless against bone wardens. They could perhaps transform and escape, but Thomas didn't know how, and Mariana's turtle wouldn't get very far.

"What are we doing?" Fiona shouted.

The only danger wrought by Wormock's spell book was the accidental collision of Fiona's wind spell with Alan's fire spell. Just as a kernel of an idea formed in Tobias's mind, the pale form of a bone warden appeared at the entrance to the alley. A nauseating howl rose from its cavernous mouth. Tobias's stomach fell as the sharp tips of its antlers barred their way.

He turned to run, knocking into Fiona again, but another bone warden dropped down behind them, blocking the rear exit. Even as the blood pounded in his ears, he worked out a possible plan.

"Fiona, do you remember the spell for growth?"

Her response came out as a shriek. "What?"

"Just trust me. Say it when I count to three."

The bone warden near the canal stroked its long fingers along Thomas's chest. Thomas became visible at its touch.

"Alan, I need you to say the fire spell on the count of three," yelled Tobias.

The warden clutched Thomas, raising him into the air. Howling, the creature opened its jaws. Thomas's eyes bulged in horror.

"One, two three," Tobias said. As his friends chanted the spells for fire and growth, he began to chant the spell for wind.

A fist-sized ball of flame blossomed above Tobias, hovering between the plaster alley walls. Fiona's spell for growth expanded it until it was two feet across. As Tobias finished the wind spell, he sent the fireball hurtling through the alleyway toward the canal. It struck the bone warden's shoulder.

Unfortunately, it also hit Thomas's back.

Roaring as fire enveloped its arm, the warden dropped the historian. Thomas landed hard on his hands and knees as flames burst from his shirt. He scrambled to get up, flailing forward toward the canal. He plunged in.

"Again!" shouted Tobias.

They called up another fireball, hurling it toward the warden. This time, they ignited its face. Its ivory features began to melt, and it shrieked toward the sky with a deafening caterwaul. It stumbled backward.

"Turn the other way, Fiona," said Tobias.

With their third recitation of the spells, a fireball hurled in the other direction, striking the second bone warden. It emitted a piercing roar, and then, with a catlike movement, it propelled itself onto the alley wall, its talons finding easy purchase in the soft plaster. With flames blazing from its head, it charged toward them. Dust sprayed from its claws where they stabbed the walls.

"Run to the canal!" Tobias shouted. "Transform!"

He heard splashes as someone jumped into the canal, and then as he reached the mouth of the alley, Fiona screamed behind him. He turned to see that the bone warden held her in its grasp above its head. Its claws pierced her neck. Blood soaked her shirt, and she let out a cry. He tried to think clearly, but the only thought that came to him was that this must have been why the banshee had screamed at him. His heart raced as the blood drained from his head—he was going to watch Fiona die.

The warden's scalp blazed, and its features melted like a candle while it screeched into Fiona's face. Thin lips curled up, revealing sharp teeth, but then it went silent, seemingly distracted. The creature pointed a sinewy finger at her neck.

"Transform!" Tobias shouted again.

Though fire deformed its face, the warden continued to point at her throat. He could see Fiona's lips move as she recited the spell, and he chanted the words along with her. His bones and skin condensed. His face protruded into a beak, and feathers sprouted from his skin. Within moments, he flew in the air with Fiona.

42

Tobias

Tobias circled over the canal, and he could see Thomas swimming toward the southern gate followed by a wolverine, a turtle, and a duck that he could only assume was an actual duck. In her bat form, Fiona swerved above him, and a trickle of blood flowed from the cut in her neck.

He climbed higher into the air, taking the lead. He directed their flight past the southern gate and lower over the marsh, but he saw no sign of the Ragmen's camp. They glided among the river birch and maple trees until they glided through the Great Swamp—the Cwag, as it was known here.

After they landed on the banks below a black locust tree, he transformed back into his human form, feeling the pain rip through his bones and muscles. He hunched over on his knees and looked up to see Fiona shift back into a girl again. She bent over, clutching her stomach and retching. Blood ran down to her waist, and there were deep gashes in her neck and shoulder.

"Are you all right?" he asked, moving toward her and putting a hand on her back.

She retched again. Her face was pale, and there were tears in her eyes. "There's a lot of blood. There's a lot of blood on me. Does it look bad? I can't see it. There's a lot of blood here."

"Slow your breathing," he said, rubbing her back while she hunched over. "I know someone nearby who can help us. That's why I brought us here."

"What do you think happened to the others?" She rose and clutched at her bleeding neck.

With his hand on her back, he led her through the trees. "It looked like the rest of them were going to make it through the southern gates. Once we transformed, the cloaking spell wore off. But the bone wardens didn't seem like they were going anywhere."

Fiona stammered, "Where did you say we're going?"

"To a friend. Simon Bandyshanks. He's one of the Cwaguns who live in the marshlands." He helped to steady her as they walked.

Her face had a pale, greenish tint. "That's really his name?"

"Yes." He smiled and looked over at the pendant at her throat. "Something made the warden pause. It pointed at your necklace, I think."

"Jack gave it to me."

He took the tiny bottle in his fingers. "It must be charmed. Quite powerfully, actually."

Her breathing was irregular, panicked. "Jack doesn't know how to charm things." She inhaled deeply, fiddling with the necklace. "I can't believe Celia. I mean, Lady Celestine. What the hell? She tried to take the skull. I mean, I know it was her cousin. But she said that whole thing about saving the larger numbers, and then she threw it all out the window when it was her own family."

"I should have known not to trust a princess."

She glanced at Tobias's empty hands. "Does Thomas have everything now? What happened to the skull?"

"I saw him swim back for it. I dropped it when it looked like…" he took a deep breath, not wanting to finish his sentence.

They walked through the shade of the birches until they came to a winding path. It led to a house constructed of uneven planks, and the upper story bulged over the lower. A twisted chimney jutted out of a mossy roof, and ivy climbed over misshapen windows. Tobias knocked on a gnarled door, and after a short delay, it creaked open. He recognized the knotted gray beard of his father's old friend.

"Tobias?" the man asked incredulously, sticking his head out and looking around.

"Simon! Can you help us?"

"I'm all-a-mort! What does thou 'ere?" he whispered, opening the door wider and motioning them in.

Fiona followed Tobias into a room cluttered with rough wooden shelves. Pots hung from the ceiling, and bundles of dried herbs dangled from hooks on the walls. Scattered all over the room were jars of dark liquids labeled with symbols— planets, animal heads, and elemental signs. A small fire burned in a hearth overhung by snakeskins.

"How are thou 'ere?" Simon asked, grasping at Tobias's shoulder. "Thy father tole me thou escaped."

He turned to look at Fiona, glowering. "Who's thess?"

"This is my friend Fiona, from Boston," said Tobias. "You know the legend of the Darkling Tunnel? It's real. We came through it."

Simon's hand flew to his chest. "Is it true?"

"The Harvesters have come to Boston." Tobias guided Fiona to a wooden stool. "We came to find the Ragmen but were attacked by the bone wardens, and Fiona's hurt."

"The bone wardens hunts ye?" He turned around again. "Hore's kitling! I did sait to thy father not to mess with Angelic magics."

"I know. You never wanted to get involved with the Ragmen. But can you help us? Can you help Fiona's neck?"

"Set down, Tobias." Simon walked over to a small cabinet. "There's no call for Angelic to fix sicknesses. A simple tinxture will do. And then ye must flitter. Rawhed scours the Cwag for Ragmen, and he wanders the woods still."

He pulled out several jars of dried herbs and a small bowl, placing them on a rough-hewn table. He began breaking up the herbs and crushing them with a pestle, spitting into the bowl to make a paste. "Oak moss's strong, rult by the earth."

There was little logic to Simon's brand of magic—herbs gathered in rutting season for the strength of the stag, flowers whose silvery petals mimicked moonlight and therefore had properties of concealment. And yet it seemed to work, and Tobias always got a strange thrill out of watching him prepare a tincture or salve. Simon poured a small quantity of brown liquid from a jar into the paste and then heated the solution over the fire.

"Was anyone I know captured?" Tobias asked, and he waited while Simon returned to the table to pour a thick black liquid into the mixture.

Simon frowned but didn't look up. "Eden."

Tobias felt the air leave his lungs. "Where is she?"

He looked up with a scowl. "Tobias, ye must flitter back to Boston. Rawhed lurks here yet."

"Where would he have taken, her though?"

Simon grunted. "To the cwod."

"To the prison? He keeps some captives alive?"

He looked back to his tincture. "Seems so. He uses them in some way." He tugged down Fiona's shirt to clean her shoulder and back. "Tobias, look thou away."

Tobias turned to the fireplace. "What do you mean, uses them?"

Simon didn't answer. He was like that sometimes—he only spoke when he wanted to. Tobias could hear his lungs wheezing as he worked.

"Have you seen my father?"

Simon sighed. "Not sense the trees was bare." He scowled. "Now ye both must scatter afore ye gets found by Rawhed. He hunts nearby."

They thanked him as he ushered them out the door and into the dappled light of the forest. They walked over the marshy paths toward a clearing as the air around them cooled. A flock of sparrows took flight from the trees, and, moments later, a group of starlings. In this part of the Tuckomock Forest, white flowers bloomed on the trees near the path, and their petals covered the ground. These were the mayflower trees.

They moved toward the edge of the clearing, and Tobias looked down at the crushed petals beneath his feet. "Rawhed uses his prisoners, he said."

"For what? Labor?" She touched her neck where it was bound. "Do you think we should transform again? Something feels wrong. I want to get out of here. We should circle overhead to look for the others."

He glanced at her. Some of the color was returning to her cheeks. "After we look for them, I want to get to the prison. I don't know what Simon meant about using prisoners, but it doesn't sound good."

A crunching noise from the other side of the clearing interrupted them, and Tobias turned. Someone was running toward them over the crumpled white petals. Why did he keep thinking about the petals?

A woman with long dark hair ran through the thicket across from them, snapping twigs. She looked terrified as she fled toward them, followed by a boy and two men.

"What's happening?" Tobias called out, but they ran past without slowing, gasping and trampling the mayflower petals.

The mayflower petals. When Tobias had asked the shew stone to tell him who'd started the Mather Adepti, it showed him a mayflower tree. The letter said the Mather Adepti's founder had gone mad. The later philosophers hadn't wanted him to find the poem.

Fiona grabbed Tobias's arm. "Tobias? Shouldn't we get out of here?"

He stared at the trampled petals as an idea formed. "The mayflower trees."

Another group came sprinting across the clearing—two women and a man.

Fiona stepped closer, inches from his face. "What the hell are you talking about?"

He grabbed her shoulders. "There's another name for them."

A woman in a red dress ran into the clearing, and someone ran close behind her. It was someone he recognized—someone from Mather. Fiona was about to shout, when Tobias clamped his hand over her mouth.

43
Thomas

Thomas kicked his way through the canal water, followed closely by Mariana and Alan in their familiar forms. Weighed down by the bag of knives and the bones he carried, he spit a stream of brown, pulpy water out of his mouth and gasped for breath.

From the canal, he'd been relieved to see Tobias and Fiona transform at the last moment. He'd circled back to grab King Philip's skull after they'd flown off while a warden had burned nearby.

Here, outside of the city, the canal flowed into a bay. In the water below him, he saw the glimmer of nippexies as he swam. He made it as far as he could from the city before his arms grew tired. When he was out of breath, he called to the others to swim toward the shore. His feet touched the ground near a wooded area, and he climbed out of the bay. Cold, filthy water weighed down his clothes.

On the rocky shore, Alan and Mariana transformed into their human forms again. They lay gasping on the rocks, and Alan held his hand over his eyes as he looked up at the sky.

Thomas hunched over, catching his breath. The fireball had burned his shirt and seared his shoulders, but his quick dive into the canal had prevented any significant damage. He squinted down at the others. "Are you guys all right?"

Mariana nodded and sat up, shielding her eyes in the sun. "What happened to Fiona and Tobias?"

"They flew." He gestured into the air, catching his breath. He stood up straight and looked at the water and the towering trees. He had no idea if they were anywhere near the Ragmen. "We should get into the cover of the forest."

He walked toward the woods, followed by the others after they'd caught their breath.

Alan rubbed his arms for warmth, drying himself off. "I think we should just perform the spell ourselves. We have the bones, and we know the words. We don't know where Tobias and the Ragmen are. And we can't stay here forever."

Thomas nodded. "You're right. I just want you both to get back home as fast as you can."

"Aren't you coming back with us?" asked Mariana.

"Eventually." He pushed his way through a thick overgrowth of mulberry bushes into a grove of old cypress and oak trees. "First I'm going to find Tobias and Fiona. I don't have parents who'll be worrying about me."

They reached a small clearing. Sunlight trickled through the leaves of oaks, and ivy vines wound up their trunks.

Thomas looked at Alan and Mariana. "Are you ready?" They nodded, and he removed the minister's sodden bones from the bag, arranging them in what he thought might be the correct form of a human skeleton, though there were lots of fiddly little bones that could be either fingers or toes. Mariana sat beside him on the ground and pulled out King Philip's skull, while Alan paced back and forth, mumbling to himself as he reviewed the mending spell.

A flicker of movement in the trees caught Thomas's eye. His throat tightened as three winged insects fluttered toward them. He took a deep breath, standing.

Alan still stared at the ground, oblivious to the creatures. "I can't remember all the words for this spell."

The bugs drew closer, and Thomas recognized the iridescent green tinge of luna moth wings, ignited by the sunlight. "Guys—we might need these." He reached into the backpack and pulled out the knives, handing one each to Mariana and Alan. "The Harvesters are here. Just—be careful."

His breath quickened as the moths hovered before them. Mariana turned the knife in her hand as she stared at them.

"Get behind me." Thomas held out his arms to either side, gripping the knife in his right hand, up in front of his face as if in a boxing stance. He squinted, the brightness of the moths in the sunlight too garish for his sleep-deprived eyes.

He had that dizzying feeling as the moths burst into their human forms, and three men stood before them at the edge of the clearing. Thomas heard nothing but his own breath.

A black-bearded man with deep gray eyes wore a brass pendant around his throat. It depicted a face formed from twisted leaves and thorns. The man stared at Thomas as the two others fanned out—older men with gray beards.

"The blasphemous Leviathan's skull." The black-haired man held out his long, thin hand.

"We should retrieve the Champion," said another.

"Druloch is with us. We can end this now," said the first.

Thomas widened his stance in front of his friends. Adrenalin pulsed in his veins as one of the older Harvesters held up his right hand. Thomas suddenly felt energized.

A ball of flame grew in the man's palm. Thomas lunged toward him, but the younger man blocked him, holding the pendant aloft. It froze Thomas in place. The Harvester whispered something into the briary face, and a blinding light streamed from its center. Thomas felt himself drift out of his body.

He was no longer in the forest, but on a night bus in London. He was home again. He couldn't remember what he'd been doing—something *strange*. Was he supposed to be fighting someone? He rubbed his eyes. He needed more sleep.

The overhead lights flickered, and his trainers stuck to something on the floor. Only one other passenger rode the bus, a man hunched over across from him. The man heaved and vomited onto his shoes.

Thomas leaned toward him across the aisle. "You okay, mate?"

The passenger looked up, and Thomas found himself staring not at a stranger, but into his own tired and aged face.

"Bloody hell!" He leapt up and ran to the front of the bus as it lurched through the dark London streets. "Let me off!" he shouted at the driver, who slammed on the brakes.

Thomas forced the doors open and stepped out onto Bethnal Green Road. Gnawed chicken bones crunched under his feet. The sky began to brighten to a cigarette gray, and newspaper sheets blew off the road and into his face, covering his eyes. When he peeled the paper off, he stared into the face of the passenger from the night bus—his own face.

"What are you running away from, Boss?" The man's eyes were half closed.

As the clouds brightened overhead, Thomas remembered

a sharper light—a blinding, green light and balls of fire. He shook his head. "I'm not supposed to be here. I'm in the woods, fighting with magic. They had fireballs."

Old Thomas laughed, a deep laugh that doubled him over.

"Fighting with magic? Fireballs? Madness. You think that's real? You're not there." He put a hand on Thomas's shoulder and looked into his eyes. "You're not anywhere."

Thomas felt the pavement fall away beneath him, and his vision went black. He was unmoored from the earth. He would forever be in this abyss. All the rules he'd thought he knew were wrong. A dull ache spread through his chest, and he drifted in the vacuum until someone screamed. Light filtered into his eyes, and he could make out the blurred shapes of trees above him and feel the earth beneath him.

"I'm here!" he shouted, though he didn't know why, and he dug his fingers into the dirt. "I'm here!" He sat up and looked around, trying to orient himself. A high-pitched noise rung in his ears. He was back in the woods with the Harvesters.

Someone sobbed. Mariana? When his eyes focused, he saw that Mariana and Alan stood before him, both holding bloodied knives. Mariana's hair and shirt were singed, and she was nearly hyperventilating, but they were otherwise unhurt. Alan's expression was one of confusion as he stared at his knife, as though he'd suddenly found himself in a murderous encounter after eating breakfast that morning.

To his right, the two older Harvesters lay unmoving on the ground. Blood pooled out from under them, seeping into the earth, and it trickled in red streams from their mouths. But the black-haired man shifted. He lay against a tree to Thomas's left, gripping his stomach. Blood poured from a gash in his side. He no longer wore his tree pendant.

Wrenched open, his eyes darted from left to right. "Help me!" He looked up toward the sky. "Help me please! Druloch! I'm going to die. Druloch!"

Thomas shook his head, trying to clear the ringing noise, and slowly stood. "You were dead before."

He grimaced and writhed where he lay. "Before. But I can't die again without claiming a life for Druloch."

Thomas moved toward him, crouching on the ground near the Harvester. "Why?"

The man gripped his stomach and choked out the words, "Isaac and Rebecca."

A small part of Thomas thought he needed to end this man's misery. "Who?"

"My children." His hands grasped at the gash, trying to piece himself together again. "Rebecca was five." He swallowed blood. "Isaac—six months. The plague. Isaac—" He coughed and spluttered. "Little hands on my beard." He shut his eyes, moaning. "Rebecca. Endless questions." He moaned again, louder this time. A glazed look overtook his eyes. "The plague. Isaac's throat turned black. Wouldn't stop crying. Rebecca—the black throat, the bleeding."

"You lost your children. When you were alive, hundreds of years ago."

"Druloch shall reunite us in the Sacred Orchard. Isaac's little arms." He wheezed. "Rebecca chasing fireflies," he whispered.

Mariana sobbed, looking at the knife in her hand. "We stabbed them. They were doing a spell. Alan punched them and the spell stopped, but I almost caught fire, and then we stabbed them."

"What do we do?" Alan's face was pale.

Thomas turned back to the Harvester. "What's your name?" He didn't know why, but it seemed like he should know it.

"Matthew." His chest heaved.

Thomas didn't know what to say to someone who was dying. "Rest now. Rebecca and Isaac will be waiting for you." He didn't know, but it could be true.

Though Rawhed's army had sprung up from the underworld, they kept their memories with them. Thomas had to remind himself that the man had already been dead once, beneath the earth of King's Chapel. When Matthew's eyes closed, his jaw slackened and his chest stilled.

Mariana's sobs only intensified, and she sat on the ground, dropping her knife. Alan stared at his shaking and bloody hands, and then he sat by her, covering his face.

Though Thomas wanted to be anywhere else at that moment, he knew, at least, that he was somewhere.

44
Adepti

Tobias was muttering something about trees, when Fiona heard a rustling and snapping noise from the other side of the clearing. Another woman ran toward them, followed by a man whose collar was up around his neck. The unruly hair almost looked like Jack's. No, it *was* Jack's unruly hair. What was he doing here? Didn't he know the danger? Fiona opened her mouth to call to him, but before she could get his name out, Tobias's hand clamped over her mouth. He held on to her, whispering something into her ear. She struggled to get free until she heard the words "hawthorn tree."

Restrained by Tobias, she watched as the lady in front of Jack dashed into the clearing, screaming. Jack sprang forward and grabbed the back of the woman's dress. He whirled her around to face him. She stared into his face and screamed again. He pulled her close and said, "Shhhhh," pressing his finger over her lips to silence her screams. He reached around her back in a tight embrace.

He pulled his arms open with a cracking sound. Long, bloody bones jutted out of his hands, and he tilted back his head, sighing with exhilaration. The woman crumpled to the ground, ribs protruding from her back like broken wings. Her body twitched. Jack bent over and plunged his hand into her back, pulling out her heart. He turned toward the clearing, closing his eyes as he bit into it. He chewed slowly, rolling his head back and moaning as though he were eating a deliciously ripe pear.

Fiona's heart seemed to stop. Even with Tobias's hand over her mouth, she unleashed a piercing scream.

Jack opened his blue eyes, staring directly at her. Blood ran down his chin. "Fiona?" he said, walking toward them.

She shook uncontrollably. Her mind couldn't process it.

Tobias held her arm. "Transform."

Fiona stared straight ahead at Jack as he whispered something. With a flick of his hand, he sent Tobias flying until he hovered by the tops of the mayflower trees. Jack stalked toward her as she stood transfixed with horror. She couldn't breathe.

He wiped his hands off on his coat. "Your Tatter friend brought you here. I told you to stay away from him."

She tried to say the word "what," but she just uttered a half-strangled noise.

He leaned against the tree, close enough to pull an errant ringlet out of her eyes. She flinched, and the sound of her own pulse roared in her ears.

"I kept him alive for you, because you seemed to like him. And really, I'm not likely to be brought down by a baker's son." He turned to Tobias, still hovering in the air, and called out. "Sorry, but it's true."

Fiona glanced up at Tobias, her eyes wide. His lips were moving as though talking, but no sound came out.

Jack sighed. "I thought I'd warned you off magic with the bone warden I sent to your séance, but apparently it wasn't enough."

Fiona finally found her voice. She stammered, "I don't understand. We came to fight Rawhed. Are you him?" She could hear the ragged edge of hysteria in her voice.

He took out a handkerchief and wiped off his chin. "I'm sorry you had to see that. It's distasteful, I know. Don't think that I enjoy it."

"You sounded like you enjoyed it."

He looked away. "There is a certain visceral thrill from corporeal nourishment, but of course I hate that it's necessary. I only consume flesh because it's what I've needed to do to stay alive over the years."

Her knees buckled as she stepped back from him. "How many years?"

"Over three centuries, anyway."

She shook her head. Is this a *nightmare*? "Tobias said something about the founder of the Mather Adepti. Is that you? Are you that Hawthorne?" She felt electrified with adrenalin and fear.

"Yes, well, Hathorne actually. John Hathorne."

Her lip trembled. "From the Salem Witch Trials?"

"Right." He shrugged, wiping the blood off his hands and face. "But it was a difficult time."

"But, he was so old. I mean, *you* were so old."

He crumpled up his handkerchief, stuffing it in his pocket, and locked eyes with her. "You're hung up on this age thing, aren't you? Eating flesh keeps me in my physical prime while I'm completing my work. The number of years I've been on this earth isn't important."

She covered her face with her hands, hoping he would disappear. This didn't make any sense. John Hathorne. Rawhed. All the same person—all Jack. "Why were you at Mather at all?"

"I was looking for something I need. If you're here to fight Rawhed, as your Tatter boy calls me, I suppose maybe you were looking for it too—the poem."

She was on the verge of tears. "I still don't understand. How could you be a witch trial judge, but you're also a witch?"

"Philosopher. Look, I can see you're upset by all this. I'll be totally honest with you, and I think you'll see my side of things." He took another step toward her, resting his arm against a tree and boxing her in. His face was clear of blood now except for one bright red drop near his mouth. "Salem was complicated. The women weren't really witches. Only men were philosophers then, but the Purgators never knew any better. At the time, we believed that if women used Angelic, they would die. Stupid, really." He rolled his eyes.

How was he able to carry on a normal conversation after he'd just killed someone? Maybe this *wasn't* a normal conversation. She couldn't tell anymore. She had an overwhelming urge to vomit.

"But it didn't matter that they weren't really *witches*, as the Purgators liked to call them." He drew even closer. "What mattered was what people said, and people said they were evil. The Purgators were powerful back then, and they wanted blood, guilty or not. They hanged Ann Hibbins when I was a student at Mather." He looked past her as he recalled the memory. "I saw her face turn purple, and her bony feet danced in the air over the Common. They left her body to rot."

Fiona shuddered. She'd seen enough hangings herself.

His pale blue eyes gazed at her again. "After I saw the Purgators kill her, I only practiced magic in secret. I left the coven and went back to Salem. I did my best to fit in. I got a wife, a bunch of land."

"You had a wife?" She shook her head. What did that matter? "Never mind. What were you saying? About turning into a three-hundred-year-old cannibalistic psychopath?" Her heart raced, but her anger gave her courage.

"I was walking in the woods one day when I was getting on in years. I saw a little sparrow with broken wings. She was writhing in pain, and her mother had deserted her. So I used a simple spell to heal the poor creature. Two girls saw me, spying on me from a thicket. I had to muddle their little minds to make them forget. They would have told the Purgators, and I didn't want my feet dancing in the air like poor old Ann's."

He stroked Fiona's cheek absentmindedly, and she shuddered.

His voice was flat as he continued. "But the spell made them insane, and it spread like a sickness, and then all of a sudden everyone was a *witch*. I had to get some control of things before the Purgators found me out. I didn't want to do it, but better that I kept the bony finger of death pointing at others than at me."

"How very noble of you." Somehow the rage stopped her from crying.

There was a look of hurt in his eyes. "It wasn't just for my own sake. I have to fulfill my destiny for all of our sakes." He sighed again. "I know, I may have gone a bit far, and the other philosophers created Maremount to escape the persecution. They locked me out of it. I'd survived the horrific purges, but as time went on, death beckoned anyway. And so I found a way to restore my youth, to continue my work."

"What destiny? What work?" She was losing patience.

He looked at her with a sudden intensity. "Let me ask you this. What do you think is the worst thing that can ever happen to a person?"

For the first time since she'd seen Jack murder someone, she let out a sob. "Having your ribs torn out of your back and being eaten."

"That's hardly the worst thing, but of course, you're such an innocent thing." He wiped a tear from her cheek. "You haven't seen the things I've seen. When I was born, entire tribes were dying of smallpox. Sometimes, just one or two people remained behind out of a whole community, people who watched as everyone they loved, and everyone they'd ever known, succumbed to a virus that turned a person's flesh black and peeled it off their body in sheets. Imagine watching all your own children die that way. And then the Christians came and told them it was their own fault for being sinners. Those who lived had to spend the rest of their miserable existences wandering alone, awaiting their own deaths."

Fiona sobbed again and glanced up at Tobias. He remained suspended in the air, yelling to her with no voice.

"What kind of a monster peels off the skin of all your loved ones right before your eyes?" Jack's voice rose in volume, and passion animated his face. "I will not submit to such a creator. People think that we're over the horror—the bodies and heads left to decay on Boston Common, spirits trapped in moldering body parts for everyone to see. People think that belongs to the past. But it's not over, because the truth is that we are the minds of angels locked in putrefying bodies for no reason at all." He choked out the last words.

"And you think you can change that."

"I know I can change it. Things got a bit messy with the Harvesters, I know. They're like a bunch of unruly children that needed to be reined in. I raised them from King's Chapel using Druloch, but now they serve him as well, which is *frustrating*. But I'm still going to rewrite the world's rules."

"How do you plan on doing this?"

"By making a new world, with new rules." He stepped back and smiled, opening his hands. "Just like they made a new Maremount. I'm really very fond of you, Fiona. You know, at the Athenæum, I really was worried for you when the Tatter assassins were sent to kill me. I hope the necklace kept you safe."

"I don't understand. What could we possibly have in common?"

"When I first met you, I thought you were sort of a curiosity. But then you seemed so sweet. It's a shame you've been trying to kill me, but you didn't know any better. You said you'd sweep the monsters away for me. No one's said anything like that to me in a long time." He shrugged and smiled faintly. "No one's tried to protect me."

She motioned at the woman's corpse and screamed, "But *you're* the monster. And you're doing all this just because you're scared to die."

"Everyone's scared of dying!" he shouted, and as he did, the sky above darkened to the color of a bruise.

Thomas placed the King's skull in a small hole in the ground. He'd insisted that Alan and Mariana find their way back to Boston. As he began covering the skull with earth, he combed his memory for what he could recall of 17th century Wampanoag burials. He thought King Philip should be buried with wampum and some corn, but he didn't have those things. At least he was able to figure out which way was southwest and to orient the skull in the proper direction.

After covering the final inch of skull, he rose and stared at the freshly upturned earth, the only sound the gently lapping waves in the bay. He rubbed his tired eyes. He'd done what he could. Perhaps it had worked, and the Tatter fighters were being strengthened as he stood.

As he turned to head north toward the city, a sharp peal of thunder cracked across the horizon. He looked up at the sky, and the hair on his arms stood on end. His heart beat faster as purplish clouds roiled above. He turned to look back at the burial spot, his body coursing with adrenalin. Within the rumbling thunder, he thought he heard a voice. Though the language was unfamiliar, he could understand the message: *I am here*. King Philip had reclaimed his voice.

He surveyed his darkening surroundings as something prickled on his flesh. The sensation of spider webs moved over every inch of his skin, into his nostrils and down his throat. He coughed, struggling with the fear of being overtaken until he felt strength electrifying his muscles, invigorating his aching body. He'd never expected this to happen. *The king's spirit is inhabiting my body.*

Lightning struck the Trimountaine Hills to the north as he raised his arms to the sky. *I am here*, King Philip's voice rang in his skull.

The sky blackened further, dark as smoke from a funeral pyre. The philosopher guided his body north again, charging his body with a crackling power. Even on his best boxing days, he'd never felt stronger. He ran back to the Fishgate entrance, and the marshy earth beneath his feet trembled with the force of an advancing army of spirits.

Fiona watched as Jack stared up at the gathered storm clouds. He inhaled deeply, closing his eyes. There was an electrified, scorched smell in the air as thunder roared through the sky.

A fat white drop of rain landed on Jack's rosy cheek. The storm clouds unleashed a torrent of rain, soaking their hair and clothes.

Out of the mayflower trees, a moth fluttered toward them. But it wasn't another luna moth. It was a large death's-head moth, like the one in her vision. It flew to Jack's ear, and he listened.

As it fluttered away, he looked at Fiona. For a moment, fear and hurt flashed in his eyes. "The King has been buried."

He tilted back his head and transformed into a death's-head moth himself. Just after he flew into the stormy sky, Tobias fell from the air, collapsing onto the ground.

Shaking, Fiona ran to him. "Are you okay?"

He sat up and gasped for breath. "You need to get back to Boston. The others must have completed the spell. All the Harvesters will be drawn into Maremount."

"We need to get back to Boston."

Tobias's hair was already plastered to his head from the rain. He stood and rubbed his shoulder. "I need to find Eden. If she stays a captive of Rawhed..." He stared at her. "I can't believe he was your *boyfriend*."

"I wouldn't say *boyfriend*." She'd hardly known him at all.

"I need to go, Fiona."

"I'll go with you."

"No. It's nothing to do with you." He pushed the hair off his face. "I can't worry about Eden and worry about you. Fly north and get back to the tunnel."

He transformed and took off. Fiona folded her arms and looked around at the muddy grove and the crumpled pile of flesh that used to be a woman. Did Tobias really think she'd let him go alone? It was clear now that she had pull with the person in charge here. And did he really think she knew which way was north? She chanted the transformation spell, her wings snapping outward, and ascended into the heavy rains. She circled until she heard Tobias's flapping wings in the distance, and followed him through the storm. As they soared over the tall pines outside the city, she glimpsed the swarms of bodies beneath their branches.

Once over the city gates, she heard the gruff shouts of the Harvesters. As the Tatter army marched toward them, they amassed in the Common.

Tobias descended near Lilitu Square, and Fiona followed. He transformed in an alley near the Throcknell Fortress and pulled the grate off a manhole. He slipped in, and she flew after him into a stone tunnel. Ahead, Tobias reached an alcove with an iron ladder that he climbed. She waited, and with a few beats of her wings fluttered up after him into an empty stone room and transformed. They were in the depths of the fortress.

From a dark corner, a stairwell led upward. She tiptoed up the stairs toward the sound of screaming, and, reaching the top, looked out from her hidden position. Candlelight wavered over a black-walled dungeon, a corridor of dingy cells. Across from her, two people lay on a hay-covered floor, and a woman slumped with her back against iron bars. Somewhere, a man repeatedly shrieked, "I don't know!"

She peered to her left. Tobias clutched iron bars of his own, whispering to someone. At the end of the row of cells stood a large wrought-iron door. From her right, she heard the sound of heavy shoes on the flagstones. She slipped back into the shadows.

Jack was Rawhed. Jack was responsible for all this.

Someone was coming. An enormous guard, almost seven feet tall, stalked past as she hid in the shadows. His palm rested on the hilt of his sword. Fiona's breath quickened. Tobias had obviously forgotten the cloaking spell, for all his demands that they practice it.

She peered around the corner again just in time to see Tobias's head swing round and spot the warden, but by then the guard had grabbed him, his hand over Tobias's mouth. Two more guards arrived, and one of them opened the cell, pulling out an emaciated girl.

"A Tatter trying to release one of the Champion's prisoners?" one of them asked, forcing Tobias and the girl toward the door. "You'll both meet the three-headed horse for this."

Fiona's stomach dropped. The guard stuffed a gag in Tobias's mouth, so he would be unable to transform. Fiona chanted the cloaking spell. Unseen, she rushed toward the guard who held Tobias. As he dragged Tobias toward the dungeon gate, she pulled the large guard's sword out of his scabbard, adrenalin coursing through her veins. The man dropped Tobias, whirling to find his assailant. The heavy sword weighed down her hand, and as she tried to lift it, a piercing pain bored through her skull. Everything went black.

There was nothing—no sound and no light—until a noise like a rushing river arose in her ears. Her clothes were wet, and she thought for a moment she might actually be in a river, but then the noise of the current was overtaken by the sounds of people shouting. She opened her eyes to blurry forms. The back of her head throbbed. She tried to ask where she was, but a cloth gagged her mouth. Her arms were tightly bound behind her back. Her stomach churned. She tried not to think of what might happen if she were to vomit while gagged. She lay on a stone platform in the open air, and rain poured from the dark clouds above.

"She's awake!" someone shouted. Her body was now visible, and she glanced down to see that someone had taken her necklace. A guard pulled her up by her shoulders and dragged her to her feet. She stood on the stony edge of the Lilitu Fountain. As her eyes focused, she saw Eden by her side, a black noose around her gaunt neck. The corpse of Celia's cousin swayed by her side. When Fiona looked up, she saw the flat, gray body of the gallows monster. One of its three heads brayed above her.

Before them, a crowd of people gathered in the muddy puddles, staring at her in sodden clothes. She scanned the skies for the arrival of a death's-head moth. Lightning seared the somber sky, but she saw no insects. Someone jerked her head backward, and she felt the weight of the noose as the executioner tightened it around her neck. The rough rope scratched her skin and her body began to shake. Her legs gave way, and hands pulled her up again so that she was standing.

Nearby, a guard read out a list of crimes for which she and Eden were condemned: "High Treason, Unsanctioned Use of Magic, Confusion of the King's Guards, Improper Use of the Sewers, Conspiracy to Aid the King's Enemies, Misuse of a Sword..." She searched the crowd, but only strangers' faces stared back at her, and the guard said the words "condemned to hang." If she could only speak, she could tell them that the Champion very much wanted her to live.

Her legs buckling under her, she glanced to the skies again. No moths. She gazed out at the grim crowd. No one jeered, or threw rotten vegetables, or seemed pleased to be there. She looked at Eden, who stared down at the platform. She couldn't see Tobias anywhere.

She closed her eyes. She knew what would happen. The gallows monster would jerk away, dragging them off the fountain, and their legs would dangle in midair as they choked to death. Their bodies would be showcased from one part of the city to another as a warning, though when Jack—when Rawhed saw them, the guards would not be rewarded. In desperation, she tried to chant the words of the transformation spell, but the gag prevented her.

She scrunched her eyes shut when she felt something sharp against her face. A crow had landed on her shoulder. Tobias was tugging off the gag with his beak. She was stunned for a moment, gasping for breath, but a shout from a guard jolted her to attention. He'd given the order for the Tricephalus to move. Her whole body trembled as she rushed through the transformation spell.

Her bones compressed, muscles cramped together, and wings erupted from her thin black arms. In her familiar form, she lifted out of the noose and circled into the air just as the gallows monster propelled itself away from the fountain.

Tobias was on Eden's shoulder below, and he'd yanked off her gag, too. But it was too late. Her legs twitched in the air.

Thomas's hands clamped around a Harvester's head from behind, snapping it to the right with a crack. The man crumpled to the wet cobblestones of Lullaby Square. A part of him felt a thrill at his power, but he also felt sick at the lives he was snuffing out. But the Harvesters had died before, right? They should never have come back. *They were the invaders.*

Tatter forces were everywhere in the alleys and streets around him, joined by remnants of the King's guards, all clashing with an onslaught of Harvesters in the storm. How many men and women had been imbued with the spirits' strength? There must be a thousand of them at least, each one glowing with a pale light and moving with the grace of a lion.

He glanced toward the fortress. In front of it, a young girl's body swung from the gallows beside Celia's cousin. The gallows-beast's heads reared back and shrieked, and its legs trampled those below it in the chaos.

Nearby, someone shouted orders. They were to cut down the bodies and then light the beast on fire. They were to burn the Harvesters' elm and the wooden doors of the fortress, and drag the invaders out into the street. They were to find the monster Rawhed and hang him in the square to end it all.

In their human forms again, Tobias and Fiona crawled through the Darkling Tunnel. He wiped a muddy hand across his eyes. Fiona kept talking to him, but he wasn't sure what she was saying. He wished she would stop. She was crying, maybe. When was the last time he'd cried? Father had told him he'd wept when his mother and sister died, but he couldn't remember anything about that. Was there something with a basket? A wicker cart on wheels, when they were sick. His father had tried to push his mother and sister to Sortellian, and their heads had knocked together—blue lips and pale faces.

His breath was shaky as he exhaled. He didn't want to think about that, about the gray skin and lolling heads. He clutched the locket around his neck, pressing his fingers into it. Fiona wouldn't stop crying, all these sobbing noises—sobbing and choking. What did it feel like to choke to death?

When they came to the end of the Darkling Tunnel, Bess wasn't there anymore.

This wasn't how it was supposed to have happened. Oswald and Eden should have come with him to Boston in December, all those months ago in the storm. It should have been the three of them together.

When he'd seen her at the prison, Eden had looked so sick, her throat and hands ashen. Even before she was hanged, there'd been a deathly shadow on her neck—the plague? Was that why he'd saved Fiona instead of her? Maybe she wasn't Eden anymore. The haunted eyes, her mouth pressed into a grim line.

He looked at his feet as he walked up the stairs. At least he'd managed to save Fiona. He wiped his eyes again with his sleeve. They were full of mud. It was everywhere.

As they climbed out of the stairwell, he was vaguely aware that Mather Academy had burned. Over blackened and dripping wood, they stumbled toward the courtyard.

Outside under the sooty sky, he walked toward the Common. Even in Boston the storm god lashed them with rain. He touched the locket at his neck—Eden's hair. His hand shook as he held it up to his face, inspecting the glass and the blond hair within.

Fiona put her hand on his arm as he started toward King's Chapel. He turned, tracing his hands over the place where the noose had been around her neck, feeling its warmth. He shook her hand off his arm and continued to the cemetery. Fiona stayed behind near the elm.

What would they do with Eden's broken body? She'd always wanted to be buried near Athanor Pond, but it was supposed to happen when she was old. A crowd in the Common shouted nearby, and the noise rung in his ears. He was alone as he approached the iron gates of the cemetery. It was where he'd come on his first day, when he'd met Fiona, when he thought he was still waiting for Eden. If he hadn't met Fiona, would Eden still be alive? Maybe he would have gone back for her sooner.

Lightning ignited the sky over Beacon Hill. His chest heaved, and rain kept getting in his eyes, streaming down his face. He pulled open the gate to King's Chapel and stumbled forward, finally crumpling to the ground beneath an oak. He pulled off the locket. She'd given it to him at the festival of the Bird King.

With all the rain, the ground was soft now. Good for a burial. He clawed into the mud with his fingers, flinging clumps away until there was a hole six inches deep. This would have to do. He shoved the locket into its grave, smearing the dirt over it. His hand shook as he mashed it into the mud. He leaned back against the oak and exhaled another unsteady breath.

After his mother had died, his father had lain in bed for

weeks. Mr. Anequs had brought over soup and bread. What was it that had lured his father out of the tangles of yellowed bed sheets and into the Ragmen? Tobias clenched his fists and took a trembling breath over the fresh little grave. Maybe he understood, finally. Maybe it was rage that had drawn him into the streets of Maremount again.

Epilogue

From his position atop one of the Trimountaine Hills, Thomas had an almost unobstructed view of Maremount. He sat on the steps of a crumbling temple, its cracked and ivory-encased columns carved with symbols of serpents and stags. The sun rose before him, and its rays slowly lit the crowded streets below. Smoke rose from many of the buildings, and in a few places fires still smoldered. Bodies lay in the streets, but the storm that had heralded the arrival of the spirits had washed away most of the blood.

That morning, the wife of a Ragman had provided a foul-smelling poultice for a burn on his shoulders. Peeking under the bandages, he saw that it looked much better now.

Had he really snapped someone's neck and driven a sword through a man's heart? He leaned back onto the stone steps, and grit pressed into his hands. He sat up and brushed it off. But they needed to die. They shouldn't have been here in the first place.

Rawhed's army had been routed in the early morning hours. With only a few Harvesters left, the monster had fled Maremount before they could hang him. No one knew where he was. After their victory, the spirit had departed Thomas's body as quickly as he had arrived.

Thomas searched the narrow streets for signs of Fiona and Tobias, but Fiona's wild hair was nowhere to be seen.

As he scanned the city, a tall man with black hair walked toward him across the cobblestone road. There was something familiar in his dark eyes.

"Are you Thomas Malcolm?"

He raised his eyebrows, exhaling. He'd become quite the curiosity among the Ragmen. "That's me."

"Thank you for helping us. I was there yesterday, in Lilitu Square."

"I'm glad I could help." He really just wanted to sleep.

"I'm William Corvin. I was told you're a friend of my son, Tobias."

He rose. "Tobias? I came here with him, but I haven't been able to find him since we were separated."

"The ravens tell me he returned to Boston through the Darkling Tunnel. He was with a friend—a girl."

Thomas exhaled. "Good. I was worried about them. Do you know what happened to Celia? I mean, Lady Celestine?"

"Reunited with her father, for now." He wiped his hand across his brow. "I wanted to follow after Tobias, but the tunnel is gone. When Rawhed escaped, he sealed it after him. I'm afraid you might be stuck here until we can find a philosopher's guide with the right spell."

Thomas's body ached. He hadn't slept in several days, and he saw trails whenever he turned his head. His fatigue dulled his reaction to the news. "So I'm stuck here."

"For now."

He closed his eyes and felt the cobblestones beneath his

feet, the sun on his face, and the breeze against his skin. He might not be home, but at least he knew he was somewhere.

Preview of

A Witch's Feast

Chapter 1

Warm water trickled down Jack's skin, and he watched the sulfurous mud slough off his body into the drain. Inhaling the shower steam, he squeezed a heavy dollop of lavender soap into a loofa and began to scrub at the mud and gore caked on his chest. Red and brown streaks swirled on the shower floor.

He felt a wave of nausea when he thought of Fiona's face after she'd seen him with the blood dripping down his chin. She'd called him a monster, as if he were Old Cratten himself. He wasn't sure what horrified her more: watching him rip out and eat someone's heart, learning of his role in the Salem Witch Trials, or realizing that he had once been an unsightly old man. He had a suspicion that she was the most repulsed by the thought of him with sagging flesh and rheumy eyes. Well, he was no longer burdened with that body. He scrubbed at the dirt on his arms, admiring the smooth skin on his muscles as he did so.

When the shower floor was clear of blood and earth, he

turned off the stream of water and stepped out. Grabbing a towel, he rubbed his black hair and aching limbs. Being hunted out of a magical city by a ghost-assisted army wasn't something that happened every day, not even to him.

He massaged his shoulders and neck with almond lotion. Fiona would come around. Of course he'd killed people over the years, but someone else had already condemned them to death. That was the point—death is inevitable. The Creator had passed its sentence. Once Jack completed his great alchemical work, everyone would be saved from the Creator's curse. Why was that so hard to understand?

When he was a boy, he had tried to save one person at a time. He had protested when he saw the women being whipped in the dirt streets at his father's orders. (What would his father have done to him if he'd known he was a philosopher and not a Puritan?)

He sighed. It had always been someone named Ann who was tormented in those days—an Ann being hanged or beaten in the streets, an Ann starving to death in a muddy jail cell, his mother Ann losing her mind and ramming a kitchen knife through her own hand. But what would happen if he *had* saved one of these Anns? A short reprieve from the corporeal punishment—no more. The creator's curse was universally applied.

He looked at his reflection in the bathroom mirror as he pulled on silk underwear. That idiot, his ancestor Nathaniel Hawthorne, had called him a *black-browed Puritan*. It was true that his eyebrows were black and severe, but beautiful blue eyes twinkled below them. He had his diet to thank for his porcelain skin and rosy cheeks. It was only unfortunate that ingesting human flesh left him with a perpetual hunger, gnawing at him even now.

Stretching his arms above his head, he loosened the muscles in his back. He yawned and stepped into his bedroom. He pulled out gray wool pants, a navy blue t-shirt, and an ashy cashmere sweater from his bureau. As he dressed, a flicker of movement caught his eye. A gypsy moth fluttered near the ceiling, but no aura glowed around it. It was an ordinary moth—not a philosopher's familiar.

After fixing himself a cup of herbal tea, he strolled into the living room. He turned on a cream-colored lamp and stretched out on his chaise lounge, content in the quiet. Steam from the tea warmed his face as he thought about Fiona's beautiful olive skin. As he took a sip of the bitter drink, a knock on his door interrupted his thoughts.

"Samael's skin," he grumbled as he walked toward the entrance. He forced himself to smile as he opened the door.

"Hi, Jack!" it was his neighbor, Elsa. She beamed at him and twirled a long strand of blond hair around her finger. She always found reasons to knock on his door. "I got a piece of your mail again."

He smiled and tilted his head. "It's almost as if you were taking it out of my mailbox."

Her smile disappeared, and he inhaled the metallic smell of cortisol. Her fear was scrumptious.

He leaned against the doorframe, taking the letter from her hand. "I was only joking." He lowered his chin and looked up at her from beneath his long lashes.

She smiled again, exhaling. "Oh."

He moved toward her. "What is that scent you're wearing? It's lovely." Lifting her wrist toward his nose, he inhaled and closed his eyes. Could he really be this hungry again?

She blushed, looking away. "Oh, I'm not—it's not anything. Just me, I guess."

Her thin wrist lay in his hand as he looked into her eyes, pulling her in slightly closer. He wanted to start with her belly. When the little ribs cracked and the blood flowed hot into his hands... but he mustn't think about it like that. It was vile, and it wasn't time to eat yet. "Do you want to come over tomorrow evening for some tea?"

"I'd love that." She pulled her wrist away. "I could come by at seven."

"I look forward to it." He rubbed her wrist before releasing it.

After casting one last glance at him with a flicker of a smile, she strutted down the hall.

He closed the door, taking his seat on the chaise lounge again and sipping his tea. A sizzling noise disrupted the quiet of the room, followed by a burning smell.

"Samael's skin!" He jumped up and peered under the lampshade.

Against the light bulb rested the moth's blackened body, and a thin tendril of smoke curled up into the air.

Keep in Touch

Readers who sign up to our mailing list will be able to buy the next book in our series (*A Witch's Feast*) for only $0.99. We'll send you an email as soon as it's released, and you'll have a 24 hour window when the book goes live to purchase the discounted book.

To join our mailing list, you can sign up on our website:

www.cncrawford.com

Finally, if you have a moment, we'd really appreciate it if you would leave an honest review on Amazon and Goodreads. Word of mouth is the number one way for new readers to learn of Rawhed and the Mather Adepti.

Yours,

Christine & Nick

Sources

We relied on a number of sources when writing this book including the Pokanoket Tribe's website; *Legends and Lore of the North Shore* by Peter Muise along with his blog; *The Name of War: King Philip's War and the Origins of American Identity* by Jill Lepore; Peter Levine, Ph.D. and his interpretation of *At the Indian Killer's Grave*; *Boston Common: A Diary of Notable Events*; *A History of the Town of Bellingham, Massachusetts;* and the *Footnotes Since the Wilderness* blog.

Acknowledgments

We thank our wonderful editor John Hart; our cover designer Carlos Quevedo; and our beta readers: Callie, Eliot, Jess, Joeleen, Meagan, Michelle. We also thank David, Geoff, James, Leslie, Peggy, Robert, Stephanie, and Will for their comments and edits, and Robin for her amazing writing advice. Thanks to Karl and Martin for their design input; Heath, Lindsay, and Audra for their marketing suggestions, the writing groups Den of Quills, The Dragon's Rocketship, and Author's Corner for their inspiration and moral support. We thank FrankandCarySTOCK for the crow-wing stock image. Lastly we thank Sean, our first ARC reviewer found through an online reading group.

Fantasy Fiction
Paranormal Fiction
Historical Fiction
(New England's
dark past)
Series Fiction
(Book #1)

For fans of
Harry Potter and/or
Sleepy Hollow!